RAVEN LAKE

ROSEMARY McCRACKEN

RAVEN LAKE
A Pat Tierney Mystery - Book 3

http://www.rosemarymccracken.com

FIRST EDITION Trade Paperback

Imajin Books - http://www.imajinbooks.com

June 1, 2016

ISBN: 978-1-77223-241-7

Cover designed by Ryan Doan - www.ryandoan.com

Praise for RAVEN LAKE

"When a rug-wrapped human body is found in a storage locker, Pat Tierney is dragged into the murky waters of ancient jealousies, financial chicanery, property rental scams and family betrayals. Watching Rosemary McCracken's smart, cool protagonist explore the depths of the mystery and swim for the surface will keep your nerves taut and your heart pounding. Don't miss *Raven Lake!*" —Gail Bowen, author of the Joanne Kilbourn Shreve mystery series

"Pat Tierney has become one of my favorite characters. She and her family feel like friends. In *Raven Lake*, Rosemary McCracken weaves an intricate story that will keep you guessing until the satisfying ending. All of her characterizations are totally believable. As usual, the rural Ontario setting is pitch-perfect." —Maureen Jennings, author of the Detective Murdoch mystery series

"*Raven Lake* is a beautifully written, heartfelt story. Rosemary McCracken weaves a compelling mystery, taking readers hostage to the action-packed conclusion." —Rick Mofina, bestselling author of *Free Fall*

"On the cusp of an exciting new turn in her life, Pat Tierney is looking forward to an idyllic summer at the cottage. Until, that is, the body of a woman is found under strange circumstances. As the mystery deepens, Pat discovers that the friendliness of neighbors and colleagues is only skin deep, and people harbor frightening secrets. *Raven Lake* kept me reading long into the night." —D.J. McIntosh, *Globe and Mail* bestselling author of the *Mesopotamian Antiquities Trilogy*

"Pat Tierney's latest adventure, *Raven Lake*, is a gripping read from start to finish. I couldn't put it down. Pat is an engaging heroine I'd love to have as a friend: she's warm, ethical and fearless. In this third book in the series, she deals with a family crisis while trying to clear a friend who has been pegged by police as a prime suspect in a murder. Rosemary McCracken draws on her financial journalism background to warn and educate us about the dark frauds at the heart of the mystery. Readers may never feel safe again in sunny cottage country." —M.H. Callway, award-winning author of *Windigo Fire*

For Ed Piwowarczyk, as always.

Acknowledgements

Many thanks to the intrepid Mesdames of Mayhem, in particular founding Madame Madeleine Harris-Callway and marketing maven Madame Joan O'Callaghan, for the opportunities they've provided to present the Pat Tierney mysteries to readers throughout southern Ontario.

Thanks to Donna and Alex Carrick of Carrick Publishing for their work and dedication in publishing the Mesdames' crime fiction anthologies, *Thirteen* and *Thirteen O'Clock*.

And thanks to the Midwives—Catherine Dunphy, Madeleine Harris-Callway, Lynne Murphy, Joan O'Callaghan and Sylvia Warsh—for their help in birthing *Raven Lake*.

Thank you, Cheryl Kaye Tardiff, publisher of Imajin Books, and her marvelous production team.

And thank you, Ed Piwowarczyk, my dear husband, my first editor and my collaborator in this wonderful book adventure.

PROLOGUE

"This locker could make one of you a millionaire," said the barrel-bellied man in the floral shirt. The metal door of the storage locker clanked as he rolled it up.

"So could the lottery ticket in my wallet," Jock muttered as he swatted at the blackflies that hovered around his head. He slapped at his neck. "Damn bugs!"

"Suck it up, big guy." Crystal swept her mane of wavy red hair back from her face. "If I can take the bugs, you can, too."

The man in the floral shirt raised the sound level on the microphone. "Jewelry, works of art, old coins. Everyone gets a quick look-see. Line up behind me and walk past the door. But don't step inside, or you're outta here."

Jock and Crystal joined about forty people filing past a storage unit the size of a small bedroom. It held a jumble of furniture—a battered rocking chair, a trunk, a headboard, a night table, and an assortment of lamps. Wooden crates and plastic containers were stacked along the sides of the locker and its back walls. A rolled-up rug, tied with rope, lay on the floor.

"Nothin' in there but crap." A man with a gray ponytail turned and pushed his way out of the crowd. "Not for me."

"I think he's right," Jock said to Crystal. "Looks like they cleared out Grandma's house. There's no market for lace doilies and crocheted afghans. Smells funny in there, too."

"Quiet!" Crystal elbowed him in the ribs then lowered her voice. "Farms, country homes, that's where you find great antiques."

Jock scowled at her. "We wasted two hours driving up here."

"Could be possibilities if the price is right. See those big crates in the back? Someone took the trouble to protect whatever's in them." She glanced around the crowd. "These hicks wouldn't know an antique from—"

A squawk from the microphone brought their attention back to the man in the floral shirt. "Okay! You've all had a look. Let's get the show rollin'."

Crystal surveyed her rivals and sniffed in disdain.

"Who'll give me one hundred? I'm bid one fifty…I'm bid two hundred…" The auctioneer fielded bids in rapid succession. "I'm bid eight twenty-five…I'm bid eight fifty. Eight fifty going once…"

"Nine hundred!" Crystal cried.

Jock grabbed her arm. "Are you crazy, Crystal?"

She shook off his hand, keeping her eyes on the man in the floral shirt.

"Do I hear nine twenty-five?" the auctioneer asked. The other bidders shook their heads.

"Nine hundred going once, nine hundred going twice…sold! To the redhead in the green dress."

Inside the locker, Crystal stared in dismay at the crates that she and Jock had unpacked. "Damn! Christmas decorations. Old photos…"

"Tried to tell you, but you had to rush in." Jock looked down a crate at his feet. "Doilies, I bet, in this mystery box."

She glared at him as he pried open the lid with a crowbar. Her face brightened as she surveyed the contents. "This is more like it. Old comic books. Could be worth something."

"Grandma the nerd. Who knew?"

"More likely her nerd son back in the sixties." She looked around the locker. "Let's check out this rug."

Jock grunted as he dragged the rug to the entrance. "Man, it's heavy. Feels like there's something in here."

He cut the rope and unfurled the rug. The lifeless body of a white-haired woman in a yellow top and blue trousers tumbled out.

Crystal gasped and held a hand to her mouth.

"Now who'd go and clear out Grandma with her furniture?" Jock asked.

CHAPTER ONE

Mist rose from the water as my canoe glided across Black Bear Lake. I glanced at my watch. I had less than thirty minutes to cross the chain of lakes between Black Bear and the town of Braeloch, or I'd be late for the morning meeting. I dipped my paddle into the water, but a noise pulled me off the lake.

I opened one eye. The clock on my bedside table told me it was six thirty. I heard the sound again. The sound of retching in the bathroom across the hall.

I was out of bed in a flash. In the room beside mine, Tommy, my eight-year-old, was sound asleep. That meant…

"Laura?" I tapped on the bathroom door. "Are you okay?"

I'd picked up Laura and Tommy when the bus from Toronto pulled into Braeloch the previous afternoon. Tommy and Maxie, our golden retriever, had a rapturous reunion, but Laura was subdued, which I put down to exhaustion after her final exams. She planned to spend a week at the lake before starting her summer job. Tommy would be with me for most of the summer.

The bathroom door opened. Laura stood barefoot in a pink nightshirt, clutching a towel. Her gray eyes met mine.

My head began to spin.

"Mom." She wiped her mouth with the towel. "They say morning sickness ends after three months so I should be over it soon."

For a few moments, I didn't know what to think, what to feel. I stood there, staring at her. *This can't be happening. Not Laura, my little girl.*

Then anger erupted. "How could you have been so stupid?"

I grabbed Laura's bathrobe from her room. "We need to talk." I handed her the robe and led the way downstairs.

She perched on a stool at the kitchen counter. I busied myself making cocoa, my mind in overdrive.

I set two mugs on the counter and called up the platitude my mother had used on me. "I'm disappointed in you."

"Sorry I don't measure up." She looked at me defiantly. "Before you go any further, I want you to know that I'm having this baby."

"And Kyle?" I assumed her boyfriend, Kyle Shingler, was the father.

"Kyle wants the baby. He wants to get married." She stared at her mug.

"Married?" I said.

"Don't worry, Mom. I already told him—marriage, no way."

Finally, some common sense. A shotgun wedding would only complicate this situation. But what a situation.

"I can't believe you could be so stupid."

She set her chin stubbornly and stared at me.

"I am so…disappointed." I didn't know what else to say.

She gave a small shrug.

"When are you due?" I asked.

"Late December. A Christmas baby."

How cute. "Laura, you are eighteen years old with zero job skills. Do you have any idea—"

Tommy burst into the kitchen with Maxie. "What are we doing today?" he wanted to know.

I put my arm around him. "Get dressed, both of you. Laura, you can take Tommy out in the motorboat after breakfast."

I tossed her a key. "The Hyundai I rented is yours while you're here."

I centered myself behind the steering wheel of my Volvo and let Schubert's "Serenade" wash over me. *It's not the worst thing that could happen. Laura is healthy and… Damn!* I gripped the steering wheel, and my knuckles turned white. "How could she have been so stupid!" *There, I said it again.*

I adjusted the rear-view mirror, catching a glimpse of myself in it. My blond hair, in its new pixie style, capped a face that was a mask of worry: downturned mouth, troubled green eyes, and forehead creased with worry lines. *Smile!*

Yeah.

I tried to focus on the hours ahead. I had two more days at the helm of Norris Cassidy's Braeloch branch. I needed to update my client accounts so I could turn them over to my replacement on Monday. I'd stay on for another two weeks to ease him into the job. Then, at the age of forty-eight, my career at Norris Cassidy would be over. I planned to open my own financial planning practice in Toronto in the fall, but I was taking the summer off.

For the past several months, I'd lived in Norris Cassidy's executive vacation home on Black Bear Lake in Ontario cottage country. It was booked for vacations throughout July and August, so I'd rented a small cottage on the other side of the lake for the summer. I planned to move into it in a few days.

I'd been looking forward to some serious downtime—reading novels and paddling a rented canoe. But after the bombshell Laura had delivered, I knew my summer would be anything but restful.

CHAPTER TWO

My computer was booting up when Paul Campbell—known as Soupy around the township—came into my office. A sour expression distorted his handsome face.

"Tomorrow's your last day in charge, Pat."

I gave him a sunny smile. "So it is."

Our junior advisor had been miffed when I took over as interim branch manager three months before. Soupy had assumed he'd be given the top job after the former manager was arrested for fraud. I'd told him he needed more experience but that his time would come.

He didn't take it well when Nate Johnston was hired as branch manager. Nate had twelve years' experience in investment management, and he'd spent the past five of them at a rival firm in Toronto.

"A city guy running this branch?" Soupy had said when Nate's appointment was announced. "Most of our clients know me. They're friends of my folks, and I went to school with their kids."

"You know this community, and that counts for a lot," I'd told him, "but our clients expect experienced money managers."

Now, six weeks later, he still wasn't happy about Nate's appointment, but it was time he got over it. "Nate starts on Monday," I said. "I'll have a barbecue next Friday night to welcome him. I've invited some of our top clients. You'll be there, of course."

Soupy scowled. "Mara works on Friday evenings."

Mara Nowak, Soupy's fiancée, was the host of *The Highlands Tonight*, the evening news program on ELK TV. But it was Soupy, with or without Mara, who I wanted at the party.

"You won't have to get your own dinner that night," I said. "Come by around seven. Casual dress."

Soupy shrugged and moved toward the office door. Then he turned to face me. "I hear Nate's rented a cottage near you on Black Bear."

I'd sent Nate an e-mail when his appointment was announced. I welcomed him and gave him the names of two realtors and a rental agency in Braeloch. He'd thanked me, but I hadn't heard anything more from him.

"He's rented it for the summer." Soupy flashed a wicked grin. "He doesn't think he'll pass his probation period."

What happened to the easygoing Soupy Campbell?

Around two that afternoon, Bruce Stohl blew into the branch without stopping at Ivy Barker's reception desk. "Mom's missing," he blurted out at my office door. His face was pale, and his eyes were filled with worry.

"Missing?" Vi Stohl had been diagnosed with Alzheimer's disease. She lived at Highland Ridge, a long-term care facility on the outskirts of Braeloch. "Since when?"

"Yesterday." He sank into the chair across from me. "Highland Ridge arranged a day trip for some of the more mobile residents. A picnic lunch at the conservation park."

"She went missing at the park?"

"No, she was on the bus on the return trip. One of the care workers who went on the outing said she was sitting beside another woman from her floor. The bus got back to Highland Ridge just after four, and everyone got off. Then Mom seems to have vanished into thin air."

I pictured a throng of elderly men and women shuffling off the bus and into the building with the help of canes, walkers, and care workers. *Where could she have gone?*

"They didn't miss her until an hour later when one of the staff went to her room to get her for dinner." Bruce slumped down in the chair, his head bent. He looked utterly dejected.

When I'd met him that winter, he had been a troubled man with a drinking problem. He'd had a breakdown a few years before, left his job as an associate professor at a university in Western Canada, and was doing maintenance work at a Braeloch church. When his father died in a fire, I thought it would send him on a downward spiral, but it had turned out to be a new beginning.

He took over his father's job as publisher and editor of *The Highland Times*. "I have no journalism background," he'd told me, "but if I could write a doctoral thesis on Nietzsche, I think I can turn out a newspaper every week."

I'd had my doubts. But the paper continued to publish, and Bruce seemed to enjoy his work.

The man who now sat across from me wore a checked shirt and a new pair of Levis. His salt-and-pepper hair had been trimmed, and he no longer sported a week's growth of stubble on his face. But he looked as forlorn as I'd ever seen him.

"I assume the police have been notified," I said.

"Highland Ridge notified them right away. They spoke to me last night, asked me who Mom knew in the township, where she might go."

My heart went out to him. "Bruce, there's nothing you can do. They'll find her."

He blinked back tears.

"Chin up, okay?"

He gave me a weak smile.

I changed the subject. "Have you decided on that property you were looking at?"

Bruce and his father had had a troubled relationship, and he didn't want to live in the house he'd inherited from him. He'd been staying at the Dominion Hotel for the past few months, looking at real estate in the township in his spare time. He'd recently set his sights on a cabin on a lake not far from Braeloch. Ted's life insurance would provide him with a substantial down payment.

I saw a flicker of interest in his eyes. "I want to buy it."

"Make an offer before someone grabs it."

"I will. As soon as we find Mom."

"You won't be the only kid in this family for long," Laura said to Tommy at dinner that evening.

"Laura!" I gave my daughter a warning look.

"He's going to notice sooner or later," she shot back, looking down at her tummy. She turned to face Tommy. "I'm having a baby in December. Around Christmas."

"A baby." Tommy seemed to weigh the words. Then he turned to me, his brown eyes wide with alarm. "Will the baby get my bedroom?"

I reached across the table and placed a hand on his. "That's your room, Tommy. Nobody will take it away from you."

We finished the meal in silence. When the table was cleared, I settled Tommy and Maxie in front of the TV screen, and put on a *Harry Potter* DVD. Then I joined Laura in the kitchen where she was loading the dishwasher.

"Tommy lost his mother six months ago," I said. "He had to leave his home and live with strangers. Considering his loss, he's settled in well with us. Now he's worried that your baby will take his room."

Laura shrugged. "That's his problem."

I saw red. My daughter, who would be a mother before the year was over, was turning her back on a frightened child. "Do you plan to raise your son or daughter yourself?"

She closed the dishwasher door and turned to face me. "If that's your way of asking whether I'll put my baby up for adoption—of course not. I don't know whether Kyle and I will be together, but we'll both be involved in raising our child."

"Really. You think you can raise a child, yet you have no patience with Tommy, and no sensitivity to his feelings. What you said at dinner was cruel."

"Tommy's not my kid."

"As I recall, you wanted him to live with us."

"Well, yeah. But he's a joint responsibility. You, Tracy, and I look after him."

"What are your plans for September?" She had been accepted into the arts program at the University of Guelph, a ninety-minute drive from Toronto. Kyle had been accepted into commerce, and they'd been talking about sharing an apartment.

"I'm not sure…with the baby coming in December."

It won't be easy to start university when you're six months pregnant. And with Kyle pushing marriage, sharing an apartment doesn't seem like a good idea.

She gave me a sidelong glance. "I could apply to the University of Toronto next year."

"And live with me?" *You expect me to raise your child.*

"It's more than a year from now. Something may…happen."

"Sure. You might win a lottery."

She just stared at me.

"You've seen a doctor?" I asked.

"Dr. Gray."

Our family doctor knew you were pregnant before me.

"She says everything is fine." Laura gave me a weak smile. "Says I'm built for motherhood."

"You should have put motherhood on hold for another ten years."

"It wasn't supposed to happen," she said. "It just…did."

"A miracle," I muttered. "Virgin birth."

"No. It must have been the day Kyle forgot his condoms. I thought it was a safe time of the month."

Spare me the details. Then I saw a tear slide down her cheek. Under her tough attitude, she was a scared little girl. I put an arm around her.

If I hadn't been in Braeloch for the past few months, Laura wouldn't have been on her own in the city. Tracy, her older sister who'd been staying with Laura while I was away, didn't get home until well past seven. Laura and Kyle had the house to themselves for hours after school.

No, this is not my fault. Laura and Kyle are responsible for getting themselves into this mess.

I withdrew my arm and stepped back. "Have you told Tracy?"

"Two days ago. She and Jamie think I should terminate, but I refuse to consider that. This is *my* baby...and Kyle's."

It had crossed my mind that Tracy and her partner, Jamie Collins, might want a child one day. Many lesbian couples raised families. But I figured that they would wait until Tracy had launched her law career.

"I'll stay here for a few weeks, if that's okay," Laura said. "I need some distance from Kyle."

"Don't the Harrisons expect you next Tuesday?" Laura had signed on to look after little Emily Harrison in July and August while her parents were at work.

"They said it would be okay to start later. Emily can go to her aunt's place."

She collapsed on a chair at the counter, the fight gone out of her.

I went over to her and took her in my arms. "We'll get through this, honey. One step at a time."

One step at a time for the next eighteen years until my grandchild went off to university. By then, Laura might be able to foot the bill.

CHAPTER THREE

I yawned all the way to work the next morning. I'd tossed and turned in bed for most of the night, thinking about Laura and the baby. Its arrival would change our lives. My life.

I felt a surge of anger. What was Laura thinking? She had years of school ahead of her, she hadn't even decided on what career she wanted to pursue. She had no idea what it would cost to raise a child, or the change in lifestyle that motherhood would bring. And there was nothing I could do except stand by and support her financially and emotionally. Make sure that she got an education and that her child was cared for while she was in school.

I turned on the car radio to distance myself from my thoughts.

"The body of an elderly woman was found in an abandoned locker at Glencoe Self-Storage yesterday afternoon." I recognized the voice of Mara Nowak, who filled in as a reporter on ELK Radio as well as hosting the evening news program on ELK TV

"The human remains were found rolled up in a carpet by Crystal King and Jock Deighton," Mara went on. "King and Deighton run an antique shop in Newmarket, and they had just purchased the locker's contents for nine hundred dollars. The party who rented the locker was several months behind in payments, and the locker's contents were put up for auction."

An image of Glencoe Self-Storage flashed through my mind. Its two rows of orange metal lockers stood out like a beacon at the intersection of Highways 36 and 123, halfway between Braeloch and Black Bear Lake.

"Police have confiscated the locker's contents and told us that an investigation is pending. They refused to say whether the deceased has been identified, or if the cause of death is known."

I thought of Bruce's visit the day before. *Could the body in the locker be Vi's?* I dismissed that as impossible. Glencoe Self-Storage was miles away from Highland Ridge.

The first thing I did when I arrived at the branch was inspect the office that Nate would occupy. I'd never liked the massive mahogany desk the previous branch manager had chosen. It put a huge barrier between advisor and clients, but it was up to Nate to decide how he wanted to furnish his office. Everything else appeared to be in order. The computer was working, and Norris Cassidy's IT department in Toronto would set up Nate's password and e-mail account on Monday.

But when Bruce dropped by the branch after lunch, one look at his face reminded me of what I'd heard on the newscast. I waited to hear what he had to say.

He sat in the client's chair and stared at my desktop for a few moments. "Mom...Mom's dead." His face was filled with grief, deep and awful.

"Bruce, that's terrible."

"They found her in a locker at Glencoe Self-Storage."

I rose from my chair. "Let's get a coffee."

Soupy came into the hall when Bruce and I passed his office. He stood watching as we stopped at Ivy's desk.

"I'll be at Joe's if anyone needs me," I told her.

We took the booth at the back of Joe's Diner and ordered coffee from Sue Tomkins, Joe's long-time waitress.

"Our front page story is about Mom," Bruce said in a tight voice. "I wrote it last night. Hardest thing I ever did in my life." His eyes glistened with tears.

I waited for him to go on.

"The police came by the newsroom around four yesterday. Not Bouchard," he said, referring to Sergeant Roger Bouchard who ran the Ontario Provincial Police's Braeloch detachment. "It was Foster, the cop from Orillia."

Detective Inspector Stewart Foster ran the homicide division at OPP headquarters in Orillia. *That meant...*

"An autopsy was held this morning. She was strangled." Bruce's voice broke on the last word.

"My God! Who would—"

He shook his head, looking miserable. "No idea. She never hurt anyone in her entire life."

That wasn't quite true. Vi had been overcome with grief many years before when her infant died of crib death. She'd snatched Bruce from his baby carriage, and she and her husband Ted had raised him as their own son.

Bruce's eyes told me he was thinking along the same lines. "That was her only slip, and it was forty years ago."

Sue set two mugs of coffee on the table. She must have known we wanted to be left alone because she didn't stop to chat as she usually did.

Bruce looked down at his mug. "Highland Ridge reported Mom missing on Wednesday. So when a body was found in the storage unit yesterday, the police called the nursing home. Someone on staff identified her."

I nodded.

"Foster and his sidekick took me to the hospital morgue." He closed his eyes. "Then we went over to the detachment. Didn't get back till after eight. Thank God for Maria Dawson. She had the inside pages wrapped up, and I wrote the front-page story."

"What did the police—"

"I seem to be a suspect. Foster told me not to leave the township without letting him know."

"You must be joking," I said.

"Apparently, I had a motive. Ted left everything to Mom and me when he died. Now that's she's gone, I inherit the whole thing."

The police hadn't wasted any time in checking out Ted's will. "Has Ted's will been probated?" I asked.

"Two weeks ago."

"Then the police have a copy of it. Once a will is probated, it becomes a public court record."

Bruce stared into his coffee mug, apparently deep in thought. "I visited Mom at least once a week," he finally said, "so the police said I'd know the layout of the building. I could easily have gotten Mom out, they said. I told them to check the sign-in register and they'd see that I hadn't been there since last Sunday. They didn't listen to that."

"They're trying to rattle you. What were you doing when Vi got off the bus at Highland Ridge on Wednesday?"

"That's another problem," he said. "I was alone in the newsroom on Wednesday afternoon. Nancy Warner, our receptionist, called in sick that morning. Maria had an interview at the conservation park. And Wilf Mathers was covering a highway accident near Donarvon."

He toyed with his coffee spoon. "There's something else."

"What?"

"I rented a locker at Glencoe Self-Storage. I'm going to sell Ted's house, and I need a place to store his furniture until I decide what to do with it."

"Why remove the furniture? The best way to show a house is completely furnished."

"That's what the police said." He shrugged. "How was I supposed to know that? I've never sold a house before."

"There are such things as coincidences," I said. "There's only one storage place around here, and you happened to rent one of its lockers."

We sipped our coffee. Bruce looked lost in his thoughts again. "Like a piece of pie?" I asked.

He shook his head.

"Well, I want another coffee." I waved at Sue and pointed to our mugs. "I never met your mom. What was she like?"

"She was a quiet woman, unassuming. Never quite adjusted to Toronto, and they lived there for forty years."

His voice broke, and he took a few moments to pull himself together. "I was kind of her world. She didn't want me to go to boarding school, but Ted insisted. I started at Central Canada College in Grade Nine."

The private school was in a town north of Toronto. Bruce would have been away from home all week.

"After I left home," he said, "Mom worked as a teller at a Bank of Toronto branch close to home. Ted wasn't happy about her going out to work, but she'd been a teller here in Braeloch before they married and she wanted to keep busy."

I smiled. Ted was an arrogant man, and a wife who worked as a customer sales representative, as bank tellers are now called, would not fit the image he had of himself as editor of *The Toronto World*, Canada's largest daily newspaper.

"How long was she at the bank?" I asked.

"Twenty years. Until her memory started going."

A forgetful bank teller wouldn't last long on the job.

"There was a problem of some kind," he said, "and she was let go. I was never clear about what happened. I was out in Alberta then."

"When was this?"

"Six years ago." He pushed the coffee mug aside. "Pat, how should I handle the cops? How can I convince them that I didn't kill Mom?"

I sat up straight in my seat. "Talk to your lawyer, Bruce. Go over to his office right now."

I told Laura about Vi before we sat down for dinner.

"In a storage locker?" Her eyes were wide with astonishment.

"She was murdered." I let her digest that for a few moments before I continued. "I'm worried about Bruce. He was devoted to Vi, and the police are treating him as a murder suspect."

"Aren't family members always suspects?"

"You're probably right. It's just that Bruce..." I sighed. "I hope this won't trigger a breakdown."

"Can we help?" Laura asked.

"I don't know what we can do."

After we'd eaten and Laura had stacked the dishwasher, she went upstairs to call her friends in the city. When I'd settled Tommy in front of the TV, I went over to the sliding doors that opened onto the deck. The wind had died down, and Black Bear Lake was a sheet of glass reflecting the various shades of green along its shores. The loon family was out, the parents swimming protectively around their two chicks in case a snapping turtle was on the prowl for dinner. A small boat moved slowly across the eastern part of the bay. I wanted to sit outside, but I knew I'd be a target for blackflies. They love my fair Irish skin.

I took a bottle of chardonnay out of the fridge to toast the end of my tenure at the helm of the Braeloch branch. On Monday, Nate would be running the show. I was about to uncork the bottle when Bruce's desolate face flashed through my mind. *What's he doing right now?*

I didn't think for a moment that he had killed Vi. He'd loved her with the simple devotion that a child has for its mother. He'd pulled his life together in the past few months, but I doubted that he could take the heat the police would apply in a murder investigation. The stress he'd be under—while he was grieving—might bring on another breakdown.

Upstairs, I found Laura on her bed, eyes closed, iBuds in her ears. I touched her arm. She opened one eye and took the iBuds out of her ears.

"I'm going into town to check on Bruce," I said. "I want you keep Tommy company downstairs. Listen to your music there."

I spotted Bruce at a table at the back of the Dominion Hotel bar. He was slumped in a chair with two empty glasses in front of him. He held a third glass in his hand.

He lifted it in a mock salute. "Rye and ginger doubles." His eyes were glassy.

I seated myself across from him. "Have you had any dinner?"

"Too busy drowning my schlorrows."

"A terrible thing has happened, but getting drunk won't make it go away." I'd be belting back a few if I was in Bruce's shoes, but I couldn't let him fall into his old ways. He might never climb out again.

"This is not how Vi would want to be mourned," I said. "She would have been very proud of you these past few months. Taking over the newspaper and looking for a home of your own. Let's find out what happened to her."

I looked him in the eye. "Let's do it, Bruce."

He stared at the glass in his hand.

"Put it down," I said. "You don't need it."

He looked up at me. I held his gaze until he put the glass on the table.

"We'll get some food." I stood up and pointed to the door to the lobby.

The hotel dining room was still open, and a waitress led us to a table for two.

I scanned the menu and ordered a steak with mashed potatoes and vegetables. "For the gentleman," I said, looking at Bruce who was slumped in the chair across from me. "With a large glass of tomato juice."

"And for you, ma'am?"

I flipped to the back of the menu. "Chocolate ice cream and a pot of tea."

Bruce had a good appetite. When he'd cleaned his plate, I ordered a piece of blueberry pie and a glass of milk for him.

When he'd finished his meal, he wiped his mouth with a paper napkin. He looked a lot better with food inside him. "Will you really help me find my mother's killer?"

"I will. We'll tell the police what we find."

He rolled his eyes. I remembered how Detective Inspector Foster had reacted when I ran into him three months before. He'd objected to anyone "interfering" with his investigation.

"And if the police don't want our help, we'll carry on ourselves." I held out a hand. "Agreed?"

He took my hand and shook it.

"What are you doing tomorrow?" I asked.

"Soupy and I are taking Ted's furniture to the locker."

Good. You need to keep busy.

"Leave some furniture in the house," I said. "Beds and dressers, and the living room furniture. Have you packed the kitchen things—dishes, pots and pans?"

"They're in boxes. The same with Ted's books."

"Put them in the locker. Anything else?"

"There's furniture from the house in Toronto in the basement."

"Take the boxes and the furniture in the basement to the locker tomorrow. I'll give you a hand. What time are you meeting Soupy?"

"Ten at Ted's place."

After Bruce had settled the bill, I followed him upstairs. His room held a bed, a dresser, a bedside table, and an old television set on a stand. The walls needed a fresh coat of paint.

"Bathroom?" I asked.

"Down the hall."

He needed to get out of that dreary room. A place of his own made a great deal of sense.

"Get a good night's sleep," I said. "I'll see you tomorrow morning."

CHAPTER FOUR

Bruce was closing the door when I pulled up in front of Ted's house in Braeloch the next morning. I opened the car window, and he came over. His face was pale and drawn.

"We're heading out with our first load. Can you take a few boxes?" He gestured toward a stack of cartons on the lawn.

Soupy gave me a wave as he closed the door of the rented cargo van.

I opened my trunk, and they loaded it up with boxes. More went onto the backseat, and one took the passenger's seat beside me.

On Main Street, I stopped to buy soft drinks and doughnuts. Ten minutes later, I pulled into Glencoe Self-Storage's yard. Two long buildings housed the metal-clad storage lockers. The office was in a smaller building to their right.

Bruce and Soupy had just taken a brown leather sofa out of the trailer and set it on the pavement in front of a storage unit. Bruce pointed at the unit directly across from it with yellow scene-of-the-crime tape across the door. "That's where they found Mom," he said in a choked voice.

"You provide your own padlock?" I asked.

"Yeah." He glanced at the lock on the unit where Vi had been found. "That's not the lock…I heard they cut it off before the auction."

Of course. The person who'd rented the locker had the key to the lock, and he hadn't paid his rent.

Soupy pointed to the roof of the building. "Surveillance cameras up there."

I looked inquiringly at Bruce.

He shrugged. "No idea if they caught anything. If they did, Foster didn't tell me."

"The time frame is easy to gauge," I said. "Between four o'clock on Wednesday and early Thursday afternoon. Probably sometime during the night. Is the gate locked at night?"

"It closes at six," Bruce said, "but we have electronic cards that let us into the yard after hours."

Keycards. The killer would have put Vi's body in the locker at night to avoid being seen. He had a keycard to open the gate.

Bruce and Soupy carried the sofa into the locker. I took the cartons out of my car and stacked them at the side of the unit. Then I walked over to the office, expecting to find it closed for the weekend.

It wasn't. "What can I do for you?" asked a brunette on the far side of fifty. The nameplate on her desk told me she was Noreen Andrews. The expression on her face said she didn't suffer fools gladly.

"I'm a friend of the Stohl family," I began.

She gave me a curt nod. "Seen you helpin' Bruce out there. You run the new financial place in town."

I didn't tell her I was no longer the branch manager; instead, I gave her my best smile. "Ms. Andrews, who rented the locker where Mrs. Stohl was found?"

She stared at me, clearly weighing whether to answer my question.

"I'm helping Bruce find out what happened to his mother," I added as I sat in the chair on the other side of her desk. "The police aren't telling him anything."

She turned to the computer screen on her desk. "The cops wouldn't want me givin' this out, but maybe you can do something with it. People gettin' knocked off is bad for business."

She clicked her mouse. "Frank Prentice. Rented the unit in November. Missed his first payment in April, and we mailed a notice to his address in Bracebridge. When he missed the second payment, we gave him a phone call. The phone was disconnected. Mailed another notice telling him that the contents of the unit would be auctioned on June 21 unless we received his payments. And we deactivated his card."

The keycard that opened the gate after office hours. "When was the card deactivated?" I asked.

"End of May, after he missed his second payment. Didn't want him to empty the unit without paying."

I turned to the window and looked at the twenty-foot-high wire fence surrounding the property. Vi's killer not only needed a key to the lock on Frank's locker, but he also needed a functional keycard to enter the yard after hours.

Noreen wrote Frank's name and address on a piece of paper and handed it to me.

"Did you meet Frank Prentice?" I asked, slipping the paper into my pocket.

"Nope. My daughter worked the office the day he first came by, but she don't remember much about him."

"How many storage units do you have?"

"Twenty-four."

"All rented?"

"Got eighteen rented now."

That meant eighteen activated cards were in circulation. "Does your security company keep track of which cards open the gate throughout the day?"

"The cops asked the security guy about that on Thursday. He said the system will be able to do that with its next upgrade. Right now, everyone basically gets the same card.

"The cops said they'd talk to all the renters," she added. "I gave Detective Foster their names."

I didn't think she'd share those names with me, but I decided there was no harm in asking.

"Sorry," she said, "that's confidential client information."

I tried a different tack. "Did the surveillance cameras have footage of what went on in the yard the night before the auction?"

"That's another question the police asked," she said. "Cameras showed no activity that night. Yard was quiet as a grave."

Her smile told me her choice of words was intentional.

I had one more question. "Do your tenants give you keys to their lockers?"

"They do not," she snapped, and her face shut down.

I was glad I'd saved that question for last.

Out in the yard, Bruce and Soupy were about to drive back to Braeloch. Bruce stuck his head out of the van window. "See you at the house, Pat?"

"You bet."

We hauled another load to the locker. When we'd arranged the furniture and boxes in the unit to Bruce's satisfaction, I took my cooler out of the trunk.

"I should've thought of that," Bruce said when he saw what I was carrying.

We sat on a bench in the yard with our drinks and the box of doughnuts.

"Noreen in the office said the cameras showed no activity the night after Vi went missing," I said.

Soupy gave a low whistle. "How did her body get into the locker?"

Bruce muttered something I couldn't make out.

"What is it, Bruce?" I asked.

"I can't believe anyone would do that to Mom."

I placed a hand on one of his, and Soupy changed the subject. "My band's playing a stag in Bracebridge tonight. Like to come along?" he asked Bruce. "We could use your help with the equipment."

"I'm not up for it," Bruce said.

"Then what do you say to a barbecue at Black Bear Lake?" I asked. "Just you, me, and the kids."

He shrugged. "Okay."

"Come by around five."

Bruce took the platter of meat from me as I was heading out to the barbecue. "Allow me," he said.

I knew that it would do him good to feel helpful. And he proved adept at the grill, delivering steaks done to everyone's satisfaction.

After we'd eaten and washed up, Laura retreated to her room and Tommy and Maxie went back outside. Bruce and I took our coffee mugs to the living room. He sat on the sofa facing the fireplace, looking bereft. "The police released Mom's body this afternoon," he said.

"Will there be a funeral?"

"At Morrison Funeral Home on Tuesday."

I smiled my approval. A funeral service would bring him some closure, although his ordeal wouldn't be over until Vi's killer was found.

"How are you feeling?" I asked.

He smiled weakly. "Mom is gone. I have nobody else." He sounded like he'd come to the end of his rope.

"You have friends," I reminded him.

He clenched his hands into fists. "I want Mom's killer found and brought to justice."

I wanted that, too. Then Bruce would no longer be a suspect. "There's one thing we know about whoever who killed your mother," I said.

His eyes bored into mine. "What?"

"He must've known her," I said.

"What makes you say that?"

"Why would anyone want to kill a harmless, confused woman. Whoever killed her must have done so because of something that happened in the past. How old was Vi when she and Ted left here?"

"Twenty-five. When they moved back a few years ago..." He looked down at his hands. "...she wasn't the same person. She couldn't look up her old friends. The only people who visited her at Highland Ridge were Lainey Campbell and me."

"It may have been someone who knew her in Toronto. Have you seen anyone at Highland Ridge who might have known her in the city?"

"I almost forgot. She had one other visitor."

"Who was that?"

"Daniel Laughton."

"Daniel Laughton, the environmentalist?" Laughton had taught at the University of Toronto. He'd had a kids' television show for years that explained the natural sciences in an easy-to-understand way. He was now the news media's go-to guy on all things environmental. Especially for his willingness to criticize governments for failing to protect the environment.

He nodded. "That's him. His family had a summer place up here, and he and Mom met when they were kids. Later, they kept in touch in Toronto. When Mom moved back here, he started visiting her at Highland Ridge."

Laughton was someone we needed to look at, although I couldn't imagine why the famous environmentalist would want to harm Vi. "Anyone else?" I asked.

"That's it."

"The locker was probably a temporary measure," I said. "The killer planned to remove Vi's body later, but he didn't know the locker's contents would be auctioned off the next day."

"So the person who rented the locker wasn't the one who...put Mom there."

"The person who killed Vi must've known who rented the locker and somehow got hold of the key. He also needed get through the gate after hours, and Noreen deactivated the renter's keycard when he missed his second payment."

That put Bruce on full alert. "Who was this guy? Superman?"

"No, he had a functional card that opened the gate. So we know something else about the killer."

"What?"

"He'd rented a unit at Glencoe Self-Storage," I said. "He's one of the eighteen people who currently have lockers that the police are talking to."

Bruce scowled. "I bet they haven't spent as much time with the other seventeen as they have with me."

He was probably right. He had a motive. He stood to inherit Vi's share of Ted's estate.

"Ever heard of Frank Prentice?" I asked.

He cupped his coffee mug in his hands and stared into it for a few moments. "Don't know anyone by that name."

"Frank rented the locker. Noreen Andrews gave me his address in Bracebridge. Let's talk him tomorrow."

CHAPTER FIVE

Laura was pecking at a piece of toast as I outlined my plans for the day. "Santa's Village?" She dropped the toast on her plate. "You've got to be kidding!"

"It'll be fun for Tommy and good experience for you," I told her.

Laura gave me a whatever-do-you-mean look.

"Entertaining your son or daughter," I said. "I assume you've given that some thought."

"Will Santa be there today?" Tommy asked.

"I'm sure he will," I said. "That's why it's called Santa's Village."

"Can Maxie come with us?" he asked.

"They told me on the phone that you can't bring dogs into the park so she'll stay with me when I drop you and Laura off."

Laura scowled. "What will you do while we're playing with the elves and the reindeer?"

"I have the address of the man who rented the storage locker where…" I glanced at Tommy's place at the table, but he was heading for the stairs to get dressed. "Bruce's mother was found. He lives in Bracebridge."

Laura wiped her mouth with a napkin. "You're playing detective again. Bruce should go with you."

"He is." I glanced at my watch. "He'll be here in twenty minutes."

"Be careful, Mom," Laura said as she pushed her chair back from the table. "This guy may have killed Vi."

"I doubt it. Why would he put her body in the locker if he knew that the contents would be auctioned the next day?"

I caught the gleam in her eyes. Vi's murder has sparked her interest.

We ate the lunch I'd packed in a park on the Muskoka River. Then I dropped Laura and Tommy off at Santa's Village's parking lot and told them we'd be back at 3 p.m. I followed the instructions on my GPS to the address Noreen had given me.

It turned out to be a white stucco house with a green metal roof. A For Sale sign was on the lawn. Bruce and I left Maxie in the Volvo and walked up to the front door. The shades on the windows were drawn, and no one answered when I rapped the brass knocker.

"No one home," Bruce said.

I rapped again. Four loud raps. No answer again.

"Maybe Frank's already moved," Bruce said.

We went around to the backyard. The shades were drawn on the back windows, and the plastic patio furniture had toppled over on the small deck.

A photo of a real estate agent by the name of Bill Vasey was on the For Sale sign. He worked for a branch of the real estate giant, Monarch Realty. We'd passed a storefront for the company on Bracebridge's main street.

"Bill Vasey may know where Frank is," I said to Bruce.

We returned to Maxie and drove over to Monarch Realty.

A blonde in a blue pantsuit was the only agent on duty. "Bill is showing a property," she said. "Can I help you?"

"I'm looking for Frank Prentice who lives at 48 Falcon Avenue. I see that his house is for sale."

A shadow passed over her face. "That's Bill's listing. You'll have to talk to him."

I took a business card from my handbag, wrote down the phone number at Black Bear Lake, and handed it to her. "Have him call me."

"Let's talk to the neighbors," I suggested when we'd left the building.

"Good idea," Bruce said.

Nobody answered the doors on either side of 48 Falcon Avenue. But a tiny old woman with thinning white hair came around from the back of the rundown cottage across the street.

"Haven't seen him for months," she said when we'd asked her about Frank. "He used to wake up the neighborhood coming home in his truck or on that big motorcycle of his. It's been nice and quiet around here since…Easter, I guess."

And now his house is up for sale.

"Did Frank own the house or rent it?" Bruce asked.

She looked surprised by his question. "Well, he put on that metal roof two years ago so he must own it."

"How long has it been up for sale?" I asked.

The woman thought about that for a moment or two. "Seven or eight weeks."

Around the last time she saw him. "Is Frank married?" I asked. "Children?"

She shrugged. "Lived there by himself."

"Frank's a roofer," she said when I'd thanked her and we had turned to go. "Prentice Roofing, the sign on his truck said."

Bruce and I crossed the street in silence. "Frank's dead," he said when we were in the car.

I searched his face. "Why do you say that?"

"His neighbor hasn't seen him in a couple of months, and his house is up for sale." He paused for a few moments. "And Mom's killer knew that he wouldn't be coming back to his locker."

"All we know is that he hasn't been seen for a while," I replied. "Maybe he found a job somewhere else and moved. Forgot about the locker."

He shook his head. "He had a business in this area. He wouldn't leave a business he'd built up."

Bruce had become quite a businessman himself in the past few months. His position at *The Times* gave him an income, a product he could take pride in, and status in the community. He had to stay tuned to everything that went on in the township, as well as keep the newspaper's advertisers happy. I hoped that would keep him grounded at this unsettling time in his life.

"Speaking of businesses, the newspaper is looking good," I said.

"Thanks mainly to Maria," he said. "She's been at *The Times* for years, long before Ted bought it. As soon as Ted's estate is settled, I'll change the masthead. Maria will be editor-in-chief."

Maria put in long hours at the newspaper. She deserved the recognition. "She'll be happy about that," I said.

"Don't go telling her yet."

Bruce took Maxie for a walk along the river while I shopped for groceries. When we returned to Santa's Village, we found Laura and Tommy waiting for us in the parking lot with big smiles on their faces.

"What's Santa doing here if he lives in the North Pole?" Tommy asked when he was in the car.

In the rearview mirror, I saw Laura tousle Tommy's hair. "This is his summer home," she said.

"Did you know Santa had a summer home, Mrs. T?" Tommy asked.

"He spends a lot of time here in the summer so I guess it's his summer home," I said.

I'd told Tommy to call me Pat, but he still called me Mrs. T. "He'll start calling you Mom one of these day," Tracy had said, but I wasn't sure about that. I could never replace his real mother.

The drive back to Black Bear Lake was a quiet one. The excitement of seeing Santa and his helpers had worn out Tommy, and he fell asleep, curled up against Laura. She spent most of the trip back with her eyes closed, her iBuds in her ears. Maxie had also flaked out on the backseat, her head on Laura's lap. And Bruce seemed to be lost in thought in the seat beside me.

We passed Glencoe Self-Storage and turned north onto Highway 123. The orange storage lockers brought my thoughts back to Frank Prentice. He hadn't been seen on Falcon Avenue for weeks. Then three days ago, Vi Stohl's body had been found in the locker he'd rented. What was the connection between Frank and Vi's killer?

I dropped Laura, Tommy, and Maxie off at Black Bear Lake and followed Bruce's Chevy into Braeloch.

Highland Ridge was at the edge of town where Main Street turns into Highway 123. It appeared to be a fairly new building. The ceilings on the ground floor were high, and large windows let in plenty of light. Plants transformed the back wall of the reception area into a tropical garden.

Bruce asked for Carol McCann, Highland Ridge's director, at the reception desk.

"Ms. McCann doesn't work weekends," the male receptionist said. "But Sheila Sommers, our assistant director, is here. Take a seat across the hall."

Five minutes later, a stout woman bundled into a tight pink suit came over to us. "Hello, Bruce. How are you doing?"

He bobbed his head and introduced me to Sheila. When we were seated in front of her desk, he told her we had some questions about the day Vi disappeared.

"I'll try to answer them," she said with a smile.

"I understand that Vi sat beside a woman from her floor on the return bus trip," I began.

"Yes, Anne Crawford," Sheila said.

"Did anyone see Vi after she got off the bus?" I asked. "Did someone take her to her room?"

Sheila looked thoughtful. "That's what the police wanted to know, and it's what I've been asking myself since she went missing. Myrna Pettigrew was in charge of the day trip, and she did a roll call on the bus on the way home. Everyone was accounted for. The bus pulled up in the driveway outside the front door a little after four. There was a rush into the building. We only have the two elevators, so some residents had to wait in the lobby for a while."

"Did your mother use a walker?" I asked Bruce.

"No," he said. "She didn't even use a cane."

While the care workers helped the less mobile residents, Vi could have wandered off outside without anyone noticing.

I looked at Sheila. "Vi never got to her room?"

She took a deep breath. "Everyone who returned to the building was escorted to his or her room."

"If Vi came into the building, she would have been taken to her room," I said. "If she didn't…"

"She may not have entered the building." Sheila looked at Bruce. "I'm sorry, Bruce, but that's what may have happened."

"Was there an event here on Wednesday afternoon that drew visitors?" I asked. "Tea party? Bake sale?"

"Nothing. We hold our big social events on weekends so that residents' families can participate."

"Were any strangers in the building that afternoon?" I asked.

"No," Sheila said. "Just a few of our residents' regular visitors."

"Who were they?" I asked.

"I gave their names to the police officers. They're talking to them."

Which meant that she wasn't about to tell us.

"Can I take Pat to Mom's room?" Bruce asked.

"I'm sorry, Bruce," Sheila said, "but the room is already occupied. We have a long waiting list. When a room becomes free, the person notified has to move in within forty-eight hours."

"I'd like to see where it's located," I said.

She hoisted herself out of her chair and took us to an elevator down the hall. The elevator stopped on the second floor, and we stepped into a small hallway between two glass doors. Sheila punched a code into a security pad on the wall, and one of the doors buzzed open.

Like the ground floor, the wing was bright and attractively decorated. Sheila waved as we passed the nursing station. The woman behind the desk smiled at her and said hello to Bruce. He led the way to a room further down the hall. "This was Mom's," he said.

The sign beside the door told us that Dorothy Baxter was now in residence. From the doorway, I saw a white-haired woman asleep in a chair beside the window.

The room's entrance was in full view of the nursing station. "Is there always someone at the nursing station?" I asked Sheila.

"Not necessarily," she said. "Staff may be with a resident, or at the morning or afternoon meetings."

"What time was the meeting on Wednesday afternoon?"

"It's always held at three o'clock when the shift changes. Staff who are leaving for the day update those who have just come on duty."

"So the meeting was over when the residents returned from their trip on Wednesday?"

"Long over."

I walked down the hall. A door with an exit sign above it was at the end of the corridor. A security pad was on the wall beside the door.

"Where does this go?" I asked Sheila and Bruce who had followed me.

"It opens onto a staircase that goes up to the third floor and downstairs to an exit," Sheila said.

"What's outside the exit door?" I asked.

"The visitors' parking lot."

The parking lot was at the back of the building where we'd left our cars.

"Do many people use these stairs?" I asked.

"Most of us take the elevator," Sheila said. "The wing on the other side of this floor has a similar set of stairs. They go down to an exit on the side of the building."

"An alarm goes off when you open the door at the bottom of the stairs," Bruce said. "I set it off one day when I tried to leave that way."

"Did the alarm sound on Wednesday afternoon?" I asked Shelia.

"No," she said. "The police asked us about that. We keep a record of any alarms that go off, accidental or otherwise."

We took the elevator back to the ground floor, and I thanked Sheila for the tour.

"Let me know if there's anything else I can do," she said. "A terrible thing happened this week. Highland Ridge was built to protect vulnerable people."

On the way out, Bruce held the front door open for an attractive dark-haired woman. "Beautiful day," she said with a smile that lit up her face.

"I don't think your mother made it into the building," I said to Bruce when we were outside. "She disappeared while the staff helped the other residents get off the bus."

"And nobody saw her." He shook his head.

"They were too busy to notice where she went."

We were standing on the driveway in front of the building "The bus dropped its passengers off here."

"There's a garden on the side of the building," Bruce said. "Mom may have gone in there."

We walked over to a trellis fence covered with honeysuckle and through an archway into the garden. Raised flower beds displayed their blooms at close range, and paved paths made it easy to move around the beds. A young couple sat chatting with an elderly man on a wrought-iron bench.

Another archway at the back of the garden opened onto the visitor's parking lot. "Not a very secure garden," I said.

"The residents come here with their families," Bruce said.

"Your mother may have gone through there." I pointed to the back archway.

He held my gaze for several beats. "Into the parking lot."

"Yes."

"Someone had to be with her, but who? And why would anyone want to harm her?"

Who and why indeed?

Laura and I were busy in the kitchen when the telephone rang before dinner. Tommy picked up the extension in the living room.

"For you, Mrs. T," he called out.

Bill Vasey was on the line. I told him I'd gone to visit Frank Prentice that day and saw that his home was up for sale. "Do you know where I can reach Frank?" I asked. "I need to speak to him about something urgent, and the phone number I have for him has been disconnected."

There was silence at the other end of the line so I repeated my question.

"Frank Prentice is dead," Vasey said. "His mother gave us the listing."

Dead. My head was reeling, but I needed to follow up while I had Vasey on the line. "How long has the house been on the market?" I asked.

"Eight weeks. Are you interested in the property? I can take you through the house tomorrow."

"No, I was looking for Frank. Can you give me his mother's name and phone number?"

"We don't give out client information, but I'll tell her you want to speak to her. I can give her your number."

"What's her name? So that I'll recognize it if she calls."

He hesitated. "I don't know if I should do this. Well, I suppose it's okay. Her name is Ella Prentice."

Laura glanced up from the chopping board when I returned to the kitchen. "You look like you've seen a ghost," she said.

"The man who rented the storage locker is dead."

Laura's eyebrows nearly hit her hairline. "He was murdered, too? What's with that locker?"

"I don't know how Frank died, but his house in Bracebridge has been up for sale for eight weeks. His mother arranged the listing."

"So he's been dead at least eight weeks," Laura said.

"Which means he had nothing to do with Vi's death."

"But somebody probably knew that he rented the locker and got hold of the key." She placed the knife on the chopping board. "Would the police know this, Mom?"

"They must. Glencoe Self-Storage would have given them Frank's address. They would've spoken to Frank's mother by now."

I wanted to speak to Ella Prentice as well. Noreen had sent an auction notice to Frank's home, so Ella knew that he'd rented a storage locker. She probably found the key to its lock in his home.

CHAPTER SIX

I heard Laura in the bathroom while I was dressing the next morning. Her morning sickness hadn't ended. When I got downstairs, she was sitting in the kitchen staring morosely at a teabag in an empty mug.

"You don't look happy," I said as I took the boiling kettle off the stove.

"Well, I'd rather not be pregnant right now. I'd rather be looking forward to going to university in September."

"You should have thought of that—"

She turned to glare at me. "Okay, I made a mistake. You must be happy to hear me say that."

I poured boiling water into her mug. "I'm happy to hear you owning up to your mistake, but it doesn't solve your problem."

"Look, I'm taking responsibility for what I did. Kyle and I both want to do the responsible thing."

"And that is?"

"To raise our child."

"But will you be able to raise this child?" I asked.

"It will be difficult...for both of us. We'll have to find jobs." She looked down at the mug of tea. "We'll have to ask our families for help."

That was my cue to tell her what I was prepared to do. I sat down beside her. "You and the baby will live with me while you're in school. You'll need to start looking at programs in Toronto that you can start next year. But you'll have to pay for child care when you're at school."

"I'll get a part-time job. And Kyle will help. He's decided he's not going to Guelph. He applied to the University of Toronto last fall, and he never turned them down."

"What do his parents say about the baby?"

"They think it's great. They're going to be grandparents." She rolled her eyes. "They want us to get married."

I'd been meaning to talk to Kyle's parents, but I wanted to discuss it with Laura first. This wasn't the right time, however; Nate Johnston would be at the branch in forty minutes.

"We'll talk more tonight." I gave Laura a hug. "Make sure Tommy has fun today."

"I'm supposed to be on holiday."

"So is Tommy. There's no reason why you can't enjoy your holiday together."

I found Soupy perched on Ivy's desk when I arrived at the branch with a box of doughnuts. "Our new manager is the last one in today," he said.

"Good morning to you, too, Soupy. Good morning, Ivy," I said. "It's just past eight thirty, and we don't open till nine."

Ivy lowered her eyes and played with a pen on her desk. I placed the box of doughnuts in front of her. "Pot of coffee, Ivy?" I said.

At eight forty-five, the front door opened and a man in his late thirties walked into the branch. He had cropped brown hair, a medium build, and a homely face redeemed by a warm smile. I recognized Nate Johnston from the photo on his former employer's website.

He walked over to me. "You must be Pat Tierney. Nate Johnston." He held out his hand, and I took it. He had a nice, firm handshake.

"This is Paul Campbell, our junior advisor." I gave Soupy a no-nonsense look. "Everyone calls him Soupy."

Nate held out his hand again. Soupy took it, but didn't return Nate's smile.

"Ivy Barker, our administrative assistant, is making coffee," I said.

Ivy stepped out of the kitchenette behind the reception area. "Hi, Nate. I know you'll like working here."

I checked that the front door was locked and the Closed sign was in the window. "Let's have some coffee and doughnuts."

While Nate settled into his front office, I stopped in to see Soupy down the hall.

"As we've discussed, I'm transferring my client accounts to Nate," I said. "Over the next two weeks, we'll bring every one of those clients into the branch, or visit them at their homes, so that I can introduce them to Nate. You'll carry on with the accounts you have."

Our previous discussions on the subject had not gone well. Soupy wanted to take over the accounts I'd been handling as much as he wanted to run the branch, but neither was about to happen. He would have to resign himself to working under Nate and managing some smaller accounts.

He scowled. "Our clients won't take to an outsider."

"Nonsense. I'm new to this community, and every client I worked with was fine with that."

"They knew you were just filling in."

I wanted to shake him. "You've been in the business long enough to know that we need experienced people to get this branch up and running."

I would have gone on, but I saw a flustered Ivy standing in the doorway. "Pat, Mr. Kulas from head office..."

Keith Kulas and Nate appeared behind her. Keith had a hand on Nate's shoulder. "The new Braeloch team leader," Keith said. "I'll have a chat with Nate in his office, then we'll all go out for lunch. Ivy, book us a table at the Winigami for twelve thirty."

That lunch reminded me why I'd decided to start my own business.

After we'd ordered from the menu and had drinks in front of us, Keith raised his wine glass. "To Nate, and the terrific job he'll do running our Braeloch branch."

The rest of us raised our glasses and took sips of our drinks. Keith raised his glass again. "And to Pat and her plans." His tone of voice made it sound like I intended to take up basket weaving.

I pasted a smile on my face.

"The Braeloch branch is doing well," Keith went on, "and Nate will make it do even better. Our goal is to have a cool million in AUM by the beginning of October."

Assets under management don't accumulate overnight. Norris Cassidy was a new player in the Glencoe Highlands, and word of mouth from existing clients was the way for it to grow. Keith was setting an impossible goal.

"We've got one more seminar scheduled for next week," Soupy said, his eyes on Keith. "Cottage succession planning, a hot topic in these parts. That'll be it for the summer, but we'll start up our seminars again in September. I've got six great topics planned for the fall."

The seminar series had been the idea of our former branch manager, but to hear Soupy talk, you'd think he was the one who'd dreamed it up. He and I had come up with those six topics together.

"The seminars have more than doubled our client base," Soupy added.

Keith smiled in approval. I felt like throwing a spoon at our junior advisor. Doubling the client base doesn't mean much when you've started the business from scratch.

"Nice job, son." Keith slapped Soupy on the back. "Shows initiative. I like that. Nate, maybe you can take a lesson from our young friend here."

Beside me, Nate said, "I expect to learn a lot here." His pleasant face gave nothing away, but I detected a trace of sarcasm in his voice.

"You'll make your mark here, Nate. A man with your credentials." Keith looked around the table. "Nate has a master's degree in business administration and an alphabet soup of industry designations."

"Good for him," Soupy mumbled.

The smile never left Nate's face. "I've been looking forward to coming to Braeloch," he said, "and building this business with you. I only wish Pat was on the team."

The last thing I wanted was to play buffer between Nate and Soupy, although it looked like that was what they needed.

"It's been wonderful having you here, Pat," Ivy put in.

"I don't know why you're leaving Norris Cassidy, Pat," Soupy said.

And if I stayed here? I'd be the one you'd be bucking.

"Our company is an industry leader," Soupy added.

"Pat has her own plans," Keith said tersely.

I took my cue from Nate and smiled at the people around the table. Then I reached for my glass and downed the wine in it.

"I hear you're on Black Bear Lake," I said to Nate when the others had turned their attention to their lobster bisque. "We'll be neighbors."

"We've rented a cottage until Labor Day," he said. "That will give my wife a chance to shop for a house. We'd like to be settled in before winter."

"Winter comes early around these parts," Soupy said.

I flashed him a killer look. Nate picked up his knife and calmly buttered the roll on his plate.

"Don't mind Soupy," Ivy said. "He's got the jitters with his wedding coming up. Three more weeks till you tie the knot, eh Soup?"

"Three weeks this coming Saturday. The party will be in this room." Soupy waved a hand to indicate the dining room where we were having lunch.

"Eleanor and I will be here," Keith said. "Wouldn't miss it, son."

I'd been looking forward to the wedding. Now, I wasn't sure I wanted to go.

Keith said goodbye to us in the Winigami parking lot. He shook my hand and gave me a brief nod. "All the best, Pat." Then he walked toward his car.

I watched his retreating back and sighed. Twenty years at Norris Cassidy, and all I got was a club sandwich and a handshake.

Back at the branch, I joined Nate in his office. He grinned as I sat down on the other side of his oversized desk. "What did you make of lunch?" he asked.

I gave a mirthless laugh. "Keith is behind you, and that's all that counts."

"And Soupy?"

I chose my words carefully. "Soupy is green, and he's ambitious."

"A dangerous combination."

I looked at Nate with new respect. "He expected to be made branch manager after Nuala Larkin..." I wasn't sure whether he knew about our former manager's get-rich-quick scheme.

"Was arrested," he said. "Quite a character, wasn't she?"

I nodded. "Soupy didn't get her job. He needs more experience, and not just in investing."

"Seems like he's out to get me."

"It's not you. He wasn't happy when I became interim manager. I didn't let him get away with anything, and he came around. I suggest you do the same."

Nate ran his hands over the big desk. "Do you mind if I switch desks with you?" he asked. "This monstrosity makes me feel like I'm a mile away from the person I'm talking to."

"Not a great way to work with clients," I said. "Sure, make the switch. I'll be at a funeral tomorrow morning so that would be a good time to do it."

We went over two of the accounts I was transferring to him. I was on my way back to my office when Detective Inspector Foster strode down the hall.

"A word, Ms. Tierney."

I stood aside to let him into my office and closed the door. We had met three months before when he was investigating a murder in the township. We'd locked horns several times, but by the end of the investigation we were on fairly good terms. But the look in his eyes now told me I was in his bad books again.

He refused to take a seat. "You're meddling." His gray eyes, behind folds of skin, bored into me like flint.

"How am I meddling?"

"You asked Noreen Andrews at Glencoe Self-Storage for information that is pivotal to our murder investigation. You did the same with Bill Vasey at Monarch Realties."

"Bruce Stohl is my friend," I said. "You've been treating him like a murder suspect."

"Vi Stohl wasn't his mother."

"But she raised him," I said. "She was the only mother he ever knew, and he's shattered by her death."

"Because of her, he never knew his real family."

I was shocked. "You're saying he had it in for Vi because of something she did more than forty years ago? I don't think he's given his real family much thought. I'm certain he didn't kill Vi and—"

"You're trying to find out who did. Stop it, Ms. Tierney. Look after your clients' investments."

I had a question to ask him. "Other than Bruce, there are seventeen people who have cards to the gate at Glencoe Self-Storage. Have you talked to them? Whoever got into the yard on Wednesday night had a functional keycard."

Foster impaled me with a look. "Leave this to us!"

I also wanted to know where I could find Frank Prentice's mother. But the expression on Foster's face told me to save my breath. He left the office, slamming the door behind him.

I pulled a telephone book out of my desk drawer. The Glencoe Highlands directory lists the residents and businesses in area, but there were no listings for Bracebridge. Then I realized that, although it was less than an hour's drive from Braeloch, Bracebridge was in another township, which had its own phone directory.

I turned back to my computer and called up Canada 411. The online phone directory listed five Prentices in Bracebridge—Frank Prentice on Falcon Avenue, Alicia Prentice on Whyte Road, and another three that were listed only by their initials, none of them an E.

I made a printout of the names and numbers and slipped it into the desk drawer. Then I punched in the number at Black Bear Lake.

"I'm about to leave the office," I told Laura when she answered. "Make a salad, and take a casserole out of the freezer."

"Kyle is here," she said.

"What does he want?"

"To see me."

I wondered what else was on his agenda. I wasn't up for an evening of arguments.

"I'll be there in half an hour," I said.

The doors to Soupy and Nate's offices were closed, but Ivy was still at her desk. "Everyone else gone?" I asked her.

"Just the two of us here, Pat."

"You'll lock up?"

"You bet."

I bought a loaf of bread at the bakery on Main Street. I was heading back to the branch for my car when I saw Bruce leave Morrison Funeral Home. I waved and crossed the street.

His face was drawn, and there were dark circles under his eyes. *Is he hitting the bottle?*

"Everything set for tomorrow?" I asked.

He nodded mutely.

"Come out to the lake with me. We'll have dinner, and I'll drive you back to the hotel."

"Not tonight. I'd like to turn in early and be at Morrison's at eight tomorrow."

Vi's service is at ten. You want to say goodbye to her, but for two hours?

"What are you doing about dinner?" I asked.

"Joe's."

I walked down Main Street with him. I'd told Laura I'd be home in thirty minutes, but I didn't care if I was late. I opened the door to Joe's Diner and led the way to my favorite booth.

Sue came over to us, concern written on her face. I smiled at her and asked for a coffee. Bruce ordered a burger and fries.

We sat in silence for a minute or two after Sue left the table. I could only imagine what was going through Bruce's mind.

"I don't know if anyone will be at Morrison's tomorrow," he finally said. "Mom and Ted lived in Toronto for years. When they returned, she went straight into Highland Ridge."

"People will come." I'd attended a funeral in Braeloch a few months before. The deceased had been a reclusive old man, but there was standing room only at the church. Like Vi, he'd been a murder victim.

Bruce looked at me hopefully. "I want to give her a good send-off. Andy Morrison suggested ordering plenty of sandwiches and pastries for the reception."

"Good idea. There'll be lots of people there. How are you doing?"

"Okay," he mumbled. "The police come by the newsroom every day with more questions. More of the same questions, that is."

I hoped he wouldn't collapse under their fire.

"Have you talked to the psychologist you were seeing?"

"No time." He croaked the words out.

"The property you're interested in, have you made an offer?"

"No."

"Go for it. There's no one living there, right?"

"That's right."

"Then you can move right in. Start fixing it up."

A spark flickered in his eyes.

"It'll be gone if you wait. Make an offer."

His shoulders slumped.

"Like me to come with you?" I asked.

He nodded.

"After the funeral." I smiled at him. "Vi would want you to have a home of your own."

Laura and Kyle said little during dinner. I talked about our move to the cottage that coming weekend and what Laura and Tommy could do help. I wasn't sure how long Kyle would be staying, so I didn't include him. I hoped he'd head back to Toronto soon.

Halfway through dessert, Laura pleaded a headache and went up to her room. Tommy took Maxie down to the lake, and Kyle helped me clean up.

"Laura's not taking this seriously," Kyle said as he stacked the dishwasher. "We've got a baby coming. We should get married."

I looked into his troubled brown eyes, and I warmed to him. I had blamed him for getting Laura pregnant, even though my head told me she'd been a more-than-willing participant. It was a natural reaction, I suppose. Mama Bear protecting her child. But now I saw that he wanted to shoulder his responsibilities. He wanted to do what he thought was right.

"What do your parents think?"

"They said we should have waited till we'd finished school and had jobs. But they're excited about the baby. They wanted to have three or four children, and I was all they got. They want me and Laura to get married."

"That's a big step to take."

He slammed the dishwasher door shut and swept his shoulder-length brown hair back from his face. "And having a baby isn't? Bringing a child into the world seems to me to be the biggest step ever. You're responsible for that little guy for the next, what, eighteen years?"

"Longer than that," I said. "But you can be responsible parents without being married. I'd say your first priority is to get a good education so you can support your child. Laura will be at university next year, too."

His face was troubled. "Do you think she...she doesn't want me?"

That was why he wanted to get married. He thought marriage would cement their relationship. He was naïve, but I felt his pain.

"Laura doesn't know what she wants right now," I said, "other than the baby she's carrying. That's what she's focused on. She's afraid to make any more changes in her life."

As soon as the words were out of my mouth, I knew I'd hit the nail on the head. Laura's world had changed dramatically, and she was afraid of everything that lay ahead of her. Kyle had to stop pushing her.

"But what about me?" His worried eyes searched my face. "Does she want me, Mrs. T?"

I took him by the shoulders and gave him a hug. "I'm counting on you to be strong, Kyle. Try to understand where Laura is at right now. Be there for her, but don't push her."

I held him at arm's length and locked eyes with him. "Whatever happens between you and my daughter, you are the father of this child. Laura wants you to be part of his—or her—life."

They had the best intentions of being good parents, but Laura and Kyle would need help for a few years, maybe for several. Like it or not, I was one of the people they would count on.

CHAPTER SEVEN

I spent an hour with Nate the next morning. I liked his questions. He wanted to know everything I could tell him about the Glencoe Highlands and how Norris Cassidy could serve its residents.

At nine forty-five, I headed across the street to Morrison Funeral Home. The chapel was packed.

My friend, Sister Celia de Franco, waved at me from the second row where she had saved me a seat. Laura was seated beside her. I'd had no idea that my daughter planned to come to the service. I raised my eyebrows, and Laura gave me a sunny smile. "Needed a change of scene," she said.

"Tommy?" I asked.

"Tommy and Kyle went fishing in the motorboat. Kyle brought rods and tackle from the city.

When Tommy had asked about fishing the day before, Laura told him she'd rather watch paint dry. Getting him a fishing rod had been on the top of my to-do list.

I turned to Celia, who'd come down from North Bay, a two-hour drive north of Braeloch, where she was a chaplain at the psychiatric hospital. She and Bruce had worked at Braeloch's Catholic church that winter, and she'd kept in touch with him after she left town. "Another murder in God's country," she whispered after we'd exchanged hugs.

We sat quietly for a few minutes, contemplating the marble urn and the framed photo of Vi on a table at the front of the room. The photographer had caught her at a happy moment, her face lit up with a smile. She looked to be in her early forties.

I glanced around the chapel. The only people I could think of who might have wanted to harm Vi were Bruce's biological parents. They were both dead, so someone else had had it in for her. But who?

A silver-haired woman dressed in a long black skirt and a white blouse sat down at the electric organ. To her right were two straight-backed chairs, an acoustic guitar leaning against one, and two microphones on stands. She frowned at the setup before launching into Bach's "Jesu, Joy of Man's Desiring."

"She's not used to sharing the spotlight," I murmured.

Celia flashed me a grin.

When the hymn ended, a side door opened and Soupy and Mara Nowak stepped out. They were both dressed in black.

Celia groaned. "The High Lonesome Wailers? Here?"

The Wailers, Soupy's band, played everything from Bob Marley to Hank Williams at dances, benefits, and stag parties. But I'd never heard of them playing at a funeral.

There was a low buzz in the chapel as Soupy and Mara sat and adjusted their microphones. Soupy strummed his guitar as Mara began to sing Vera Lynn's wartime hit "We'll Meet Again." The congregation was silent at first then began to hum along with her.

"Hardly a dry eye in the house," Celia said as the final notes died down.

Bruce entered by the side door, accompanied by a fair-haired man I recognized as Andy Morrison, the funeral director's son. Bruce wore the dark gray suit he'd bought for Ted's funeral. His face was haggard, and I saw him take a deep breath as he looked at the large crowd. He walked slowly over to the table that held the urn and the photograph and placed a white rose in front of Vi's photo. Then he took a seat in the front row.

Andy went up to the podium, gave a brief summary of Vi's life, and called up Lainey Campbell. Soupy's mother had been Vi's close friend when they were young, and she shared a few stories about Vi as a teenager.

"After high school, Vi took a job at the Highlands Savings Bank here in Braeloch," she said. "Not long after that, she met Ted Stohl, a rookie reporter at *The Highland Times*. They were married the next summer."

Lainey faltered and looked down at her notes. She was probably thinking about the early years of the Stohls' marriage, and their infant son. I was relieved when she lifted her head and went on.

"When I heard that Vi and Ted were returning to Braeloch, I looked forward to seeing my friend again." Her voice caught. "Sadly, it wasn't the reunion I'd hoped it would be. Vi had retreated into her own world, and we never caught up with each other. But I'll always treasure my memories of my girlhood friend."

Lainey's husband, Burt, was up next. Like his wife, he'd gone to school with Vi. "In Grade 8, Vi and I were neck-and-neck contenders in Glencoe Highlands Spells, the township's big spelling bee. The winner went on to the provincial contest, and I was hell-bent on representing the Highlands in Toronto that year. But pretty little Vi pulled the carpet from under me with the word *chameleon*—I forgot the *h*. After that, I always called her Chameleon. She pretended she hated it, but it was my way of reminding her that she was a champ."

Several people around us chuckled. "I'm next," Celia whispered and glanced at the sheet of paper she held. "Oh, dear."

Before I could see what had upset her, she was called to the podium.

"A reading from the book of Ecclesiastes." Celia cleared her throat and continued. "There is an appointed time for everything, a time for every affair under the heavens. A time to be born, a time to die…"

I recognized the words as the lyrics of "Turn! Turn! Turn!", a golden oldie when I was growing up. I hadn't realized it had been adapted from Scripture.

After the reading, Celia spoke of Vi's devotion to Bruce, followed by a prayer for the repose of her soul.

"O God, who hast commanded us to honor our father and our mother, in Thy mercy have pity on the soul of this mother, Violet, forgive her her trespasses, and when his hour comes, have her son, Bruce, reunited with her in the joy of everlasting brightness. Through Christ our Lord, Amen."

"What a choice," Celia whispered when she returned to her seat. "'Forgive her her trespasses?' We're commemorating Vi here, not recounting her sins. What's wrong with Psalm 23?"

"Which one is that?" I asked.

"You know, 'The Lord is my shepherd…'"

"Let it go," I said. "It's Bruce's way of mourning his mother."

Andy returned to the podium. "Bruce invites you for refreshments in our lounge upstairs. But before we leave the chapel, please join Soupy and Mara in one of Vi's favorite songs, 'Amazing Grace'."

Celia smiled. "That's more like it."

As the hymn ended, an attendant opened the double doors at the back of the chapel, and the organist struck up "Over the Rainbow." She didn't look happy about being upstaged by Soupy and Mara.

We stayed in our seats as people filed out of the chapel. "You're looking lovely, my dear," Celia said to Laura. "Positively radiant."

Laura's pregnancy wasn't showing yet, but her skin was glowing and her fair hair was thick and glossy.

"I'm three months' pregnant," she said, looking pleased with herself.

Celia blinked, but showed no other sign of surprise. "A new life is always a blessing." She turned to me. "You'll be a grandmother, Pat."

I could have given her an earful. Instead I said, "Around Christmas, I've been told."

Celia put an arm around Laura. "Fine time of year for a child to be born." Then she turned to me. "Bruce looks badly shaken."

"He's lost his mother and the police are questioning him," I said. "He was alone in *The Times* newsroom when Vi went missing at Highland Ridge. And he comes into her share of Ted's estate."

"So he's a suspect." There was worry in her eyes. "Will he hold up under the stress? I hope he hasn't started drinking again."

I pictured Bruce's haggard face. "He was doing well until this happened. He seemed happy at *The Times*, and he was looking to buy his own home. But now..."

She nodded. "I'll talk to him."

She hurried to the side door that Bruce and Andy had taken. Laura and I left the chapel by the main doors and took the stairs to the second floor.

Foster approached us as soon as we entered the lounge. "Well, Ms. Tierney, another funeral."

"They're customary when someone dies," I said. "And when the cause of death is murder, the investigating officer attends."

The hint of a smile crinkled the skin around his eyes, but it vanished when Bruce and Celia came into the room. "Excuse me," he said.

I felt a flash of irritation as he approached them. *Can't he leave Bruce alone on the day of his mother's funeral?*

Laura and I joined the queue at the buffet table. The red-haired woman in front of us turned around. "Did you know Vi Stohl?" she asked us.

"We didn't know her," I said, "but her son's a friend."

"We found her." She inclined her head toward the dark-haired man at her side.

"Found her?" Laura asked.

"Rolled up in a rug in the storage locker," the man said.

"I'm Crystal King," the woman said, "and this is Jock Deighton, my guy."

Before I could introduce myself and Laura, Crystal launched into the story of how they'd purchased the locker's contents and found Vi's body. "Creepiest thing that ever happened to me. We find all kinds of things in storage lockers, but I never thought—"

"Been following it on the news," Jock put in. "Thought we'd come up here and pay our respects."

"We haven't got the goods we bought yet," Crystal grumbled. "Paid $900 and the cops are still holding onto them."

"It's been less than a week," I said. "The police will probably turn them over to you soon."

When we'd filled our plates, Jock invited us to join them at a table. I couldn't think of an excuse to refuse. "We'd like to pay our respects to Mrs. Stohl's son," he said when we were seated. "You said he's a friend of yours."

"We heard he runs the newspaper here," Crystal said. "Maybe he could do an article on how we found his mother. And mention our shop in Newmarket."

Jock placed a hand on hers. "Not the time for that, babe."

I jumped in to stop her. "Bruce isn't working today. You saw how shaken he was at the service."

"Bruce is the guy who put the flower on the table?" Crystal asked.

"Let him have the rest of the day to remember his mother," I said.

But my heart sank as I saw Celia and Bruce heading in our direction. "May we join you?" Celia asked.

I nodded, and Bruce sat down beside me. "I'll get some sandwiches," Celia said and went over to the buffet.

I introduced Bruce to Crystal and Jock, and hoped for the best.

"We bought the contents of the locker where your mom was found," Crystal announced to Bruce.

There was no stopping her. "Jock picked up a rolled-up rug, and a body fell out of it. Scared me out of my boots!"

Jock gripped her wrist. "We're real sorry for your loss, Mr. Stohl."

Bruce had turned pale, and a film of sweat glistened on his upper lip.

"You'll have to excuse us," I said. "Bruce isn't feeling well." I rose from my seat, and motioned for Bruce to get up, too.

We met Celia coming toward us with two plates in her hands. "We need to get Bruce away from those two," I whispered to her.

"We'll sit with the Campbells." She led us to the table where Soupy and his parents were eating.

"Bruce," Lainey said, "that was a lovely service."

As Bruce sat down with the Campbells, Foster approached Celia and took her aside. *What does he want with her?*

I returned to Laura, Crystal, and Jock. "You upset Bruce," I said as I sat down.

"Crystal sometimes gets carried away," Jock said.

She scowled at him and turned to me. "Laura was telling us that the locker was rented by a Frank Prentice."

I nudged Laura's leg with my foot. "Ever heard of him?" I asked Crystal and Jock.

They both shook their heads. "We don't know nobody in these parts," Jock said. "Thursday was the first time we been up here. We saw the auction advertised on a newsletter we subscribe to, and Crystal thought we might find some farm antiques. From now on, we'll keep to the south of the province."

"We'll go where the money is, big boy," Crystal said.

"Frank Prentice is dead," Laura said.

Crystal and Jock looked surprised, but I watched them carefully.

"That's why he wasn't payin' the rent," Jock said.

"Any connection to Vi being killed?" Crystal asked.

"Frank didn't kill her, if that's what you mean," Laura said. "He died eight weeks ago, but we don't know how he died."

I gave her a harder kick under the table. Crystal and Jock didn't need to know all this. "You went through some of the locker's contents before you found the body," I said to them. "What was in there?"

"Christmas decorations, old photos, tablecloths, doilies," Jock said. "Really disappointing."

"There was a box of old comic books that might be worth something," Crystal said. "I hope the police will let us take it back with us."

"I wouldn't count on it, babe."

Just then Foster joined us. "I'd like a word with Ms. King and Mr. Deighton," he said. "A private word."

"You think they killed Vi?" Laura asked as we crossed the room.

"No. They paid nine hundred dollars for the contents of the locker. They wouldn't have done that if they'd put her in there."

"Maybe the murderer wanted the body to be found."

That was something I hadn't thought of. I was pondering that possibility when I felt a hand on my shoulder. I turned to see Celia beside me.

"I'd like to spend the day with Bruce and hear about Laura's plans," she said, "but I have to get back to North Bay. I'll come down for a weekend later in the summer."

"Where is Bruce?" I asked.

"Over there." She pointed to the doorway where he was talking to a small group of people. I recognized George Packard, *The Times'* business manager.

I looked at the table where the Campbells had been sitting, but they were gone. A lot of people had left. Their curiosity more or less satisfied, they'd gone back to their routines.

"Let's hang with Bruce today," Laura said to me. "You don't have to go into work. The branch has a new manager."

It was a good idea. Bruce would have company, and Laura could focus on something other than her problems. And Nate didn't really need my help to look over his new accounts. "I'll have a quick word with Nate," I said. "I'll meet you and Bruce here in 20 minutes."

I gave Celia a hug. "What did Foster want?"

"He asked what I was doing last Wednesday afternoon." She grinned. "Told him I was tied up with the criminally insane."

Nate was in his office with a prospective client. "Her name's Tess Watson," Ivy told me.

"Missed her by a whisker," Soupy said with a frown on his face. "Got back here moments after Nate lured her into his den."

"You and Nate are on the same team," I said. "If Ms. Watson brings us her business, she'll probably spread the word. Her family and friends may become your clients."

Soupy shrugged. "Meanwhile, Nate pockets commissions on everything he sells her."

I'd had enough. "Soupy, you're twenty-eight years old and about to get married. Will you start acting like a professional?"

His nostrils flaring, he turned and stalked down the hall to his office.

Ivy gave me a "what can you do?" look. I scribbled a note for Nate and handed it to her.

Bruce and Laura were waiting in Morrison's lobby. Bruce looked better than he had at the service. Chatting with people had done him good. Over the past few months, he'd made friends in the township, although no one had thought of keeping him company that day.

"Why don't we check out that property you're interested in?" I said brightly.

He nodded, but without much enthusiasm.

"Rosso Realty has the listing?" I asked him.

"Yup," he said. "It's on Raven Lake."

"Let's see if your dream home is still on the market."

Laura took his arm. "Raven Lake, that's a cool name. I love that poem where the raven keeps saying, 'Nevermore'."

"Edgar Allen Poe's 'The Raven'," Bruce said.

Laura smiled at him. "Awesome."

I followed them down Main Street, amused by Laura's sudden interest in helping Bruce. Kyle had probably forgotten my advice and was pushing marriage again. Pushing Laura away.

CHAPTER EIGHT

Rosso Realty operated out of a storefront between Danny's Butcher Shop and Braeloch Bread and Buns. A young woman with a punk hairdo was seated behind a desk in the small office. "I couldn't get to your mom's funeral," she said to Bruce. "I'm real sorry for your loss."

He acknowledged her condolence with a bob of his head. Then he introduced us to Amy Perkins. "I'd like to show them the Raven Lake property," he added.

"A great place," she said. "A family in Toronto is coming up to see it on Saturday."

It was the oldest sales trick in the book, but Bruce swallowed it. "D'you think we could go over now?" He sounded worried.

Amy looked at her watch. "My colleague will be here in fifteen minutes. I'll drive you over then."

"Bruce, why don't you change into something more comfortable?" I said. "We'll meet you here in fifteen."

Bruce left for the hotel, and I turned to Amy. "Why is the owner selling?"

"She's a retired teacher who's spent summers at the cabin for years. She now finds it's become too much work for her."

Laura and I went into the bakery next door. We took the bagels we bought over to the Volvo. Bruce was back at Rosso Realty when we returned, dressed in jeans and a short-sleeved shirt.

Amy took us to the gray minivan she'd parked on Main Street. On the drive to the lake, she delivered her sales pitch. I tuned her out and took in the countryside from the window beside me. Laura stuffed her iBuds into her ears.

Ten minutes down the highway, we pulled onto a side road. A mile or so down that, we turned into a lane. "The roads are plowed all winter, but you'd have to clear this lane yourself," Amy said. "A snow blower would do the job."

"This place is heaven," Laura said as we pulled up in front of a log house that overlooked a sparkling blue lake.

"Neighbors on both sides, permanent residents on the south side," Amy said. "You can't see their homes now with the trees in leaf."

It was a great location. On one of the prime lakes in the township. A fifteen-minute drive into town. Privacy, but with people nearby.

The cabin itself was a fixer-upper. Two small bedrooms, a small living and dining room, and a tiny kitchen. The windows were small, which made the interior dark on that sunny afternoon. The cabin's best feature was a fieldstone fireplace that took up an entire living room wall.

Bruce ran a hand over the fireplace stones. The haggardness had left his face, and his eyes looked dreamy.

"Is the furniture included?" I asked Amy.

"All included. The owner has taken the items she wanted. What you see is what you get."

The furnishings weren't fancy. An old leather sofa, a wooden table and four chairs, beds and battered dressers in the two bedrooms. But they would suit Bruce just fine. He didn't want Ted's furniture.

"How is the house heated?" I asked Amy.

"There's the fireplace," she said, "and a wood-burning stove in the kitchen."

"You can't stay here in the winter," I told Bruce.

"Maybe not this winter," he said, looking out the window at the lake, "but I can have the crawl space under the house dug out and a furnace put in."

I was about to point out how expensive that would be, but one glance at him stopped me. He looked relaxed, content, at home. And he would come into considerable money when Ted's estate was settled. He could probably afford a home in town, and this place for the summer.

"It's a great place, Bruce," Laura said. "You can fix it up as you go. Are you good at that?"

"I can do a fair bit. What I can't, I'll pay to have done over time."

"This place is a steal," Amy put in. "It's on a great lake, and it will only increase in value."

"I'll repair the chinking between the logs this summer," Bruce said. "Mice have got in. I saw droppings in the cupboard under the sink."

I winced, wondering what the mice situation was like at the cottage I'd rented.

"Nothing a few mousetraps won't fix," Amy said.

We stopped at the top of a steep flight of stone steps to look at Raven Lake, which was dotted with white sails that afternoon. Bruce led us down the steps to a pebble beach.

"You gotta buy this place, Bruce!" Laura cried.

Amy beamed at her.

"I'll need a canoe," Bruce said.

"And a raft," Laura added.

He'd clearly made up his mind, and his happy face swept away any doubts that I had. When Amy headed up the steps, I took him aside. "Come to a decision?"

"I'm going to make an offer when we get back to town." He told me the price at which the property was listed. It sounded reasonable, but I suggested he come in a little under that.

"And make your offer contingent on a professional property inspection," I added. "You need to know what you're up against. Faulty wiring, a bad septic system, who knows what there might be."

"I don't want to lose out to that family in Toronto."

"I'm sure an inspection can be done before the weekend."

Bruce made his offer back at Rosso Realty's office with Laura and me along for moral support.

Amy called the owner and left a message. "I'll try her later, or she may get back to me first," she said to Bruce. "If she accepts your offer, you should be able to get an inspection done tomorrow or Thursday."

"I could move in on the weekend," Bruce said.

"If you're satisfied with the inspection." I turned to Amy. "Who is the owner?"

She glanced at the document on her desk. "Tess Watson. She lives here in Braeloch."

The woman who came into the branch that afternoon. She'd have a sizable sum of money to invest with the sale of her cabin. I hoped Nate had sold her on Norris Cassidy.

Outside, I turned to Bruce. "I hope you're not going to work today."

He smiled. "Maria and George ordered me to take the day off."

"Would you give me a hand for an hour or two? I have the key to the cottage I've rented. I'd like to take a few things over today."

I wanted to keep him busy. I'd packed up everything we wouldn't need in the next few days. It would take an hour or so to bring the boxes to the cottage on the other side of the lake. Then Bruce could join us for an early dinner.

"No problem. I'll be over in about thirty minutes." He gave us a salute and walked down Main Street toward the Dominion Hotel.

Laura glared at me. "Back to Black Bear? I'll go for a drive."

"Not today," I said. "I want you to keep Bruce company."

A black sports car was parked in front of the house. I heard the door of Laura's Hyundai slam shut behind me. Moments later, she was standing beside my car window. I rolled it down.

"Whose Ferrari is that?" I asked.

"Kyle's mother's." Laura groaned. "This should be fun."

Kyle opened the front door of the house. Maxie ran out, barking loudly, with Tommy behind her.

I took a dog leash from the glove compartment, and thrust it at Laura. "Take Tommy and Maxie for a walk."

They'd vanished around the side of the house when a couple joined Kyle at the door. I'd met Yvonne Shingler on a handful of occasions. The attractive brunette was turned out in a turquoise sundress that probably had a designer label. I assumed the ruddy-faced man behind her was her husband.

She took a few steps toward me. "Lovely place, Pat." She turned to include the man. "My husband, Russell. Russ, this is Pat Tierney, Laura's mother."

"Where did Laura go?" Kyle asked.

"She and Tommy took Maxie for a walk."

"I hope she won't be long," Yvonne said. "We drove up here to talk to both of you."

I moved toward the door. "You can start with me."

Inside the house, I led the way to the living room. "Something to drink?" I asked.

"Water, please," Yvonne said. "Bottled. You can't be too careful about water out in the country."

I got bottles of Evian water for the Shinglers and took a seat on the sofa in front of the fireplace.

"We're going to be grandparents, Pat," Yvonne said, sitting down beside me. "We need to get the kids settled. In a nice condominium, Russell and I thought."

She looked up at her husband, who was standing beside his son. Russell held up his hands in a gesture of helplessness.

"And we need to nail down the wedding plans," she went on. "A small, tasteful wedding. Around fifty people. A short ceremony followed by a luncheon."

I gave them a smile. "This is the first I've heard about a wedding."

"We've been talking about getting married for weeks," Kyle said.

"I understand that *you've* been talking about getting married," I said to him.

Yvonne put a hand on mine. "I know they're young, Pat, but young people can make a go of it. I was just twenty when I married Russell."

From what I'd gathered from Laura, Yvonne had never earned a penny in her life although her clubs and charitable causes kept her constantly on the go. But I hadn't brought my girls up in that lifestyle. I wanted them to have careers and be able to pull their own weight.

I heard a car door slam outside. The front door opened and Laura, Bruce, Tommy, and Maxie trooped into the house.

"Laura!" Yvonne cried. "How are you feeling, my dear? Morning sickness over?"

"Hi, Mrs. Shingler. Mr. Shingler." Laura introduced them to Tommy and Bruce.

Tommy came over to me. I put an arm around him. "Heard you went fishing," I whispered.

His brown eyes sparkled. "Kyle put a worm on my hook, but a fish took it off."

"Your mother and I have been talking about the wedding," Yvonne said to Laura.

Laura looked gobsmacked. "Mom?"

I held up a hand. "Laura has something to say to you, Yvonne."

Bruce headed for the door. "I'll be outside."

"Young lady, you're going to be a mother in, what, six months?" Yvonne's voice had climbed an octave. "Of course, you're going to get married. And you couldn't do better than Kyle. He's a kind, generous boy who's going places and will take good care of you. One day, he'll run his father's company."

"Kyle's cool," Laura said, "but I don't want to get married yet…to anyone. Not till I finish school and have a good job. I don't want to be taken care of."

"You and Kyle need to be settled before the baby comes," Yvonne went on as if Laura hadn't spoken. "Russell and I have been looking at condominiums in Guelph, and we found one you'd like. It's close to the university so Kyle won't have to spend a lot of time commuting."

"Mrs. Shingler." Laura's voice was strong and decisive. "I'll be living with my mother in Toronto for the next few years. I'll take this year off and start university next fall."

"So, you see, everything's settled," I said.

Yvonne stared at us, her mouth open. "Now, just a minute! Everything is not settled. In fact—"

"So what can I pack, Mom?" Laura asked.

"You'll have to excuse us," I said to Yvonne and Russell. "We're moving. We're taking clothes and books over to our new place right now."

Yvonne was still fuming, but she recovered her composure as she stood up. "I'll call you in a few days, Pat. When you've had time to think about what Russell and I have said." With that, she turned on her heel.

Russell and Kyle followed her out of the house.

Laura rolled her eyes. "'What Russell and I have said!' Russell doesn't say a word when she's around. Neither does Kyle."

We went to the front window. Russell was seated in the Ferrari. On the driveway, Yvonne was saying something to her son. Kyle listened in silence, his head bowed.

"I told you," Laura said.

We piled suitcases and boxes into Bruce's Chevy and my Volvo. I asked Kyle to stay behind with Maxie.

"Pretty small place," Laura said when I pulled up in front of the gray clapboard cottage that I'd rented from Maria and Ross Dawson.

Tommy raced through it, inspecting every nook and cranny. I followed him upstairs. "This room's mine!" he said, standing in the doorway of the smallest bedroom. I peeked in and saw a large, framed *Star Wars* poster on the wall.

I ruffled his hair. "Good choice, Tommy."

The cottage didn't impress Laura. "Pokey," she said. "And I assume there's no internet here."

"There's no internet tower on Black Bear Lake," I replied, "but we have three bedrooms and a great screened porch. We'll spend most of our time out there."

There were also plenty of windows that opened to let in the breeze from the lake. And I didn't see any signs of mice.

I hung up my clothes in the bedroom that faced the lake. It had twin beds so Tommy could bunk in with me when we had a guest. From the window, I spotted a shed near the waterfront that I hadn't looked into on my previous visit. Laura and Tommy followed me out to it.

The shed door was locked, but one of the keys on the chain Maria had given me opened it. Inside, a red kayak on foam blocks took up most of the space.

"A kayak!" Tommy said.

"Paddle's on the wall." Laura pointed to a wooden paddle resting on two metal brackets.

I made a mental note to ask the Dawsons if we could use the kayak.

"Can I go fishing in it?" Tommy asked.

"We'll need a two-person boat for fishing," I said. "We can rent a rowboat."

As we walked back to the house, I saw houses through the trees on both sides of the property. I wondered where on the lake Nate and his wife were staying.

Dinner was tense that evening. Laura was still keeping her distance from Kyle, and they ate in silence. She seemed to have forgotten her intention of spending the day with Bruce.

Fortunately, the cabin he'd made an offer on was at the top of Bruce's mind. "I'll move in as soon as the sale goes through," he said.

Tommy couldn't wait to move across the lake. "D'you think there's fish over there?" he asked.

"It's the same lake that we're on here," I said. "Same fish, I expect."

After we'd finished eating, Bruce and Kyle took Tommy for a ride in the motorboat.

"Yvonne won't rest till Kyle and I are married," Laura said as we tidied up the kitchen. "She has to have everything her way."

Another reason not to marry Kyle.

"I never realized till today that she's the one who's been pushing marriage," Laura said.

"She's afraid she won't be part of her grandchild's life. You need to tell her that won't be the case."

Fifteen minutes later, everything was in order and Laura retired to her room. Bruce opened the sliding doors and came into the house. "Thought I'd give Amy a call. She can't reach me on my cell out here."

I pointed to the phone beside the sofa and left him to make his call.

"I'm a property owner," he said when I returned with two mugs of tea. "Or I will be if the bank approves my mortgage."

I handed him a mug and sat down beside him. "Congratulations. Don't forget to arrange a property inspection."

"Amy is setting one up." The anxiety lines had returned to his face. "It's been quite the day. I said goodbye to Mom and bought myself a home. Six months ago, who'd have thought I'd be a newspaperman and a homeowner?"

He gave a hollow chuckle. "And a suspect in a murder investigation. My life's been full of ups and downs. Learning about my parents was a turning point."

I looked at him closely. He'd never spoken to me about his real parents.

"By some miracle," he said, "I bumped into Soupy the night I found out about my other family, and we spent hours talking. Actually I did the talking, and he listened. No opinions, no advice, just a solid presence."

Soupy had been a good friend when Bruce needed him.

"I didn't sleep much that night, and when I did I had weird dreams," Bruce went on. "The next morning, I resolved to get myself together. Soupy had told me about Dr. Reynolds, a relative of his. I called him, made an appointment, and Soupy's dad lent me his spare car. I started seeing Reynolds once a week, and he gave me a letter asking my family doctor to get me on Prozac. Well, I didn't have a family doc, but I took it to Mom's doctor and he gave me a prescription." He paused. "Hope you don't mind me unloading on you like this."

Bruce was usually a man of few words. He'd said more in the past few minutes than I'd ever heard him say at one time. "Go on," I told him.

He looked down at his hands and spread his fingers. "I'd been depressed for years, suicidal on a few occasions, but Reynolds said I'm not manic or psychotic." He looked up at me with a sad smile.

Suicidal? My head was spinning.

"Ted's death freed me to become myself," he continued. "I wanted his love, I couldn't understand why he was cold to me. It finally made sense when I found out I wasn't his real son. He must've thought I was a poor replacement for the boy who'd died."

He gave another hollow laugh. "I survived both my families, and I've managed to turn my life around."

But he didn't look at all happy. He had also survived Vi, who he'd loved. I thought of the log cabin above Raven Lake and how happy he had looked there. The sooner he made it his home, the better.

CHAPTER NINE

The next morning, I decided to find out how long Kyle would be with us. "Laura told me you have a summer job," I said. "When does it start?"

"Next Tuesday."

Does that mean you'll be here for the next six days?

"I'm working at Dad's company," he said. "I could ask for the whole week off."

"Kyle, remember what we talked about. Laura is overwhelmed by what's ahead of her."

"I'll help her get through it."

"Let her have some time to chill. She'll be back in Toronto in two weeks. You'll see plenty of her this summer."

He looked at me mournfully. "Does that mean you're asking me to leave?"

"I'd like you to give Laura some space. She needs a breather before she starts her job."

He lowered his eyes. "When do you want me to go?"

"Today would be best. Talk to Laura when she comes down for breakfast. Keep it upbeat, and she'll have happy thoughts of you when you're in the city."

I smiled ruefully as I headed out to the Volvo. I never thought I'd be counselling couples.

I spent an hour with Nate. Then I went into my office, closed the door, and sat down at the huge mahogany desk that took up almost the entire room. I starting dialing the numbers I'd found on Canada 411. As Noreen had said, the late Frank Prentice's phone had been disconnected. I reached voicemail at two of the numbers, but I didn't leave messages.

A third was answered by a young man who said he thought Frank was "a cousin or something," but that I should talk to his mother when she got home. Alicia Prentice said she was a distant cousin of Frank's. I asked her how I could reach Frank's mother.

"Last I heard, Ella lived in Barrie," she said, naming a city north of Toronto.

"Do you have her phone number?"

"I haven't seen her in years. She never took to our family."

"You don't have her phone number?" I persisted. "Or an address?"

"Afraid not."

"Would she be listed in the phone directory? Or would the listing be under her husband's name?"

"Ella's a widow, or she was the last I heard of her. She might be listed as Eleanora Prentice. Ella is short for Eleanora."

I scribbled Eleanora in the notepad on my desk then tried another question. "Did you see much of Frank? He lived in Bracebridge."

"I saw him around town from time to time, and we said hello. But as I said, we're distant cousins—our fathers were first cousins—and we didn't see much of each other when we were growing up. I only found out he'd died when *The Examiner* ran an article about his motorcycle accident."

I'd learned two things from Alicia: where Ella lived, and how Frank had died.

I called up Canada 411 and searched for listings of Ella, Eleanora, or E Prentice in Barrie. Nothing came up for any of those combinations.

A search for Frank Prentice on *The Bracebridge Examiner*'s website brought up an article dated April 20. Eight weeks earlier, around the time his house went up for sale.

A color photo of a tanned, smiling man astride a massive motorcycle accompanied the article. He was squinting against the glare of the sun.

Two weeks before the article ran, Francisco Prentice had taken his Harley-Davidson Road King for a weekend spin through Ontario lake country. He was on his way back to Bracebridge on a Sunday afternoon when he skidded on a patch of oil on the highway south of Algonquin Park. He lost control of the machine and was thrown over the handlebars. He had died before an ambulance could get to him.

I skimmed the paragraphs about Frank's volunteer work with the Boys and Girls Clubs of Canada and Habitat for Humanity, and read the tributes from his friends more carefully. One of them said Frank "loved the Toronto Blue Jays, the Boston Bruins, good food, and the stray cats that found their way into his life." He sounded like a nice guy.

The last paragraph said he was survived by his mother, Ella Prentice, of Newmarket, Ontario. Newmarket, another city north of Toronto. Not Barrie.

Canada 411 gave me Ella Prentice's address in Newmarket. It provided a map of her neighborhood and a link to driving directions. I made printouts of both.

I spent the rest of the morning with Nate. Laura called around noon, saying that Kyle had left for the city. "Thank you, God!" she added.

Ivy was up to her elbows at the photocopy machine in the kitchenette, so I scribbled a note and propped it against her computer screen. I left the building by the back door.

Ella had been a beauty in her prime, and she was still an attractive woman in her early sixties. The tiny Filipina's colored and coiffed hair, her buffed skin, and her toned body told me she did her share to keep the beauty industry running.

She sized me up with shrewd eyes as I rattled off the reason for my visit at her front door. "The real estate agent said you wanted to speak to me," she said.

But she hadn't bothered to contact me.

"You knew the woman they found in Frank's locker?" she asked.

"No, I didn't, but her son is a friend of mine. I'm trying to help him."

She pursed her lips and held the door open. "Come in."

I follower her trim, Spandex-clad figure to a room at the back of her bungalow where an exercise bike and a treadmill looked out on a lush garden. We went through a set of sliding doors onto a shady deck. She took a chair at a round table and pointed to another.

"I'm sorry about your son's passing," I said when I was seated.

A flash of pain crossed her face. "How can you be sorry? You didn't know Frank."

"You're right, I didn't know him. But I'm sorry for your loss."

She gave me a curt nod, took two glasses off a trolley, and filled them from the jug on the table. "Iced tea. No sugar."

"Thank you." I took a sip from the glass. The tea was strong and tart with plenty of lemon. I gulped down half the contents of the glass.

Ella sipped her tea, clearly waiting to hear more from me.

"Vi Stohl lived in a nursing home in Braeloch. She suffered from dementia," I said. "It's a mystery why she was strangled, and why her body was put in a locker outside of town."

"Well, Frank didn't put her there. That's what I told the police."

"No, he didn't. He died in April, and Vi was killed last week. Did you check out his locker?"

"I haven't been to Braeloch in years. And I didn't know he had a storage locker up there until the police told me last week."

"Frank lived in Bracebridge. Why did he rent a locker that was miles away from his home, in another township?"

She took a deep breath. "He told me he'd been given some furniture that belonged to Carrie, his grandmother, after she died, but he didn't say what he did with it. Carrie lived in Braeloch. That must've been why he stored it there."

Noreen had mailed reminders to Frank when he'd missed his payments, and a final notice about the auction. Ella must have seen them.

"You didn't find a rental contract for the locker in his house?"

"I went through all Frank's stuff. I'm his beneficiary." Her voice was frosty. "There was nothing about a locker."

"Glencoe Self-Storage mailed reminders to Frank when he missed two payments. And a notice that the locker's contents would be auctioned on June 21. You didn't come across them?"

"I just told you, no." She rose from her chair. "You'd better leave now. My personal trainer will be here any minute."

On the way front door, I tried one more question. "Did Frank have a girlfriend?" The article in *The Examiner* hadn't mentioned a wife, and Ella had said she was Frank's beneficiary.

"Frank always had some babe on his arm, but would he settle down? Give me grandchildren? No!" She didn't look happy about that.

"Did any of his friends have keys to his house?"

"Ms. Tierney, the only people who have been in Frank's house in the past two months are real estate agents. And the people they've showed it to."

"Anyone go through it before you put it up for sale?"

She opened her mouth to say something then looked down at her polished fingernails. "I had a woman in to clean before it went on the market, but I'd removed anything important by then."

"I don't know why you didn't receive the notice about the auction."

"Goodbye, Ms. Tierney."

My mind was clicking as I drove into Toronto. Ella must have found the rental contract, the key, and the keycard in her son's home. And she would have seen the notices of the missed payments. Surely she would have wanted to see what was in the locker.

I left the Don Valley Parkway at the Eglinton Avenue turnoff. Ten minutes later, I was parked on a residential street behind my favorite bistro. It was just after five, and there were still tables available at

Milo's. I claimed my usual spot at the bay window and sat down to wait
for my daughter.

When Tracy arrived, a few heads turned to look at her. A pretty girl,
she looked especially attractive in a pale yellow suit with her wavy
brown hair held back from her face with combs.

She gave me a big hug. "Jamie sends her love. She's working late
tonight."

She sat down across from me and slipped off her jacket. "How's
Laura?"

"I was the last to know."

"Parents usually are. It goes with the territory." She took my hand in
hers. "I'm sure your parents were the last to know some of the things you
were up to."

I gave her a wobbly smile. "She's decided not to go to Guelph this
fall. She and the baby will live with me, and she'll go to the University
of Toronto next year."

"Kyle still pushing marriage?"

"Oh, yes. Along with his mother."

"I hope Laura doesn't cave in. The last thing she and Kyle should
do is get married."

"Laura has other options," I said. "A place to live—"

"And someone to help raise her child. But what about you, Mom?
You took Tommy in few months ago, and now you'll be raising a
grandchild."

"I intend to make Laura independent. She'll get an education that
will hopefully lead to a good job."

"It's still a lot for you to take on."

Tell me about it!

The waitress handed us menus, and I ordered a bottle of wine.

"Fill me in on the woman who was murdered in Braeloch," Tracy
said when we'd studied the menus. Her eyes were twinkling. "Are you
playing detective again?"

"Vi Stohl was Bruce's mother. No one knows why she was
murdered or why her body was put in a storage locker." I told Tracy that
Frank Prentice from Bracebridge had rented the locker and that he'd died
in a highway accident weeks before Vi went missing.

The waitress returned with the bottle of wine. After she'd filled our
glasses and taken our dinner orders, I clinked glasses with Tracy.

"Go on about Frank," she said.

"His home has been up for sale for the past eight weeks," I said.
"His mother had it listed."

"And you talked to her, right?"

"I visited her this afternoon. Ella Prentice lives in Newmarket, and she was at home when I came by."

"Do you think she…?"

"I can't imagine why. But she claims she didn't know that Frank had a storage locker, which I find hard to believe. The woman who runs the storage business sent notices to his home when he missed his payments."

"The police must have talked to Ella by now," Tracy said.

"They have." My mind sped back to something Ella had said. "Her mother-in-law lived in Braeloch."

Tracy looked thoughtful. "There may be a connection between Ella and Vi. Ella's mother-in-law probably knew Vi, and Ella may have met her."

I shook my head. "Vi and her husband spent forty years in Toronto. They returned to Braeloch a few years ago, but Vi was suffering from dementia by then. Her husband placed her in Highland Ridge."

"You told me that Bruce's parents lived in Braeloch before they moved to Toronto," Tracy said. "They may have known Ella's in-laws back then. And Ella's husband. Are Ella and her husband still together?"

"Ella's a widow."

A light went on in my head. Jamie grew up in Braeloch, and her mother still lived there. "Would Jamie's mother—"

"Have known Ella's husband and her mother-in-law? I'll ask her. What were their names?"

"Ella called her mother-in-law Carrie so I assume she was Carrie Prentice. I don't know her husband's first name."

Our meals arrived, and Tracy told me what she was up to at work. Earlier that month, she'd joined the law firm where she'd spent her articling year. I was bursting with pride as she told me about the case she was working on.

Over dessert, our conversation returned to the murder in Braeloch. "Who would want to kill Vi?" Tracy asked. "A confused old lady."

"Vi had a life before her illness," I said.

"What do you know about her, Mom?"

I told her what Bruce had told me, including that she'd been let go from the bank.

"Someone at the bank might remember her," Tracy said.

"It's been several years since she worked there."

"There may be people there who were her friends. Or who know who her friends were," Tracy said.

We were grasping at straws. The truth was we knew very little about Vi.

Tracy took a taxi to the condo she shared with Jamie on The Esplanade. I drove over to my home in Moore Park. Everything was more or less in order, except for the kitchen where unwashed dishes filled the sink and the floor needed scrubbing. Our absence had given our housekeeper an opportunity to slack off. I grabbed a bottle of Evian water from the fridge and went out on the back deck.

Whoever had killed Vi knew that Frank had rented a locker at Glencoe Self-Storage. That person had been in Frank's home, before or after his death, and had gotten hold of his key. His keycard had been deactivated long before Vi's body was put in the locker so her killer had used someone else's card.

I sighed in frustration. Other than Bruce, who had rented storage lockers?

I sipped my water and went over everything Bruce had told me about Vi. She had been working at a bank in Braeloch when she met Ted. Later, when Bruce went off to school, she took a job at a Bank of Toronto branch in the city. She held that job for twenty years. Then there was a problem, and she was let go.

Twenty years on the job. The bank would have a file on Vi's work performance. I thought of Marnie MacRae, a senior executive at the Bank of Toronto who'd been my tennis partner a few years before. Could she access those files, or did she know someone in Human Resources who could? I quickly dismissed that idea. I wouldn't help anyone who asked me to pull a file on a Norris Cassidy employee.

Tracy thought that someone at the bank might remember Vi. It was a long shot but I couldn't come up with a better idea.

A glance at my watch told me it was five to eight. I didn't like to leave Laura and Tommy alone at Black Bear Lake. *Now if Kyle was there...*

I had to smile. A week earlier, I would have raced up north *because* Kyle was there with Laura. What a difference a week can make.

I went into the house and picked up the telephone in the kitchen. "How did it go today?" I asked when Laura answered.

"Kyle wasn't happy when he left, but I told him I'd be in Toronto in two weeks."

His mournful face flashed through my mind. "I'm sure Kyle will be fine. How did you and Tommy spend the day?"

"Nothing too exciting. We went for a swim after lunch. We worked on the dog paddle today. He's getting the hang of it."

Tommy hadn't spent much time around water, and he needed swimming lessons. I was pleased that Laura was teaching him the basics.

"Then I sat in the shade, and Tommy played on the shore," she went on. "A woman came by in a canoe. Her name is Zoe. We talked for a while."

"Someone your age?"

"Older than me, but way cool. Hey, where are you, Mom?"

"In Toronto. I have something to do here in the morning, so I'll spend the night at the house."

"Okay. We'll see you tomorrow evening?"

"Yes. Lock the doors and make sure the ground-floor windows are closed."

"Mom, we've got AC here. Remember? We keep the windows closed."

"Don't open the doors for anyone."

CHAPTER TEN

I called Laura at eight the next morning. She and Tommy had survived the night at Black Bear Lake without me, but Tommy had developed a bad case of sunburn. Laura said his back and shoulders were red and painful.

"Why didn't you tell me this last night?" I asked.

"He didn't complain about it until this morning."

"You didn't make him wear sunscreen at the beach?"

"I made sure he wore a hat," she said. "The top of his head and most of his face are fine."

"Is he running a fever?"

I drummed my fingers on the table while she went to check Tommy's forehead. She should have known better than to let him play in the water without sunscreen.

"Doesn't seem to have a fever," she said.

"His forehead's cool?" I asked.

"Yup."

"Spread aloe vera gel over his sunburned skin. Gently. No swimming lessons today. Have him stay in the shade with a shirt and a hat on."

"Anything else, boss?" There was an edge to her voice.

"He needs plenty of fluids. Lemonade. I should be there around noon."

I groaned as I put down the receiver. I'd be running interference for years while my grandchild grew up.

My next call was to Bruce. I wasn't sure whether he'd be at *The Times* that early in the morning, but he picked up on the first ring.

I told him that I was in Toronto and that I planned to visit the bank where Vi had worked. "Have you told the police about her job there?" I asked.

"It never occurred to me that it was important. It was a long time ago."

I wanted to remind him that Vi had been let go because of a problem at work and that we needed to know what that problem was. But I figured that should be obvious to him. "Someone may remember her," I said, "and that may lead to something."

"Maybe." He sounded doubtful.

"I might as well give it a try. Where is the branch located?"

"Corner of Queen and Paxton in the Beach. If it's still there."

At five past nine, I walked into the Bank of Toronto branch on the Beach's bustling Queen Street strip. I gave the redhead at the information desk my business card and asked to speak to the manager.

Peter Demetriou was studying my card when the receptionist brought me into his office. "Pat Tierney," he said when I was seated across from him. "We met at the Socially Responsible Investing Conference last year. We sat at the same table."

I recognized the flashy dresser. "I remember."

I told him I'd been out of town for several months running a new Norris Cassidy branch in cottage country. In the town of Braeloch, where a woman had recently been murdered. A woman who had worked at this branch six years before.

Peter looked startled. "The woman who was found in that storage locker up north?"

"Yes."

"She worked here?"

'That's right. Her name was Vi Stohl, and I'm helping her son look into her death."

"Go on," he said.

"We thought someone here might remember her. She was a customer services representative for twenty years."

"What exactly do you want to know?"

"The kind of person she was, her interests, that sort of thing. Vi suffered from dementia in recent years, and I haven't been able to locate any of her friends in Toronto. She and her husband moved up north a few years ago, and she was living in a nursing home. She didn't have a chance to make friends in Braeloch."

He looked thoughtful for several moments. "I've only been here for two years, but Irene Hounsell may be able to help."

He picked up his telephone receiver. "Have Irene come to my office."

A few moments later, a woman appeared in the doorway. She was in her fifties with gray hair fluffed out around her head like a dandelion gone to seed.

"Come in, Irene," Peter said.

When she was seated, he introduced us and asked if she remembered Vi Stohl.

A cloud passed over her face. "I heard what happened to Vi. Terrible." She turned to me. "Are you with the police?"

"No, but I'm asking a few questions on behalf of her son. I'm trying to get a sense of who Vi was. Peter said you worked with her."

"We were both tellers here. I transferred to this branch a few years before Vi left."

"What was she like?" I asked.

"Quiet and reserved," Irene said. "Our clients liked her. She was a good listener, and she did her best to help people."

"Excellent skills to have," Peter put in. "This is a people-centered business."

"She was well liked by the staff?" I asked.

"Very much. Vi brought in homemade cookies and squares. Offered to stay late or work weekends if someone else couldn't." Irene's face fell. "I can't imagine who would want to hurt her."

We were silent for a few moments as we thought about that.

"What were her interests?" I asked.

Irene smiled. "Vi was a homebody. Her husband, her son, her home, and her garden were her main interests."

"I understand that there was a problem here," I said.

Peter sat up straight in his chair and searched my face.

Irene took a deep breath. "Vi started forgetting things. I was able to cover for her a few times, but there are lots of details to a teller's job. Not to mention the continual learning curve. New products, new computer systems…"

Peter was looking worried. I figured that he was concerned about employee confidentially—even though the person in question hadn't been a bank employee for years and was no longer alive.

"Vi Stohl was murdered," I said to him. "There may be a connection between what happened here and her murder."

"I need to talk to head office," he said.

"Money went missing," Irene went on. "I'm not sure how much it was, but I heard it was a considerable amount. Vi was let go. We all assumed it was because of the missing money."

Peter held up a hand. "We can't go any further with this. Irene, please return to your workstation."

"Did you keep in touch with Vi after she left?" I asked her.

Peter spoke first. "Irene." He inclined his head toward the door.

She got up from the chair and left the office. Peter followed her to the door and held it open for me.

I considered returning after the bank had closed for the day and approaching Irene when she left the building. I wanted to know the names of everyone who was at the branch when Vi worked there.

But what would I do with those names, I asked myself when I was out on Queen Street. The police needed to know about the missing money and that Vi may have been let go because of it. They could make the bank release the employees' names.

But before I did that, I had to check on Tommy and get back to work. I had appointments with two clients that afternoon.

I called Laura as I walked down Queen Street. She said Tommy's face was flushed, and his forehead felt warm.

I didn't like the sound of that. I told her I was on my way.

I hit the pharmacy on the next block from the bank. Then I got into the Volvo and didn't stop driving till I reached Black Bear Lake.

I found Laura chatting with a tanned brunette on the deck. I smiled at the visitor and turned to Laura. "Tommy?"

"He's on the sofa," she said. "I was about to make his lunch."

The brunette unfurled her long legs and stood up. I remembered seeing her at Highland Ridge. Bruce had held the door open for her as we left the building.

"I'm Zoe Johnston." She held out her hand. "Laura told me you worked at the Norris Cassidy branch in town so I knew right away who you were. Nate's my husband."

I shook her hand. "Nate said you're spending the summer on this lake. Where's your cottage?"

"Over there." She turned to face the lake and pointed to the right. "It's set back from the water so you can't see it from here."

"You'll have to excuse me," I said. "I need to check on my son. He got too much sun yesterday. We'll talk more at the party on Friday night."

Tommy was indeed running a fever. I consulted the instructions that came with the medicine I'd bought. "It's cherry-flavored," I told him. I gave him a spoonful of syrup, and he washed it down with water.

I had chicken noodle soup warming on the stove when I heard Laura call out. I went over to the sliding doors and saw Zoe waving from a yellow canoe.

Tommy managed to eat half a bowl of soup and drink some lemonade. I settled him back on the sofa and returned to the table.

I put the thermometer and the bottle of syrup in front of Laura. "Take Tommy's temperature in an hour." I showed her how to do it. "Tommy's a child. You can't expect him to remember to put on sunscreen."

She looked repentant, so I asked, "Did you have plans for the day?"

"Zoe wanted to take me out in her canoe."

"Another time."

Soupy was seated at Ivy's desk, talking to a woman with wavy silver hair. "Pat," he said when he saw me, "I sent Ivy off for lunch. Would you mind her desk while I..." He inclined his head in the direction of his office.

I was no longer the branch manager, but I wasn't the receptionist. I turned to the woman. "I'm Pat Tierney. You're...?"

"Tess Watson," she said. "I stopped by two days ago, and I'm back with my investment portfolio."

Tess was the vendor of the property Bruce had bought. "You met with Nate Johnston, our branch manager." I caught the look on Soupy's face, and it wasn't pleasant. "Nate has a lunch appointment, but he'll be back at two. Would you...?"

"I have errands to run," Tess said. "I'll be back to see him at two."

As soon as she'd left, Soupy got up from his chair.

"Sit down," I said.

He did as he was told, but with ill grace.

I locked the door, hung the Closed sign in the window, and shut the blinds. I sat on Ivy's desk, and we stared each other down for what seemed like minutes.

I was the first to break the silence. "You were trying to poach Nate's client."

"Tess isn't Nate's client. She talked to him the other day because he was the only advisor here at the time. But he didn't sign her up."

I threw him an exasperated look. "How many times do I have to tell you that we are a team? You'll handle some of the business Nate brings in. And vice versa. What don't you get about that?"

He smirked.

I struggled to control myself. "You're in this for the long term. You're building a business, not grabbing quick sales. To do that you need a strong team of people you trust, and who trust you. You make a move on Tess behind Nate's back, and you'll alienate him. Don't forget that he's the manager. Any new clients you sign up need to go through Nate, and he sends that information to headquarters."

I thought of Soupy's new Porsche, his Rolex watch, and his spiffy suits. His wedding was coming up with all the expenses an occasion like that entailed. He was probably carrying a hefty credit-card debt.

"Money problems?" I asked.

He shrugged. "I'm waiting for those juicy commissions and fees to roll in."

Norris Cassidy paid him a small salary, and it was up to him to supplement it with commissions for selling investments and with fees for his advice. Probably not enough income to support the lifestyle he wanted.

"You left a good job to come here. You knew this was a start-up operation."

"My girl lives here, and so does my family. This is my turf."

"Soupy, the more clients this branch attracts, the better you'll do."

His green eyes flashed. "I'd do just fine if Nate Johnston wasn't standing in my way." With that, he got to his feet and went into his office.

Ivy arrived just then. "Chuck and Gracie Gibson will be in to see me in a few minutes," I told her. "And Tess Watson will be here to see Nate at two."

In my office, I brooded over how I could turn the Soupy situation around. Tess would talk to Nate at two, so one disaster had been averted. But there was nothing I could do about Soupy's feelings of entitlement or his spending habits. When I left the branch, its two advisors would be yoked together for better or for worse. Probably for worse.

But it wasn't my problem. I was out of there in another week.

I was booting up my computer when my telephone rang. "Mr. and Mrs. Gibson are here, Pat," Ivy said.

The Gibsons had retired to their vacation home on Raven Lake ten years earlier, but the last time I saw them they were talking about moving back to Toronto. "This business of growing old is the pits," Gracie had said. "I'm afraid of falling on the uneven ground. And we need to be closer to our doctors."

Ivy brought them into my office. Chuck helped Gracie into a chair in front of my desk then took the chair beside her.

I smiled at them. "Have you reached a decision on your home?"

"Gracie wants one last summer at the lake," Chuck said." We'll put the property on the market next spring."

Gracie sighed. "We have another problem."

"Someone's advertised our place on a vacation rental website," Chuck said. "On Sunday, a woman from Cleveland showed up with her kids. She thought she'd rented the house for a week. Wired money to some guy who'd posted the ad on Cottage Getaways."

"They were so disappointed after coming all the way up here," Gracie said. "I felt sorry for them, but what could we do? We pointed them to the tourist office. Hope they found something."

"That's not all," Chuck said. "Another family drove up yesterday. They weren't as understanding."

"The husband certainly wasn't. He had to be restrained by his wife," Gracie said. "He was waving his arms, said he'd 'punch out' Chuck. He threatened to call the police and sue us. I called his bluff. I held out my cell phone and said, 'Go ahead.' He backed off, and they left in a huff."

She glanced at Chuck. "I hope they don't come back."

"We looked up the listing on our computer." Chuck took a printout from a plastic case he was carrying. "It has photos of the exterior and the interior of our house."

The Gibsons had internet access on Raven Lake, while Black Bear was still in the dark ages, I thought as I looked at the printouts of their fieldstone fireplace, their country kitchen, and the view of the lake from their porch.

"Did you take these photos?" I asked. "Post them on a website or on Facebook?"

"No!" Gracie said. "We don't have a camera, we don't have a website, and we're not on Facebook. Whoever took them came into our home when we weren't there."

"We want this to stop," Chuck said.

"You told the police?" I asked.

"Oh, yes," Gracie said. "And a lot of good that did. Sergeant Bouchard told us this is a popular scam in other parts of cottage country. He said they'll be looking into it. Looking into it, ha!"

"I e-mailed Cottage Getaways," Chuck said. "The fellow who runs it has pulled the ad, and he says he's blacklisted the person who placed it. But how many others have been taken in by it?"

"Some hothead will think we're behind the scam," Gracie said, "and goodness only knows what he'll do to us. We're isolated at the end of our long lane."

Their home was broken into. They don't feel safe there anymore.

I went over their investment portfolio with them. Little had changed since the last time we'd looked at it.

"We're real sorry to see you leave, Pat," Chuck said as they got up to leave.

I heard Nate's voice in the hall. "I'll miss you, too, but I'll introduce you to Nate Johnston, the new branch manager. You'll be working with him when I leave."

Tess Watson arrived soon after the Gibsons left, and Nate took her into his office. When the door closed behind them, Soupy stormed out his office and left the building, banging the door behind him.

I considered going after him, but what more could I say to him?

I called Black Bear Lake. Laura told me that Tommy was sleeping, and his forehead felt cooler. I told her to give him a drink when he awoke.

My work at the branch was nearly finished. The following week, I'd introduce Nate to the rest of my clients and that would be it. He didn't need any more hand-holding. He'd make an excellent branch manager if Soupy would let him do his job.

The police needed to know what had happened at the Toronto bank where Vi had worked, but if I told them they'd think Bruce had withheld that information. It was Thursday afternoon, and I knew Bruce was busy putting *The Times* to bed. Editing and page layout, he'd told me, sometimes went on into the early hours of Friday morning. I thought of waiting until the next day to talk to him, but I decided against it.

I said goodbye to Ivy and walked down the street to *The Times* building. I asked for Bruce over the intercom at the front door, and the door buzzed open. I told the security guard in the lobby who I was and that I wanted to speak to Bruce. He picked up the telephone on his desk.

"Mr. Stohl will see you." He pointed to an ancient elevator. "Second floor."

The Times newsroom held about a dozen desks with computers. Bruce and Maria Dawson sat at a grouping of six desks in the center of the room.

"Pat," Bruce said as I approached them, "is something wrong?"

"I know you're on deadline," I said, "but could we talk for a minute?"

He motioned toward an office at the back of the room. When we were seated, I told him about my visit to the bank and what Irene had said about the missing money.

"Mom would never have taken money," he said. "Ted had a good job, and she was just working to pass the time."

"The police have to be told. Vi may have seen or heard something that got the thief worried. That could be a motive for murder."

"That money went missing years ago. If the thief thought that Mom knew he'd taken it, why would he wait until now?"

"I don't know. But the police need to know about the missing money. If they find out about it, they'll say you were withholding information."

Bruce squared his shoulders. "You're right. I'll go over to the detachment now." He threw me a sidelong look. "Would you come with me?"

"It can wait till tomorrow. This is your busy day."

"I should get onto it now. Wouldn't want Foster to think I'm withholding information."

Foster had set up shop in a back office at the Braeloch detachment. Whiteboards were mounted on two walls. Photos and newspaper clippings were taped to them, and lists of names and places had been written with black and red markers.

He looked up from the papers on his desk and glowered at us.

"Detective Foster," I said as Bruce and I took chairs facing his desk, "we've found out something you should know."

"You have, have you? I told you to look after your clients' investments."

Bruce and I exchanged glances.

"Well?" Foster barked. "What did you find out?"

"I got to thinking about the people my mother knew before she got sick," Bruce began. "As I told you, she led a quiet life. But when I went off to boarding school, she got a job at a bank close to where we lived in Toronto."

"What bank?" Foster asked.

"Bank of Toronto. She was a teller at one if its branches for twenty years."

Foster glared at him. "You didn't tell us this."

"I didn't think it was relevant," Bruce said. "She took the job for something to do, and it was close to home. Then her memory started slipping, and she was let go."

"She was let go?" Foster asked.

"There was a problem before she left," I said. "I visited the branch today—"

Foster started to rise from his chair. "You did what?"

"I was in Toronto this morning. Bruce had told me his mother worked at a bank in the Beach, so I went over there to see if anyone remembered Vi."

Foster sank back in his chair. I told him I'd talked to Peter and Irene, and what Irene had said about the missing money. "Vi took the blame for it. It may have something to do with what happened to her last week."

I let Foster digest that for a few moments. "The bank will give you the names of everyone who worked at that branch six years ago," I said. "Maybe one of them was in Braeloch last week."

"What makes you think Vi Stohl didn't take the money?" Foster asked.

"Mom would never have taken money," Bruce said. "Someone else did."

"You should look into it," I said. "Peter Demetriou, the manager, wasn't there six years ago, but Human Resources will have employment records."

Foster's face had turned an unhealthy shade of red. "You're the one with the motive, Stohl. With your mother gone, you inherit Ted Stohl's entire estate." Then he looked at me. "Stop wasting our time."

As we got up to leave, I couldn't resist asking, "Have you spoken to the people who have keycards at Glencoe Self-Storage?"

His eyes darted to a list of names on the whiteboard on his left. Then he turned his head and fixed his eyes on us. "Will you let us get on with our work?"

As soon as we were outside the building, I asked Bruce, "Did you catch any names on that list he looked at?"

"Doug Beecham and Ray Otter."

"The first two names on the list. The third is Meredith Hunter, but that's all I caught. Do you know these people?"

"Ray Otter is the maintenance guy at *The Times*. Never heard of the other two."

Someone on that list had a card to open the gate the night that Vi was put in the locker.

Bruce took me down to the basement of *The Times* building where a wizened man with a leathery face was tinkering with a computer tower. Bruce introduced me to Ray Otter.

"Do you have a locker at Glencoe Self-Storage?" I asked.

Ray looked startled, and for a good reason. What right did I have to throw questions at him?

But he answered me. "I've had a locker out there for the past year. Sold the house after my Molly died, and I've been storing the furniture till my daughter finishes college. She may want it when she sets up her own home."

He looked at Bruce. "This is something to do with what happened to your mother, right?"

"We have the names of a few people who have keycards to the gate," Bruce said. "We were wondering…"

"If one of them put your mother in that locker," Ray said. "The police asked me what I was doing the night before she was found. I told them I was playing euchre at the Legion, and that Tom McKinnon gave me a lift back to the room I rent here in town. I don't have a car no more so I would have needed another ride to get over to the storage place."

I asked if he knew Doug Beecham and Meredith Hunter. I said they were also renting lockers.

"Don't know either of them," he said.

We thanked him and took the stairs to the ground floor. "I think we can eliminate Ray," I said.

I was driving down Main Street ten minutes later, when I saw a small woman in a smart white suit hurrying along the sidewalk.

It was Ella Prentice, and she looked worried.

I drove around the block and parked in the public lot behind the Dominion Hotel. But by the time I returned to Main Street on foot, Ella had vanished.

CHAPTER ELEVEN

Shirley Corcoran arrived at the house early the next morning. She and her husband Hank were the caretakers of Norris Cassidy's vacation home, and I'd asked them to help with the party. Shirley had gone shopping the evening before, and I helped her carry boxes of food and beverages into the house.

"I should be back by five," I told her when we'd got everything into the kitchen. "The guests will be here around seven."

Tommy's temperature was normal, but his sunburn was still sensitive. His grandmother had called the night before, asking if he could spend the Canada Day weekend with her. I'd jumped at the chance to keep him out of the sun for a few days. Her driver would pick him up later in the morning.

I gave him a hug and told him I'd see him on Monday. "We'll be at our new place," I said, "so you'll be swimming on the other side of the lake."

The Friday before the Canada Day weekend was a statutory holiday, but I found Nate in his office when I got to the branch at ten. He handed me a schedule of our client meetings for the following week. I went into my office and called Lainey Campbell.

Soupy's mother said she'd be delighted to meet me for lunch. I spent an hour tying up loose ends on my computer. At eleven, I headed over to the Winigami Inn.

Lainey was seated at a table with a view of the lake. The deep purple of her summer jacket brought out the silver in her salt-and-pepper hair.

"I'm worried about Bruce," I said when I sat down across from her.

Her face was troubled. "We should have had him over to the house these past few days, but I've been helping Mara's mother with the bridesmaids' dresses. That's no excuse but..." She held up her hands.

"You've been busy." I leaned over the table. "Lainey, the police don't seem to be looking any further than Bruce in their investigation. Whoever put Vi in that locker needed a keycard to get into the yard after hours."

Her eyes widened.

"Noreen Andrews won't give me the current renters' names, and neither will the police. But I know two people who were renting lockers when Vi was found. Doug Beecham and Meredith Hunter. Do you know them?"

She shook her head. "Never heard those names. They may be cottagers."

"Maybe they are. There's something else you can help me with," I said. "Can you tell me more about Vi? I can't get a handle on who she was."

"She was a sweet girl back in high school, always tried to do the right thing. I was more of a hell-raiser."

"Did she have a particular interest? A hobby?"

"She liked kids, and she did a lot of babysitting when we were in our teens."

That didn't tell me much. "Other than you and Burt, who were her friends before she left Braeloch?"

"Are you looking for a friendship that went sour? That would be a long time to hold a grudge, but I honestly can't think of anyone who didn't like Vi."

"Not necessarily someone she didn't get along with," I said. "Just someone who could tell me more about her. Perhaps a different side of her than you knew."

Our roast beef sandwiches arrived, and we tucked into them. After a minute or two, Lainey looked up from her plate. "I know who you can talk to," she said. "Ronnie Collins."

"Ronnie...Veronica Collins? Jamie's mother?"

Lainey smiled. "Of course, you know Ronnie's daughter."

"And I've met Veronica a few times." Like Lainey, Vi would have been in her late sixties, but I'd put Veronica down as a good ten years younger than that. She would have been a child when Vi and Ted married.

Lainey must have read my thoughts. "Ronnie's younger than Vi and me," she said. "Vi was her babysitter. She looked after Ronnie and her brother Harlan in the summers while their mother was at work. Harlan was older than Ronnie, and he took summer jobs after a year or two, but Vi continued to take care of Ronnie. They'd hit it off from the start. Vi called Ronnie her little sister, and Ronnie was a flower girl at her wedding."

"Did they keep in touch when Vi moved to Toronto?"

"I doubt it. Vi and Ted cut all their ties when they left Braeloch."

We looked at each other for a few moments, thinking about why the Stohls had turned their backs on Braeloch.

"Ronnie and I were never close," Lainey went on. "There's the age difference, of course, and she was uppity when she came back from secretarial school in Huntsville. Got herself a closet full of new clothes and an assortment of airs and graces."

A smile flickered across her face. "She's friendlier these days. When Soupy got his job at the Norris Cassidy branch, I told Ronnie and she went to see him. He's managing her money now."

I took the opportunity to ask about her son. "How's Soupy holding up? His wedding's coming up soon."

"The reception will be in this room." She looked around the dining room and sighed. "He's been acting strange lately. Pre-wedding jitters, I figure, but it's not like him to be nervous about anything. He's always been laid-back. And he and Mara have been going together for years, since they were in high school. It's about time they got married."

"He may be worried about money. The wedding will cost them a fair bit, and Soupy told me they're building a home on the lake where you have your cottage."

"Mara's an only child, and her parents are paying for the wedding. But the cottage will set them back some. Burt and I gave them the land, but we think they should wait a few years before they build a summer home. They have their bungalow in town to finish paying for."

She shrugged. "I expect he'll settle down after the wedding."

Veronica's white frame house was picture-pretty that summer day. Well-tended flower beds lined the walkway, and baskets of fat pink geraniums hung from the roof of the veranda. I smiled as I got out of my car, thinking about what Lainey had said. I wouldn't have described Veronica as uppity—rather, she was a perfectionist with little patience for the weaknesses of others.

"What brings you here, Pat?" she asked when she came to the door. Then the smile left her face. "Is Jenny—are the girls okay?"

"They're fine," I said, "and extremely busy. I had dinner with Tracy on Wednesday, but Jenny was working late and couldn't join us."

Jamie's given name was Jennifer, and her mother called her Jenny as she did when she was growing up. I called her Jenny, too, when I was with Veronica. There was something about Veronica—her perfectly coiffed blond hair, the string of pearls she was wearing on that weekday afternoon, and her perfect home—that put me on my best behavior.

She invited me inside. "We'll sit out back," she said.

I followed her down the hall and out the sliding doors at the back of the dining room. She led the way to a wrought-iron love seat that faced a rose garden.

I told her that I was helping Bruce look into his mother's murder.

"Poor Bruce," she said. "I heard he was doing really well until this happened."

Bruce had rented Veronica's basement apartment the previous winter. She'd evicted him when she caught him smoking.

"He was doing well," I said. "He enjoyed running *The Times*. But now…"

"You're afraid he'll go back to his old ways."

I met her eyes. "It's a concern. That's why I want to get to the bottom of what happened to Vi. Bruce needs something to focus on right now, and he needs to have closure."

She nodded, and I knew that she'd help me. She'd felt badly about turning Bruce out of the apartment, but she'd told him she didn't allow smoking in the house. And when Veronica made a rule, no one was permitted to break it.

"I understand you were close to Vi before she and Ted left Braeloch. What she was like then?"

She looked up at the branches of the large maple tree at the back of her yard. "She was fun to be with. We had wonderful adventures at the lookout above town." She chuckled. "We pretended we were Laura Secord and her maid walking through the forest to warn the British that the Americans were about to attack."

I tried to picture Vi taking a little girl on outdoor adventures. That was a whole new side of her.

Veronica seemed lost in thought, so I said, "You were in Vi's wedding party."

She smiled. "Imagine how exciting that was for an eleven-year-old. I wore my first long dress. Pale blue with rosettes along the bottom."

"You were probably too old to have a sitter by then, but you kept in touch with Vi."

"She was a good listener, and I had a lot of insecurities at that age. She was the older sister I never had."

She paused again. This time I waited for her to go on.

"When she had her baby, Bruce, I offered to babysit. She never took me up on it."

I wasn't sure if Veronica knew who Bruce's real parents were, and I wasn't going to bring it up.

"And then she was gone." Her face twisted. "To Toronto. Never even said goodbye to me."

"You didn't hear from her after she left Braeloch?"

"Not a word. I hadn't thought about her for years when Ted moved back here. I visited her once at Highland Ridge, but she didn't know who I was. It was too painful."

"Do you remember any of her friends?"

"Lainey was her best friend. And she started dating Ted when he arrived in town to work at *The Times*. I thought their courtship was terribly romantic."

"Anyone else you remember?"

"A fellow sometimes joined us with his dog at the lookout."

"A boy from Braeloch?"

"I never saw him around town, only at the lookout. His name was...let me see...Daniel. And his dog was Angus."

Could that be Daniel Laughton? "What do you remember about Daniel?"

"Tall, gawky fellow, but nice. He knew all about animal tracks, plants, minerals in the rocks. Took the time to explain them to me."

"Bruce told me Daniel Laughton, the environmentalist, had been a friend of Vi's when they were young. Could that have been him?"

"Daniel Laughton, who had that TV show?"

"*The Wonders Around Us.*"

She looked astounded. "It never occurred to me, but that could have been the boy we saw at the lookout. He knew all about the outdoors."

"Were he and Vi dating?"

"I don't think so. Just friends."

"Is there anyone who would have wanted to harm Vi?" I asked.

Veronica looked shocked. "No one around here."

At the front door, I thought of something else. "Do you know the Prentice family? Carrie Prentice? I believe she died last year."

She looked at me as if I were slow-witted. "Carrie Prentice was my mother. And, yes, she died last fall."

Carrie was Ella's mother-in-law, so Ella was married to your brother, Harlan. "I met Ella Prentice a few days ago, but I didn't realize she was your sister-in-law."

Veronica didn't comment as she followed me onto the veranda. But the expression on her face told me that she and Ella weren't close.

"I asked Ella about the storage locker where Vi was found," I said. "Her son rented it."

"Poor Frank, I didn't know he'd rented that locker. The article in *The Times* didn't mention it."

"Ella thinks he stored his grandmother's furniture in it."

"I gave him some pieces after my mother died. I always liked Frank, and he was Mum's only grandson." Her eyes widened. "But he wouldn't have killed—"

"No, Frank died weeks before Vi. Did you see much of him?"

"Not much since my brother died, but he came to my mother's funeral with his girlfriend."

"Girlfriend?"

"I assumed she was his girlfriend. Christine, I think her name was, or maybe it was Celine. Didn't catch her last name."

"Ella was in Braeloch yesterday."

"No way. Ella hasn't set foot in town since Harlan died. She didn't even come to Mum's funeral."

"I saw her walking down Main Street."

"I can't imagine what brought her here."

I glanced at my watch as I drove away from Veronica's house. My guests would arrive in three hours.

Back in my office, I punched in the phone number of Tracy and Jamie's condo. When I got voicemail, I figured the girls were spending their holiday at work. I reached Jamie at her office at Optimum Capital, the Toronto brokerage house where she worked as legal counsel.

After we'd exchanged greetings, I asked, "You've heard about the woman who was found in a storage locker up here?"

"Found murdered in a storage locker," she said. "It's been big news for days, Pat."

"Your cousin, Frank Prentice, rented that locker."

"Frank?" She sounded surprised. "He was killed in a motorcycle accident in April."

"The killer knew about his locker. And got into it."

"Frank probably told a lot of people that he'd rented it."

"Maybe. I was speaking to your mother today. She said she gave him some furniture."

"That's right. Frank was at Gran's funeral with his gal, Crystal."

"Crystal?"

"Crystal King, a tall redhead. At least, she was taller than Frank. He seemed to have a thing for tall women."

"A redhead by the name of Crystal King bought the contents of Frank's storage locker last week," I said. "She found Vi Stohl's body."

"She knew what was in the locker," Jamie said.

"The furniture your mother gave Frank."

"That's right. Mom took Frank and Crystal to Gran's apartment after the funeral. She hoped that he'd take some of the furniture."

"Your mother knew Vi when she was a child. Vi was her babysitter."

"Braeloch is a small town, Pat. Everyone knows everyone else up there. And many of them are related."

I could hear the smile in her voice.

"I have a meeting to go to," she said. "Talk to you later."

My mind sifted through the new information as I drove to Black Bear Lake. Now I knew why Crystal had been willing to pay $900 for the contents of Frank's locker. That furniture Veronica gave Frank must have been pretty special.

CHAPTER TWELVE

The Corcorans were in full stride when I arrived at Black Bear Lake. Hank was on the deck setting up a barbecue he'd brought over to supplement the one that was already there. I opened the door and gave him a wave. He grinned back at me.

Shirley and Laura were making salads in the kitchen. Shirley greeted me cheerfully, but Laura didn't seem to be enjoying her role as sous-chef. I was about to ask, "Where's Tommy?" when I remembered he was with his grandmother for the weekend.

Maxie followed me to my bedroom where I changed into jeans and a sleeveless blouse. I hesitated before the phone on the bedside table. I had another question for Jamie. I punched in the number of the girls' condo and left a message asking Jamie to call me.

Downstairs, I helped a glum Laura carry plates and cutlery to the buffet table. We were setting up a bar on the counter between the kitchen and the dining area when a car came up the drive.

Shirley looked at her watch. "Not quite six. Guests are early."

At the front door, my heart fell when I saw Yvonne and Russell Shingler getting out of their black Ferrari. Yvonne saw me and waved.

"Excellent news, Pat," she said when she'd crossed the driveway. "I found a delightful place that does weddings. The Sandy Cove Inn on the other side of this very lake. And guess what? It had a cancellation for the last Saturday in July. Russell and I drove up this afternoon and made a deposit."

I stared at her, speechless.

She put an arm around me. "So it's all set. Four weeks from tomorrow. They'll take care of everything, even arrange for a justice of the peace. All we have to do is draw up a guest list. Can we put our heads together now on who to invite?"

I was stunned by her nerve, but I didn't have time to argue with her. "Not now. I have guests arriving in an hour."

She followed me into the house. "Is Laura here?"

Minutes before, Laura had been helping Shirley, but she'd beat a hasty retreat when the Shinglers arrived. "She's around somewhere," I said. "Down at the lake most likely."

Yvonne went over to the doors to the deck. "A barbie, what fun!"

"A welcome party for the new manager of the branch where I've been working," I said. "Several of our clients will be here." No outsiders, I was trying to say.

"Russell and I can help," Yvonne chirped. "He's a marvelous bartender, and I'll assist him. It will be no trouble for us because we're staying at the Sandy Cove tonight."

My first thought was to turn her down flat, but I realized I could use the help. With Hank manning the barbecue and Shirley organizing the food, I'd planned to ask Laura to serve drinks but she looked out of sorts.

And I didn't want to be needlessly rude to Yvonne. Her son would be part of my grandchild's life. And so would she. "That's a good idea," I said. "Thank you."

I turned to Shirley. "Russell will run the bar. Will you show him where everything is?"

Russell joined Shirley behind the counter.

"We can talk tomorrow morning, Pat," Yvonne said. "Russell and I will come over after breakfast."

"Sorry, tomorrow's not good either," I said. "We're moving right after breakfast."

"Oh, there you are, Laura!" Yvonne said to my daughter, who'd come in with Maxie.

"Hi, Mrs. Shingler."

Yvonne went over to her and gave her a hug. "Dear Laura, you must call me Yvonne. Russell and I have found a lovely place for the wedding. We'll tell you about it later when your mother's guests have gone."

Laura looked ready to explode so I steered her to the front door. Outside, she gave a strangled cry. "What the hell was that about?" she asked. "What wedding?"

"They've booked the Sandy Cove across the lake for the last Saturday in July."

Laura's face took on a look of horror.

I put a hand on her arm. "Don't worry, you're not getting married. Let me get through this party then I'll tackle Yvonne."

I drew her to me. "Chin up, sweetie. Why don't you take Maxie for a walk along the lake?"

She gave me a ghost of a smile.

By eight, the party was in full swing. Hank was flipping meat on the barbecues, and Russell was pouring wine and beer. Many of the guests had gathered on the deck. Several had wandered down to the lake.

I went over to the sofa where Laura and Zoe were seated. I noticed that there was no meat on their plates. "There's steak and chicken and sausages on the barbecue," I said.

Zoe held up a hand. "Thanks, but I'm a vegan."

"Laura?" I asked.

She ran a hand over her abdomen. "I find meat hard to digest these days."

Zoe shot her a curious look.

"I'm three and a half months pregnant," Laura told her.

Zoe blinked several times.

"The couple behind the bar are my boyfriend's parents," Laura said. "They've booked a wedding for us next month."

"Laura," I said in a warning tone.

Zoe was about to say something when Nate came up and put a hand on her shoulder. She looked up at him and smiled.

"I hear you and Zoe have met," he said to me.

"Laura, my daughter, met Zoe a few days ago," I said. "Laura, this is Nate Johnston, Zoe's husband. Nate's the new Norris Cassidy branch manager."

"I was just telling Zoe about my wedding," Laura said to Nate. "It's at the Sandy Cove Inn four weeks from tomorrow. You can come if you like."

Nate's eyes widened in surprise.

"Laura," I snapped.

"I'm sure Yvonne has my wedding dress picked out," she went on. "Something white and frothy and ultra-feminine. But will it fit over my baby bump four weeks from now?"

Yvonne joined us. "I saw an exquisite little number on Queen Street West, Laura. Strapless, with a beaded bodice and a full organza skirt. When will you be back in the city, my dear, so I can arrange a fitting?"

Laura jumped off the sofa, toppling her plate on the floor. She fled upstairs with Maxie at her heels.

"Should I go after her?" Yvonne asked me.

"No," I said, picking the food off the floor.

"So much is happening so quickly." Yvonne gave a happy sigh. "It's understandable that she's a little overwrought."

I could cheerfully have gone after Laura and smacked her. And I wanted to smack Yvonne even more.

An hour later, I'd doused myself with DEET and was circulating among my guests on the deck.

"Soon as the weather warms up, I'm outside every chance I get," a tanned and brawny client of Soupy's told me. "Tomorrow I go camping for a week."

I smiled at him and flapped a hand at a blackfly that was buzzing around my ear.

"The bugs stay away from us natives," Soupy said to me. "Hey, here's Bruce."

I turned to see Bruce climbing the stairs to the deck two at a time. I'd told him to drop by if he was free, but I hadn't expected him to show up. One look at his face told me he wasn't in a mood to party.

"Excuse me," I said to Soupy and his client, and crossed the deck.

"Foster came by the newsroom this afternoon," Bruce said in a low voice. "He was out at my cabin, and he found a woman's cardigan on the porch. He thinks it was Mom's."

"Let's go inside." I led him to the study at the front of the house.

"How did the police know you'd bought a place on Raven Lake?" I asked when the door was closed behind us.

Bruce sank into the sofa. "They could've heard it from anyone. I haven't exactly kept it under wraps."

I sat on a chair and tried to picture the porch on Bruce's cabin. "Was the cardigan on the porch when we were there on Tuesday?"

"No. I would have noticed it."

"Did Foster show it to you?"

He nodded. "He had it in a clear plastic bag. He's sending it to Orillia for testing."

"It was Vi's?"

"I'm not certain. It looked familiar, maybe because it was Mom's favorite color. Pale blue." He paused for a few seconds then continued in a voice husky with emotion. "The staff at Highland Ridge said she was wearing a blue cardigan on the day trip. She didn't have it on when she was...found."

Our eyes met, and silence stretched between us.

I was the first to speak. "Have you moved into the cabin?"

"Tomorrow. I took stuff over the past two nights."

"I take it the cardigan wasn't there last night."

He shook his head.

"Foster found it today?" I asked

"That's right." He had tensed right up.

"Don't let the police rattle you. We'll find out who put it on the porch. And when we do, we'll know who killed your mother."

I took him over to the table and handed him a plate. While he was helping himself to the food, the telephone rang.

"Mom," Laura called out, "it's Jamie."

I picked up the extension in the study.

"We just got in and heard your message," Jamie said at the other end of the line.

"I have another question for you. Do you know what pieces of furniture your mother gave Frank?"

"I wasn't with her when she took Frank and Crystal to Gran's place, but I called her before I left work tonight. She gave him a slant-top desk, an old armoire, a table and four chairs, and a few other pieces. Gran had kept a lot of her parents' things." Jamie chuckled. "Lovely old furniture, but, as you know, I'm not into antiques."

The girls' condo was done up in minimalist style with sleek stainless steel and leather furniture.

"Was your grandmother's furniture valuable?"

"Probably, if you knew where to go. But Mom wanted Frank to take whatever he liked. He was the only grandson."

Tracy got on the line. "Jamie and I were thinking of driving up there tomorrow. Is there room for us at the new place?"

"There is, and we'd love to see you. I'll put both of you to work, though."

I gave her directions to the cottage. She said they'd arrive after lunch the next day.

In the living room, Bruce was talking to Laura who had returned to the party. "Bruce moves into his cabin tomorrow," she said when I joined them.

"I take it the inspection went well?" I said.

He gave a curt nod. "A few issues, but nothing I can't deal with."

"This time tomorrow," Laura said to him, "you'll be in your own home."

He didn't reply. I knew he was thinking about the cardigan and Foster breathing down his neck.

Laura threw me a worried look. Just then Nate and Zoe came over. Laura introduced them to Bruce, adding that he'd bought a home on a nearby lake.

"We're looking for a place on a lake," Nate said. "We should talk to your real estate agent."

"Ask for Amy at Rosso Realty," Bruce told him. "I'll be off now, Pat. Thanks for the food."

We watched as he slid the doors to the deck open.

"That was Bruce's mother who was found in the storage locker," Nate said.

"My God!" Zoe said. "His mother?"

Nate patted her arm. "We should get going ourselves."

By eleven, the guests had all left and Shirley was running a final load in the dishwasher.

I was taking a breather on a sofa, with Maxie stretched out beside me. Laura sat down on my other side. "Mom, can you handle Yvonne? I'm not up to it."

I looked into her eyes and nodded.

Yvonne crossed the room with her handbag slung over a shoulder. "We have to work on the guest list, Pat. You, too, Laura. Would later tomorrow be good? After you settle in?"

Russell stood behind her, jiggling a set of keys in his hand, a thoughtful expression on his face.

Laura shot me a pleading look.

"Thank you, Yvonne and Russell, for your help tonight," I said. "I really appreciate it."

Yvonne beamed at me. "It was nothing. We're family now."

"Sit down for a minute," I said.

I waited until they were seated across from us. "There won't be a wedding at the Sandy Cove or anyplace else. Laura isn't ready to get married, and I don't think Kyle is either. It's not happening."

Beside me, Laura shifted her weight on the sofa.

"Pat—" Yvonne said.

Russell put an arm around her shoulder. "Listen to what Pat is saying, hon. The girl isn't ready."

"Russ, they're having a baby in December."

"There's no hurry," he said. "Kyle will go to university in the fall as planned."

"And Laura will go next year," I said.

"Maybe they'll marry later on," he said, "and maybe they won't. But these days an unplanned pregnancy shouldn't be a reason for a lifetime commitment."

Yvonne looked like she was about to burst into tears. "But the deposit we made at the Sandy Cove—"

"We can afford to let it go, Yvonne." Russell's tone was sharp. "It's not worth any unhappiness for the kids."

She gave him a sidelong look. "It was difficult for you, wasn't it? Finishing your degree with a baby at home."

He stroked her cheek.

"What will happen when the baby arrives in December?" she asked me.

"Laura and the baby will live with me while she's still in school," I said.

"It's Kyle's child, too," she said.

"Of course," I said. "The child will always be a part of Kyle's life. And yours."

She didn't look convinced.

"As you said, we're family." I smiled at her. "Even without a wedding."

Laura reached over and grasped my hand.

CHAPTER THIRTEEN

I locked the door behind us the next morning and said a silent goodbye to an era in my life. After spending four months in that house, I wasn't the least bit sorry to leave it. It was at the end of a long drive with dense woods separating it from its neighbors. On more than a few occasions, I'd felt extremely isolated there.

A few miles down the highway, I made a left-hand turn onto a side road. The gray clapboard cottage was basking in the morning sunlight. Maxie barked her approval. She gamboled around the building, stopping to sniff at its corners.

"You can take Tommy's room tonight," I said to Laura as we unloaded the car.

She winked at me. "A double bed for the girls. Better treatment than Kyle and I get."

She was in high spirits, no doubt because the wedding had been called off, so I let her comment pass. I left her to put the food away and drove into Braeloch for more groceries. Tracy and Jamie didn't eat meat. I was thankful they'd recently broadened their diet to include fish because I didn't have many recipes for soya beans and lentils.

On the drive into town, I thought about the conversation with Jamie the night before. She'd said her mother....*Veronica!* I was sure Veronica would like to spend some time with her daughter that weekend. When I finished my shopping, I drove over to her house.

She was perfectly turned out in a cotton skirt and a matching jacket. She looked as if she was expecting visitors, but by then I knew that she dressed up every day. Maybe she was expecting visitors who never came.

"The girls are coming up this afternoon," I told her, "and they'll head back tomorrow afternoon. Join us for dinner."

She looked surprised, and I realized she'd had no idea that her daughter would be in the area that weekend.

I gave her directions to the cottage. "Come around five," I said.

She was closing the door, when I said, "Jenny told me that Crystal King was the woman Frank brought to his grandmother's funeral."

"I thought her name was Christine."

"Crystal bought the contents of Frank's storage locker. She paid $900 at the auction. Those pieces you gave Frank must have been valuable."

She put a hand up to her face. "I had no idea they were worth anything."

"Crystal runs an antique shop so she would have known their value. There's big money in old furniture," I said. "Well, we'll see you this afternoon."

I passed the Dominion Hotel as I drove through Braeloch, and it made me think of Bruce. He would have checked out of his hotel room by then and was probably settling into his new home. I hoped the police would let him enjoy it.

At the cottage, I found Laura and Zoe drinking tea on the porch. Zoe had paddled over in her canoe again.

"The house is small," Laura was saying as I joined them at the table, "but this is a terrific porch. A great view of the lake, and the bugs can't get you."

"I told you we'd spend most of our time out here," I said.

Zoe stretched her arms over her head. "I could sit here for days. We've rented a great place, but it doesn't have a screened porch. That's something I want our new home to have."

"Come over here any time you like," Laura said.

"Have the police found out who killed your friend's mother?" Zoe asked.

"His name's Bruce Stohl," Laura said, "and it's a mystery what happened to his mother. A little old lady. Why would anyone want to hurt her?"

Zoe shook her head.

"Do you plan to look for work around here?" I asked Zoe.

She appeared surprised by the question. "Maybe. I haven't given it much thought. I'm too busy looking at properties."

"What kind of work do you do, Zoe?" Laura asked.

"A bit of this and a bit of that, but I haven't worked since we got married last year. I quit my job to focus on the wedding, and I never went back to it."

"Where did you meet Nate?" Laura asked.

"We worked at the same company."

"You're a financial planner?" I asked her.

She shook her head. "Nate is, of course. I was the receptionist."

We were throwing out a lot of questions, but her answers told us very little about her. So I tried something else. "You looked familiar when Laura introduced us. Then I remembered that I saw you at Highland Ridge."

"My aunt lives there. I try to visit her every week."

"It's great to have family in the area," I said.

"It certainly is," she said with a smile. "If we could find a home on a lake, everything would be perfect. But winterized lakefront properties seem to be out of our price range."

"Bruce plans to spend the winter at his cabin," Laura said.

"I wouldn't bet on that," I told her. "He'll be pretty cold there unless he gets proper heating."

"He's looking into that," Laura said. "And he'll start chinking the walls next week."

"Where is Bruce's place?" Zoe asked.

"Raven Lake," Laura said.

"You must've seen the listing," I said. "He only bought it a few days ago."

"Raven is a beautiful lake," Zoe said. "Another aunt has a home on it. But Bruce's cabin sounds like a summer place, and we're looking at winterized homes. We're not as handy as your friend."

"My sister and her partner will be here soon," Laura said. "Why don't you and Nate come for dinner?"

I wondered how we'd all fit around the porch table.

"That would be great," Zoe said, "but we'll be at my aunt's place this evening."

"The aunt at Highland Ridge?" I asked.

Zoe smiled. "No, her sister. She has the place on Raven Lake."

"Another time then," Laura said. "We're practically neighbors."

Chuck and Gracie Gibson also lived on Raven Lake. I thought about telling Zoe that they planned to sell their home the following year, but I decided against it. She and Nate needed a place for the coming winter. Besides, the Gibsons' property had been targeted in a cottage rental scam. That would have to be cleared up before Chuck and Gracie could sell it.

Tracy and Jamie arrived around two, and I greeted both of them with hugs. It had been weeks since I'd seen Jamie, and she had a fabulous new hairdo. The same burgundy color she favored, but cut in a wavy bob that accentuated her cheekbones and her almond-shaped green eyes.

"What's new in the city?" Laura asked behind me. "Two power women like you must be close to its pulse."

"We're happy to get out of it for a while." Petite Tracy grinned up at Laura who towered over her. "It's a steam bath these days."

Laura took them to their room. They came out wearing their bathing suits then went down to the lake.

I followed them and took the kayak out of the shed. Maria Dawson had told me I was welcome to use it. Jamie came over to help as I dragged it over the grass. We lifted it over the rock that sloped down to the water and set it in the water.

"You got a kayak, Mom," Tracy said from the inflatable mattress she was stretched out on.

"It belongs to the owners of the cottage."

"I had a kayak when I was a teenager," Jamie said.

"Give me a lesson," I told her. "I've never been in one."

"Ready to go out now?"

I was wearing an old pair of shorts and a T-shirt, and I didn't care whether they got wet. "Sure." I returned to the shed for the paddle and a lifejacket.

"How do I get in?" I asked as I kicked off my sandals at the edge of the water.

"First, put on the life jacket."

I did what she told me.

"This shallow water is perfect for launching," she continued. "Lay the paddle across the front of the cockpit, and hold it there to steady yourself. Step in, crouch down...sit."

When I was seated, she pushed the boat out a few feet. "Stretch out your legs and put your feet on the footrests. Relax your shoulders. Keep your weight balanced in the center of the boat."

She showed me where to grip the two-bladed paddle. "No need to hold on so tightly. Each stroke is a downward pull while your upward arm pushes the shaft away from you. There! You're making a figure eight."

Tracy hand-paddled her mattress over to us.

"You turn the kayak by paddling on one side," Jamie said.

"Mom, put this on. And this hat." Tracy handed me a tube of sunscreen and her baseball cap.

I spread sunscreen over my face and arms and handed the tube back to her. "You have another hat?"

"Two more in the house."

"Put one on," I told her.

"Wait here a moment." Jamie ran over to the shed and returned with a whistle on a nylon string and a small plastic pail. "Blow the whistle if you need help. The pail is for bailing out water."

She pushed me out farther. "You'll find your rhythm. Bon voyage!"

It didn't take me long to get the hang of the paddle, and soon I was skimming over the water. I kept close to the shore where I wouldn't come face-to-face with a speedboat, although the lake was quiet for a Saturday afternoon.

I paddled by a stretch of undeveloped lakefront. Cedars grew close to the water, providing cooling shade. A family of ducks saw me and changed their direction. Beside a stand of bulrushes, a man was fishing from a small outboard. He raised a hand, and I waved back at him.

The rhythm of the paddle helped my mind unwind. My thoughts drifted to the blue cardigan that had been left on Bruce's porch. *Who would want to frame him?*

I'd been on the water about ten minutes when I came to an Alpine-style chalet. A yellow canoe was tied to the dock. I remembered that Zoe had visited Laura in a yellow canoe.

I rested my arms on the paddle, and a door opened onto the second-story veranda. "Is that you, Pat?" I recognized Nate's voice.

I waved at him.

"I'll be right down." What seemed like moments later, he appeared around the side of the house and walked down the path to the lake.

I paddled closer to the shore.

"Come in for a drink," he said. "Zoe's gone to Braeloch, but she'll be back soon."

"Thanks, but I have to get back and start dinner. Maybe we'll see you with Zoe the next time she paddles over."

He chuckled. "You'll never get me in a canoe. I can't swim. Zoe's the adventurous one. She's been exploring far and wide in that canoe of hers."

"So it's Zoe who wants a home on a lake," I said.

"You got it." He gave me a smile. "A house in town would suit me fine."

Back at our waterfront, I forgot what Jamie had said about keeping the kayak balanced. I leaned to the right as I tried to get out and toppled the boat and myself into the water. I climbed out, thankful that no one was watching, and pulled the pail out of the cockpit. Now I knew what it was for.

CHAPTER FOURTEEN

We were sipping sangria on the porch an hour later when a car drove up the lane. "That must be your mother," I said to Jamie. "I invited her for dinner."

Jamie sucked in a breath and squared her shoulders. I'd never been clear about her relationship with Veronica. I knew they didn't see much of each other, but I'd put that down to Jamie's job in the city. Now Jamie looked like she was girding herself for battle.

Veronica gave Jamie a peck on the cheek and turned to my daughter. "You must be Tracy."

It wasn't much of a leap for her to take because Jamie had an arm around her. What surprised me was that Veronica hadn't met her before. The girls had been living together for months.

"Good to meet you at last, Mrs. Collins." Tracy turned to me. "We've talked on the phone."

"My name's Veronica, dear, but call me Ronnie." She turned to me. "You, too, Pat. I suppose we're family now."

How much more family could I handle?

Jamie offered to barbecue the salmon steaks. Ronnie followed her onto the deck outside the porch. Tracy and I went into the kitchen.

"I thought Jamie and Ronnie would enjoy some time together," I said to Tracy. "But Jamie seems..."

"Jamie and her mother don't see eye to eye on very much."

"We can't choose our parents."

Tracy smiled. "Or our children, Mom."

I gave her arm a playful punch. "Kids have a way of getting on with their lives, don't they?"

She held up her hands in mock surrender.

Over dinner, Laura related the drama with Yvonne the previous night. Tracy and Jamie stared at her, apparently at a loss for words.

"She does have a point, dear," Ronnie said to Laura. "You're expecting a baby so you should get married. Do you love this fellow?"

"Mom." Jamie gave her a stern look. "It's none of our business."

"It's always better for a child to have two parents," Ronnie went on. "And they sound like nice people. Not every boy's parents would be so accepting."

I escaped to the kitchen to dish up strawberry shortcake. When I returned to the porch with our dessert, the topic of conversation had moved on from marriage and babies.

"It's Canada Day," Laura was saying, "and there's a fireworks show in Braeloch tonight. We should all go."

Jamie's eyes met mine, and I nodded. "It's an annual event at the fairgrounds," she said. "Might be fun."

"A great idea," I said.

We arrived at the fairgrounds at dusk. A crowd had gathered on lawn chairs and blankets in front of the bandstand where Mara Nowak stood holding a microphone.

"Over here." Jamie led us to a low bench at the edge of the clearing.

I took a seat, pulled up the top of my hoodie, and tucked my hands in my sleeves. I'd forgotten to bring insect repellant. Beside me, Ronnie pulled her skirt over her knees and her jacket sleeves over her hands.

"Something to drink?" Jamie asked us. "Your choice is coffee or soft drinks."

We gave her our orders, and she headed for the food and drink concessions.

On stage, Mara took off her Stetson and waved it over her head. "Think small towns are slow towns? Not ours, and especially not on Canada Day. We had loads of fun out here today, didn't we? C'mon, people, make some noise!"

The crowd whooped and clapped in response.

"Now before we light things up with the Highland Firefighters' show, I'd like you to welcome some friends of mine. The High Lonesome Wailers! Take it away, guys."

The crowed gave a noisy welcome, and Soupy and three other members of the band trooped out on stage. They waved at the audience, took their places beside their instruments, and struck up the opening chords of Bachman-Turner Overdrive's "You Ain't Seen Nothing Yet." Soupy played lead guitar, and a fellow with a shaven head did the vocals.

"Soupy's band's not bad," Laura yelled.

"Let's hear it!" Mara cried, prompting cheers and whistles from the crowd.

"And now Braeloch's annual fireworks extravaganza," she said, "thanks to the Highland Firefighters. They're making sure it all goes off safely. Let's hear it for our firefighters!"

The crowd applauded.

"First up, the spectacular Spider formation." Mara gestured toward the night sky.

A bang that sounded like a gunshot rang out, and a burst of radial lines, like the legs of a spider, lit up the sky. The audience hooted its approval.

"Tommy would love this!" Tracy shouted.

Ronnie sat rocking on the bench beside me, her arms wrapped around her middle.

"You okay, Ronnie?" I raised my voice so she could hear me.

"I'm fine." She cringed when a whistle pierced the air.

"You must have seen a few fireworks shows here," I said when the noise had died down.

"It's my first time here in years. Herb and I brought the girls every Canada Day when they were small. But when they got older, they wanted to go with their friends."

"They can't wait to leave us when they're teenagers."

"Some of them leave and never come back." She pulled her jacket tightly around her.

A sparkling Catherine Wheel was spinning through the sky when Jamie returned with a cardboard tray of drinks. "Sorry, I took so long. I saw a few people I knew." She turned to her mother. "And I saw two of Frank's relatives. I couldn't remember their names, so I didn't approach them."

Ronnie shrugged. "They're part of Ella's gang. She has a huge family—sisters, nieces, nephews, cousins," she said to me. "Never could keep track of them all."

Jamie handed us our drinks. "And I saw Crystal, Frank's friend."

"Crystal!" I said.

"She's over there." Jamie waved at the crowd of people who were lined up in front of the food concessions.

I jumped up. "I won't be long." I wanted to find out more about Frank's furniture.

"Now the Chrysanthemum," Mara announced from the bandstand. Colored stars floated through the sky, followed by a crackling sound.

I scanned the faces in the crowd as I approached the concessions. I couldn't see Crystal, but I spotted Lainey and Burt walking hand in hand.

I felt a tap on my shoulder and turned to see Bruce and a heavy, dark-haired man who was holding a serious-looking camera with a zoom lens.

"I thought you'd be having a quiet evening at home," I said to Bruce.

He held up a notepad. "On the job. It's a big night in Braeloch. Fortunately, I was able to team up with Wilf here. He takes much better pictures than I do. I'll write the copy, and he'll supply the art."

He introduced me to Wilf Mathers, *The Times'* reporter-photographer. At least I assumed that's what he was. "Two-way man" was what Bruce called him, and I didn't think he was referring to Wilf's sexual preference.

Wilf patted his sizable paunch. "Need to do some running around tonight to burn up the chili dogs and butter tarts I put away today."

Bruce told Wilf to get some shots of the fireworks. When he'd moved off, Bruce and I joined the lineup in front of one of the concessions. Mara announced the next display, and the sky erupted into a giant spray of light.

"I'm officially in residence at Raven Lake," Bruce said when the noise had subsided. "Moved my stuff this morning then I went for a swim. Foster was waiting for me when I got back to the cabin."

Foster had to ruin his first day in his new home. I waited for him to continue.

"He had more of the same questions. What was the cardigan doing on my porch? I told him that if I'd killed my mother I wouldn't have left her clothing out in plain sight. He didn't see my point."

"They know it was Vi's cardigan? They had it analyzed?"

"I asked him that, but he wouldn't give me an answer. I've heard it takes some time to test for DNA."

"Have you asked your neighbors if they saw anyone at your place?"

"When Foster left, I went over and introduced myself. Nobody noticed anything out of the ordinary, but there are a lot of trees between the houses."

We gave our orders to the woman behind the counter. Bruce paid, and we walked over to a picnic table with our ice-cream cones.

He sat down across from me and shook his head. "I thought I'd bought a piece of paradise then Foster arrived as soon as I moved in."

I was stumped. Someone was trying to frame Bruce, and there wasn't a thing we could do. Whoever had left the cardigan had taken a bold step to implicate him. That person was worried. And dangerous.

We finished our cones, and I gave Bruce's hand a squeeze. "Get back to work," I said. His job at the newspaper was his lifeline.

As I made my way back to our group, a series of popping noises sounded, followed by a bang, and a bouquet of light filled the sky. When the noise subsided, I heard someone call my name.

Crystal was right behind me. "We met at the funeral," she said. "Crystal King. And you're Pat... Sorry, I don't remember your last name."

"Tierney, Pat Tierney. What brings you back here, Crystal?"

"Some business I need to sort out."

"To do with the storage locker? Have the contents been released?"

A shadow crossed her face. "Yes, but they're disappointing. One of the reasons I'm in town is to talk to the guy who runs the newspaper. Bruce Stohl. Now that some time has passed, I thought he'd want to write an article on me. About how I found the body in the locker. It would make a great human interest story, don't you think? Bruce wasn't at work when I dropped by the newspaper building this afternoon."

"It's Saturday. He generally takes weekends off." The last thing Bruce needed was to see Crystal again.

"You said you're a friend of his. Where does he live?"

I had to get her off Bruce's trail. "Let me see if I can arrange something."

"What are you, his keeper? Just tell me where I can find him."

"He moved this week, and I haven't been to his new place. Are you in town all weekend?"

"I drive back to Newmarket tomorrow. I'm at the Dominion Hotel tonight."

"Let me see what I can do." Another lie, but I wanted to talk to her about the locker. "I'll meet you for breakfast in the hotel dining room. Nine o'clock."

"You'll take me to Bruce?"

"Nine o'clock in the hotel dining room."

Crystal shrugged. "Nine o'clock." She turned and walked away.

I hoped she wouldn't bump into Bruce before she left the grounds.

I was approaching our group when I realized that the banging and popping had stopped. Mara was huddled on the bandstand stage with Foster and two OPP uniform officers. I went over to Laura and put an arm around her.

Mara picked up the microphone and cleared her throat. A murmur ran through the crowd.

Her voice floated over the fairgrounds. "Folks, I'm sorry but...there's been...we have to end the fireworks."

Groans greeted her announcement.

"What's the matter?" a woman cried.

"There's been…an accident and a man's been hurt." Mara's voice shook a little.

Foster took the microphone from her. "Ladies and gentlemen, there's been a shooting."

The crowd gasped. I pulled Laura closer to me.

"That's all we can say for the moment, but we need to talk to everyone here," Foster said. "Don't leave the fairgrounds without speaking to a police officer. We'll have more details for you shortly."

Foster stopped in front of me on his way to the fairgrounds gate. "Well, Ms. Tierney, trouble seems to follow you. We know where to find you, but you'll still need to have a word with one of the officers." He turned and walked toward the gate.

"Stay with Laura," I said to Tracy. "I'll be back in a few minutes."

I walked through the fairgrounds, circling the groups of people who were huddled together. *Where is Bruce?*

The rest of the evening was a waiting game. We lined up at one of the six interview stations the firefighters had set up on the fairgrounds. When I reached the front of our line, I gave the officer my name, told him where I had been in the fairgrounds during the fireworks, and how I could be contacted. "Who was shot?" I asked him. "Is he okay?"

"Sorry, ma'am, I'm not at liberty to say. Next, please."

While I waited for the others, I checked out the people who were still lined up to talk to the police officers. I spotted Hank and Shirley in one lineup. Ivy waved at me from another. I went over to her, and she introduced me to her young man.

"Have you seen Bruce Stohl?" I asked her.

"We saw him with Wilf Mathers before the fireworks started," Ivy said. "Wilf took a picture of Glenn and me, and we told Bruce that we've spent Canada Day at the fairgrounds for as long as we can remember. Bruce wrote it all down."

Glenn put an arm around her. "We may be in *The Times* next week."

"Did you see Bruce after the fireworks ended?" I asked.

They looked at each other and shook their heads.

CHAPTER FIFTEEN

When the alarm clock buzzed at eight the next morning, I wanted to pull the covers over my head. Instead, I dragged myself out of bed and into the car. On the drive into Braeloch, I caught the news on ELK Radio, but there was no mention of the shooting at the fairgrounds.

I claimed a table in the Dominion Hotel's dining room and gave the waitress my order. A few minutes later, Crystal joined me.

"What a rigmarole they put us through last night," she said as she reached for a menu. "I didn't get back here till after midnight."

She watched the waitress place a bowl of yogurt and berries is front of me. "Is that all you're having? I couldn't face the day on that." She ordered a fruit cup, fried eggs, ham, hash browns, and a double order of toast.

I'd be fifty pounds heavier if I ate a breakfast like that every morning, but Crystal looked great—a big-breasted woman with a tiny waist. Add masses of red hair and a pretty face to that, and you had a gorgeous woman. Until she opened her mouth.

"Do you know who was shot last night?" she asked.

I thought of Bruce, but I pushed that thought away. "No. There was nothing about it on ELK Radio this morning."

"It could have happened while we were talking."

I met you just after I'd left Bruce. Where did he go?

Crystal's breakfast arrived, and she gave it her full attention, leaving me free to worry about Bruce. *If he was shot, how serious are his injuries? Or was he...?*

"I'm ready for my day now," Crystal said when she'd polished off the last piece of toast slathered with raspberry jam. "I'll have another coffee, and we can head out."

I signalled the waitress to refill our cups.

"You think Bruce will be at the newspaper now?"

"I doubt it." I poured milk into my coffee. "It's Sunday morning. Sunday is his day off."

"But there's been a shooting. Wouldn't he go in for a big story like that?"

"*The Times* is a weekly," I said. "Its deadline is days away. More details will be available by then."

I took a sip of my coffee. "Crystal, you knew Frank Prentice, the man who rented the locker where you found Bruce's mother."

Her eyebrows shot up. "Who told you about Frank?"

"Frank had family in Braeloch. His father grew up here. You were with Frank at his grandmother's funeral last fall."

Her gray eyes narrowed. "So? Jock was away that weekend, and Frank was an old friend. Jock never understood about Frank."

I wasn't interested in her love life. "Frank's aunt took both of you to his grandmother's home after the funeral. To look at some furniture she wanted to give Frank."

"He was going to drive up with his truck the next week and put it in storage."

"Was this furniture valuable? Antiques?"

"Old Canadiana pieces." She closed her eyes for a moment or two. "I told him what he should take. A lovely old Quebec armoire. A table and four chairs, a cradle, and a cherrywood slant-top desk."

"That was why you bought the contents of his locker."

"Hey, I felt terrible about poor Frank, but I needed a hit. He'd shown me the storage place outside of town where he was going to put the furniture. 'I'm not going to tell nobody about this,' he said. 'You find a buyer, babe, and I'll give you a twenty percent commission.'"

She stared at me defiantly. "I did nothing illegal. When I heard Frank had died, I started to watch the auction listings. I saw one scheduled for Glencoe Self-Storage, and figured it had to be Frank's locker. I went to the auction and paid $900 for the contents."

"Last night you said the locker was disappointing. No antiques?"

"One end table, that was it. I hate to speak badly of the dead, but Frank screwed me around."

"His locker was probably gone through after he died. His mother must've found the rental contract among his papers."

"Yeah, I suppose she took the good stuff and didn't bother to pay the rent." Crystal took another sip of coffee. "Well, crying about it won't bring those pieces back."

She set her mug down on the table. "We're off to Bruce's place?"

"Bruce is out of town today." Which I hoped he was—settling in at Raven Lake.

She glared at me. "Why didn't you say so?"

"I didn't want to spoil your breakfast."

I picked up the bills the waitress had left on the table and took them to the cashier at the front of the room.

Crystal couldn't say I'd left her hungry.

I turned on the car radio to catch the 10 a.m. news.

"A man was fatally shot last night during the Canada Day fireworks show in Braeloch," a male newscaster said. "The body of the Glencoe Highlands resident was found face-down at the northeast edge of the fairgrounds at approximately 10:15 p.m. The fireworks were called off, and police spent the next several hours questioning everyone on the grounds. The man's identity is being withheld until his family can be notified. We'll have more details later today."

Bruce. I pulled onto the side of the road. My hands were shaking. Whoever had tried to frame Bruce for Vi's murder had killed him. With evidence now pointing to Bruce, the killer hoped the police would close the case.

I turned the Volvo around and headed for Bruce's cabin.

Bruce's Chevy wasn't in the driveway, and the front and back doors of the cabin were locked. I scanned the lakefront from the top of the stairs. There was no one in the water or on the beach.

I broke the speed limit driving back to the cottage.

"What's the matter, Mom?" Laura asked when I joined the girls on the porch.

"The man who was shot at the fairgrounds last night...he died." I told them what I'd heard on ELK Radio. "I think it was Bruce."

"It wasn't Bruce," Jamie said. "You said last night that he was with a photographer. No one would shoot him in front of a witness. With all that banging and popping, the man could have been shot anytime during the show."

I was sure it was Bruce. "He was on his own when I last saw him. He'd told the photographer to take some pictures."

"Does he have a cell or a phone at his cabin?" Jamie asked.

"I don't think his landline is connected yet." I rummaged in my handbag and pulled out a notebook. "Here's his cell number."

"I'll check it out." Laura took the notebook and went into the house.

I was right behind her. I poured myself a coffee in the kitchen and listened as she left a voicemail message.

"He's not answering his cell," she said when she got off the phone, "and there's no listing for him on Raven Lake. I called the newspaper, but no one's there. Don't newspapers always have reporters around to cover the news?"

"*The Times* is a weekly," I told her. "The next issue won't be out for another five days."

"Well, I left a message telling him to call us."

Lunch was a quiet meal. We were all thinking about what had happened the night before. The phone rang as we cleared the table. We looked at one another.

"I'll get it." Laura ran into the house.

"For you, Jamie," she called.

Jamie joined us on the porch a few minutes later. "Mom's in the hospital. She had terrible abdominal pains during the night—she's had gallstones before—and she took a taxi to the hospital. The staff there sent her to Peterborough." Her shoulders slumped.

Tracy reached for her hand. "I take it that Peterborough has a larger hospital than Braeloch."

Jamie nodded and gave her a weak smile. "She's going for tests now. I thought we could drive down to Peterborough."

"I'll get a bus to Toronto from there," Tracy said. "You should be with your mother."

"They may have the test results when you get to the hospital," I said.

I went for a paddle after Tracy and Jamie had driven off. It was another quiet afternoon on the lake, so I ventured away from the shoreline. My arms were soon working up a steady rhythm with the paddle, but my mind was speeding along in another direction.

Bruce isn't at home, and he isn't at the newspaper. I tried to focus on the rhythm of the paddle dipping into the water.

Crystal is a regular at storage auctions. She'd know that when Frank hadn't paid his rent on the locker, the company would have sent reminders to his home. And, later, a notice about the contents being put up for auction. She must have figured that his mother had seen those notices and cleared out the locker. So why did she bid on it?

And what about Ella, who claimed she hadn't received an auction notice? Why was she lying?

I entered the bay where Nate and Zoe's cottage was located and continued on to the Norris Cassidy vacation property. A new family was in residence. A woman was sunbathing on the dock, and two kids were in the paddleboat.

I paddled over to the creek that links Black Bear to another lake. The kayak floated down the creek and came out on the other lake. I couldn't remember its name.

I'd travelled this route on a snowmobile four months earlier. A network of creeks links Black Bear to three lakes, and the last lake in the chain is Serenity where Braeloch is located. Turning the kayak around, I promised myself that I'd explore the chain that summer. Then I paddled back up the creek and over to our cottage.

Bruce was on my mind the whole time.

"Feel like going for a drive?" I asked Laura, who was reading on the porch.

"Where to?"

"Over to Raven Lake."

"You're really worried about Bruce."

"I guess I am."

"Let's go."

The cabin looked exactly as it had that morning. The door was locked, and Bruce's Chevy wasn't in the driveway.

"He may be visiting friends," Laura said as we stood at the top of the stairs looking down at the beach.

No. He moved in yesterday morning, and he worked last night. He wanted to settle in here today.

"Or he may be with the police," Laura went on. "They probably think he had something to do with the shooting."

She'd put her finger on the other worry I'd been pushing to the back of my mind.

We'd just opened the cottage door when the telephone rang. It was Jamie, calling to tell us that her mother was scheduled for laparoscopic surgery the next morning to remove her gallbladder. She sounded tense and worried.

"Your mom will recover faster after a laparoscopy than with open surgery," I told her.

"That's what the doctor said. Tracy's on a bus to Toronto, and I have her car. I'll drive Mom to Braeloch when she's discharged, which will probably be Tuesday morning. I'll stay with her for a week."

"Jamie will be in Braeloch for a week!" Laura cried when I relayed what Jamie had said.

"She'll be helping her mother."

"I'll give them a hand."

"Tommy will back tomorrow," I reminded her. "He won't want to be indoors when he could be out on the lake. The rowboat I rented will be delivered around ten in the morning."

"We'll go out on the boat tomorrow," Laura said. "But Tommy may want to go into Braeloch on Tuesday."

She was getting bored with her vacation.

Mara Nowak was in her element on *The Highlands Tonight* that evening. The shooting at the fairgrounds was big news in the township.

"Wilfrid Mathers, a lifetime resident of the Glencoe Highlands, was found dead at the Canada Day fireworks show last night," she said, looking solemnly into the camera. "Police are calling his death a homicide.

"An employee at *The Highland Times* for sixteen years, Mathers was taking photos at the fairgrounds for the newspaper. His body was discovered at the edge of the grounds at approximately 10:15 p.m., and police questioned everyone who was there until the early hours of this morning. The investigation continues, and Bruce Stohl, *The Times'* publisher, is assisting the police with their inquiries."

Relief washed over me. *Bruce is alive.*

But he was with the police, and that wasn't good.

Mara vanished from the screen. She was replaced by a close-up of Wilf's smiling face, with the years of his birth and his death under the photo.

"The cops will really be on Bruce's case now," Laura said.

CHAPTER SIXTEEN

I stopped at Bruce's cabin on my way to work the next morning. Nothing had changed—no Chevy, and no answer when I pounded on the front door.

When I got to Braeloch, I asked for him over the intercom at *The Times* building.

"Mr. Stohl hasn't come in yet," a male voice said.

"Is Maria Dawson there?"

"I'll buzz you in," he said, and a buzzer sounded.

"Good morning, Ms. Tierney," the security guard said when I entered the lobby. He pressed a button on the telephone. "Pat Tierney here to see you."

He pointed to the elevator. "Second floor."

In the newsroom, a dozen men and women huddled in chairs they had drawn into a semicircle. A gray-haired woman in her sixties was crying into a tissue. I waved to Maria, a slender woman with closely cropped dark hair, and she came over to me.

"We're all in shock," she said. "Wilf...he was like a brother to us."

I grasped her hand. "A terrible thing."

"It is, but that's not why you're here." She didn't say it unkindly.

"I'm worried about Bruce. Did you speak to him yesterday? Or this morning?"

A frown creased her face. "No. I tried to reach him when I heard about Wilf yesterday, but he wasn't answering his cell."

"I went over to his place twice yesterday, and again this morning," I said. "He wasn't there."

"That's odd." She frowned. "He said he'd be working on the house on Sunday. But he should be here soon. I'll have him call you when he comes in."

My next stop was the OPP detachment. The officer at the front desk told me Foster was on his way in from Orillia.

I gave the officer my card. "Tell him I'll be at work."

At the branch, Soupy had pulled up a chair beside Ivy's desk. "Saturday was the first time we played it," he was saying as I walked in.

"Morning, Pat," Ivy said.

Soupy gave me a smile and turned back to Ivy. "So what did you think?"

"Hmm, why did you stutter when you sang it?"

"Ivy, the stutters in 'You Ain't Seen Nothing Yet' are famous. Randy Bachman was poking fun at his brother, Gary, the band's manager. Gary stuttered. Randy never intended to release the song, but when the record company—"

Ivy folded her arms across her chest, and gave him a stern look. "I'm sorry, Soupy, but Wilf Mathers was killed on Saturday night. That's all anyone will remember about this year's Canada Day celebrations."

Soupy got out of the chair, deflated.

"Let's get a coffee at Joe's, Soupy," Nate said from his office doorway. "I've got forty minutes before the Robinsons arrive for their appointment."

I watched them leave, happy to see Nate reaching out to Soupy.

"I don't know why anyone would want to kill Wilf," Ivy said to me.

I took the chair Soupy had just vacated. "Tell me about him. I know he worked at the newspaper for many years, but what was Wilf like?"

"A nice, ordinary man. That's what makes it so weird. He was a Scout leader, belonged to the Rotary Club, and he grew up here in Braeloch. He had a freelance business shooting wedding photos. My mom says he never harmed a soul in his life."

A nice, ordinary person like Vi Stohl. "Wilf was taking photos on Saturday night," I said. "Maybe he took a photo of someone who didn't want his picture in the paper."

"Everyone likes to have a photo in *The Times*."

"The news reports didn't say whether the police found his camera on him."

As if on cue, the front door opened and Foster walked in, brandishing my card. "You were looking for me, Ms. Tierney."

I led him down the hall to my office.

"Well? Where is Stohl?" he asked when he'd seated himself across from me.

"*The Highlands Tonight* said Bruce was helping the police with the investigation. That meant he was with you."

"We questioned Stohl on Saturday night. But we haven't been able to locate him since then."

My heart sank. "I've been out to his house three times. He wasn't there. And he wasn't at the newspaper when I stopped by a half hour ago."

"Is that what you came to tell me?"

"No. I ran into Bruce and Wilf at the fairgrounds on Saturday night."

That got his attention.

"It must have been about fifteen minutes before the fireworks ended," I added.

"And?"

"Bruce wanted to talk to me so he sent Wilf off to take photos."

"Where did Mathers go?"

"I wasn't watching."

"Did Stohl say what kind of photos he wanted? People shots?"

"He told him to get photos of the fireworks."

"Then you and Stohl talked."

"We lined up and bought ice cream," I said.

"I don't care what you ate. What did you talk about?"

"He told me you came by his place that morning."

"Did Mathers come back while you were with Stohl?"

"No. We watched the fireworks for a while then Bruce went off to find Wilf. I was on my way back to my family when Mara Nowak announced that there'd been an accident."

Foster sat there in silence.

"What I'm saying," I went on, "is that I was with Bruce from the time Wilf left to take photos to just before Mara made her announcement. He couldn't have killed Wilf."

"That's for us to decide, Ms. Tierney."

Of course. "I'm worried about Bruce. Where could he be?" I was thinking aloud.

"That's what we want to know."

"Did you find Wilf's camera?" I asked. "Was it on him?"

Foster's face shut down, but I pressed on. "He must have taken a photo of something or someone his killer didn't want to appear in the newspaper."

"Let me know as soon as you hear from Stohl."

If I hear from him.

Ivy came into my office as soon as Foster had left the building. "Did they find the camera?"

I looked at her round, earnest face. "Detective Foster wouldn't tell me."

"They didn't find it," she said. "The killer didn't want anyone to see a picture that Wilf took."

"The police may be looking at what's on the memory chip."

"No," she said. "They didn't find the camera."

"I think you're right."

Who or what did Wilf photograph? And where the hell is Bruce?

"How did it go with Soupy?" I asked Nate between appointments that morning.

"He started out being his usual abrasive self."

"I told you he thought he was in line for your job," I said. "He can't seem to accept that he needs more experience."

"I'm aware of that, but it doesn't make it any easier to work with him."

"I can't figure it out. He's headstrong, but he's not stupid."

"Well, he left Joe's happy. I gave him two of the accounts you turned over to me."

I must have looked surprised because he added, "The Callows and Mike Molloy." Neither investment account had much in the way of assets, but both had plenty of potential.

"Don't let Soupy get to you," I told him. "Whatever's bothering him probably has nothing to do with you."

As soon as we broke for lunch, I walked over to *The Times* building. Another security guard was on duty, this one a tight-lipped blonde. She told me that Bruce wasn't available.

I was turning to leave when the old elevator came grinding down from an upper floor. Its metal doors opened with a clang, and Maria Dawson stepped into the lobby.

"Has Bruce been in?" I asked her.

"Not yet. Detective Foster was here this morning." She exhaled loudly. "He asked us about the camera Wilf was using on Saturday. Whether we had it. We don't."

The police didn't find his camera.

"Wilf had a camera with a zoom lens when Bruce introduced us on Saturday night. Did it belong to *The Times*?"

"It was probably his Nikon D4. He preferred to use his own equipment."

"If the police were asking whether you'd found the camera, that means they're looking for it."

"That's right." Worry filled her eyes. "I drove out to Bruce's place after you left this morning. No one's there. I'm afraid whoever killed Wilf—"

I put up a hand. "Don't even think that."

I was seriously worried. As Maria had been about to say, whoever killed Wilf may have wanted Bruce out of the way, too.

Or had he gone AWOL? Bruce had left a tenure track position at a university a few years before and wandered aimlessly before coming to Braeloch where Ted and Vi had relocated. He might have dropped everything and hit the road again.

I decided to eat lunch at my desk in case Bruce, or somebody who knew where he was, called. I'd taken the first bite of my sandwich when the telephone rang.

"I'm back, Mrs. T!" Tommy said at the other end of the line. "Maxie's really happy to see me."

"Did you have a good time with your grandmother?"

"It was okay, but I missed Maxie."

"I'll give you a big hug when I get home. Put sunscreen on before you go into the water."

I'd just returned to my sandwich, when Ivy brought Russell Shingler into the office.

"Please go on eating," he said when I put the sandwich aside.

I covered it with foil wrap and dropped it into its paper bag. "How can I help you?"

He sat back in the chair across from my desk, a smile on his ruddy face. He was a handsome, fair-haired man who looked as if he spent a lot of time on the golf course.

"I've come to a decision, but I haven't run it by Yvonne yet."

I had a feeling I wasn't going to like whatever it was.

"We couldn't have more children after Kyle was born, and that saddened Yvonne immensely. Laura isn't ready to raise a family, so I've decided that Yvonne and I will raise our grandchild. We'll pay Laura a substantial sum of money when the baby is born."

"You want to pay my daughter to give up her child?"

"And we'll take care of Laura's education expenses. University tuition, residence or rent, and living expenses until she finds a job in her chosen field. All she has to do is make Kyle the custodial parent."

I didn't know whether to laugh or throw my paperweight at him. "You want to buy my daughter's child."

"I want to compensate Laura for any inconvenience."

"You want my daughter to give up her baby. For money."

He shifted in his seat. "I wouldn't put it that way. I just want what's best for our son, your daughter, and their child. I want to secure their happiness. I don't want to 'buy' the baby."

I had to bite my tongue to curb my outrage. I hadn't been happy to learn that Laura was pregnant, but I had come to accept that there would be an addition to our family at the end of the year. Now Russell Shingler was flashing his money and talking about procuring a baby for his wife. And this wasn't any baby he was talking about, it was my grandchild.

"Mr. Shingler, Laura is going raise her child with my help. Kyle can be as involved as he wants to be."

He looked astonished. "You need some time to think about what I said. Laura's education will be paid as long as she wants to stay in school. Law school, medical school, post-graduate studies, whatever she wants to pursue will be taken care of."

"Mr. Shingler, get out of my office."

"Think it over," he said as he rose from his chair. "Discuss it with Laura."

I did not discuss it with Laura. She was in good spirits at dinner, relaxed and happy. I saw that she'd gained a little weight. Her face and breasts were fuller, and her hair was thick and glossy.

"I feel like a load's been lifted off me since we sent Yvonne and Russell packing," she said. "No more wedding talk."

"Wedding?" Tommy asked. "Are you and Kyle getting married?"

"No, Tommy. We're not getting married."

"I've never been to a wedding," he said.

"I haven't heard from Kyle since his parents were here," Laura went on, "and I don't care."

"When am I gonna see Bruce's new place?" Tommy asked.

I smiled at him. "Soon, I hope."

"Have you heard from Bruce?" Laura asked me.

"No. He wasn't at work, and he's not at his cabin." Maria had called before I left my office. She told me that The Times' business manager had just returned from Raven Lake. No one was at Bruce's place.

"Where can he be?" Laura asked.

"I wish I knew," I said.

"He said we'd go swimming at his beach," Tommy said.

I got up from my chair and put an arm around him. "Bruce hasn't been seen since Saturday night. We're worried about him."

"Where did he go?"

"Nobody knows," I said.

"Think, Mom," Laura said. "You know Bruce better than most people around here. Who are his friends?"

"He sees a fair bit of Lainey and Burt Campbell. But Lainey called me this afternoon when she couldn't reach him at The Times."

"Soupy?"

"No. I've been talking to Soupy and Ivy about Bruce all day."

"Think, Mom. He must've mentioned someone."

"After Ted died, Bruce began seeing a psychologist who's a relative of the Campbells. I asked Lainey if Dr. Reynolds had heard from Bruce. She called me back to say he hadn't seen or heard from him in a couple of weeks."

"There must be someone else."

"No one I can think of."

We were clearing the table when Jamie called to say that her mother's laparoscopy had gone well. She planned to drive Ronnie home in the morning.

"Tommy and I can go over tomorrow and help them," Laura said when I told her Jamie's news.

"The best thing you can do is let Ronnie rest," I told her. "She'll be exhausted after the drive from Peterborough."

It was time for Laura to get back to her life in the city.

After the dishes were put away, she curled up on the sofa with a book.

"A game of Chinese checkers, Mrs. T?" Tommy asked, a grin on his face.

"Sounds good to me."

My thoughts were on Jamie and her mother as I watched him set up the game board on the dining room table.

"You can go first, Mrs. T."

I moved one of my marbles into an empty hole on the board. Tommy took his turn, and we began to move across the board. I let my thoughts drift, and something Ronnie had told me surfaced. Years ago, she and Vi had explored the trails around the lookout above Braeloch, and sometimes they met up with a young man called Daniel.

"Mrs. T, you're not concentrating," Tommy scolded.

I hopped my marble over the one beside it and smiled at him. We continued advancing across the board until all Tommy's marbles were in the triangle directly across from his starting point. "I win!" he cried.

He looked at me and shook his head. "That was too easy, Mrs. T. You were far away."

After I'd tucked Tommy into bed, I sat beside Laura on the sofa. "Like to get back to the city?" I asked.

"I'll go back on the weekend. I need to start my job, and you'll have left work by then."

I nodded, grateful that she'd be with Tommy until I left the branch.

"Kyle will come and get you?"

"That's not a good idea. I can take the bus."

"I'll drive you down on Saturday. Tommy can spend the night with his grandmother."

"You're the best, Mom!" She planted a kiss on my cheek and went off to bed.

I poured myself a glass of chardonnay and took it out on the porch. Frogs were croaking down by the lake. I sipped my wine and looked up at the star-studded sky.

Bruce met Daniel Laughton at Highland Ridge. Are they still in touch?

CHAPTER SEVENTEEN

I dropped into Highland Ridge the next morning. Sheila Sommers greeted me with a smile when I was taken to her office. "What brings you back here, Ms. Tierney?"

I told her that Bruce hadn't been seen for a few days and that I was worried about him.

The smile left her face. "The man at *The Times* who was killed on Saturday night…"

"It's been a bit much for Bruce. His mother and now Wilf Mathers. He probably needs some time to himself, but I want to know if he's okay."

"How can I help?"

"I'm trying to come up with the names of friends of his family, any people he might be staying with. Can you tell me who visited Vi while she was here?"

"Vi didn't have many visitors. Her husband, of course, and Bruce. Lainey Campbell was a regular, and she sometimes brought her husband with her. Veronica Collins visited when Vi first arrived, but she stopped coming. Some people aren't comfortable around people with dementia."

She closed her eyes for a moment or two. "And Daniel Laughton."

"*The* Daniel Laughton."

"Yes, the environmentalist." She smiled. "He's a wonderful man. I so enjoyed his books on Canadian wildlife and that TV show he had. The world needs more people like him."

She snapped out of her reverie. "Anyway, Dr. Laughton came to see Vi about once a month. He sent her a lovely floral arrangement last Christmas."

"He knew Bruce?"

"Oh, yes. I saw them leave the building together not long ago."

"Does Dr. Laughton have a place around here?"

"He has a vacation home on Raven Lake."

After our client meetings that morning, I went into my office and flipped open the Glencoe Highlands phone directory. It had a telephone listing for an R. Laughton, but gave no address. There was nothing for a Daniel or a D. Laughton

I tried the number for the R. Laughton, who turned out to be Daniel's son Rob. He was reluctant to give me his father's number, but I told him I wasn't an admirer wanting a selfie with the great man. And I wasn't a reporter. I couldn't say what it was about, only that it was urgent that I speak to Daniel. Rob could have called my bluff, but he didn't.

I punched in the number he gave me, and a woman picked up.

"Laughton residence."

"My name is Pat Tierney. May I speak to Daniel Laughton?"

"How did you get this number?"

I didn't want to get Rob into trouble. "I'm not at liberty to say, but it's important that I talk to Daniel."

There was silence on the other end of the line.

"Hello?" I held my breath, hoping she wouldn't hang up.

"I'm afraid he's can't come to the phone now. What's this about?"

"I'm looking for someone Daniel knows, a man named Bruce Stohl. He's missing, and I hope Daniel can tell me where he is."

"There must be some mistake. I don't know what you're talking about."

"If you could ask—"

"Goodbye." She hung up the phone.

Seething at her rudeness, I grabbed my handbag and left the building.

I was approaching Joe's Diner when a maroon van pulled into a parking space on Main Street, narrowly missing the bumper of the vehicle in front of it. Chuck Gibson was at the wheel of the van, and Gracie was beside him. I waited for them to get out.

"Good to see you, Pat," Chuck said, coming around to open Gracie's door.

"How's everything going?" I asked when they joined me on the sidewalk.

Gracie shook her head, and I saw that she looked shaken. "A couple showed up this weekend."

Chuck put an arm around her, and she went on. "When we told them our home wasn't for rent, they weren't at all nice about it. The man wanted his $1,500 back. We told him we had nothing to do with the ad he'd answered, but he didn't believe us. Said if they didn't get their money back, he'd break our picture window. "

"I got Sergeant Bouchard to come over," Chuck said.

"Good thing we'd called the police before and they knew about our problem," Gracie continued. "Sergeant Bouchard told the couple that our home has been targeted by those con men."

"The couple backed off?" I asked.

She nodded. "They weren't happy, but they left. They could come back, though, and other people will probably arrive, too. The police haven't put an end to it."

"The ad was on a different site this time. VacationSpots," Chuck said. "Posted by a different fellow, too, Sergeant Bouchard said. But no one seems to know who these people really are. They can set up e-mail accounts under any names they like."

"That couple threatened to break your window so it's no longer just a nuisance when renters show up," I said. "I wonder if the police had the rental sites release the IP addresses of the computers that posted the ads."

Chuck and Gracie looked at each other in dismay. "IP addresses?" Gracie said. "This is getting much too complicated."

We wrapped up our client meetings around four. I was gathering up my things to head out to the lake when the phone on my desk rang.

"Mrs. Shingler is here to see you," Ivy said.

"Send her in." I knew this wasn't going to be fun.

Yvonne had a smile on her face. "Have I caught you at a bad time?" she asked.

"Come in and close the door." I pointed to the chair in front of my desk.

She perched on the edge of the seat, her arms wrapped around her handbag. "Last night, Russell told me what the two of you discussed. I decided I had to speak to you myself."

I waited for her to go on. I wasn't about to make this any easier for her.

"You were tied up in meetings all afternoon," she said. "I would have gone to see Laura, but I don't know where your new place is."

Thank God for that.

"Russell told you that we want to raise Kyle and Laura's child. We'd compensate Laura financially, and we'd give the child every advantage."

"And Russell must have told you my answer."

"He said you needed some time to think about it."

"My answer was and still is no."

"Pat, I couldn't have any more children after Kyle, although we desperately wanted to. We considered adopting. What troubled us about adoption was that we wouldn't know the child's family background. But this would be perfect. Our son is the father, and we know Laura and her family."

"Mrs. Shingler—"

"Yvonne."

"If someone wanted you to give up Kyle when he was born, you would have been outraged. You never would have considered it. So you will understand how Laura would feel if she knew what you were asking. She's looking forward to being a mother in a few months, and she intends to bring up her child to the very best of her abilities."

Her violet eyes bored into me. "But will that be good enough for the child? A child needs a father and a mother, and Laura doesn't want to get married."

I tried staring her down. "Laura isn't ready for marriage, and neither is Kyle. A rocky marriage would be terrible for a child."

"That's why Russell and I will raise our grandchild."

"Laura will live with me while she finishes school. I've brought up two children, and I still have a young boy at home. My daughter Tracy will be a big part of the child's life. So will Kyle, and you and your husband. Our grandchild will have lots of people to love and nurture him."

Yvonne hadn't taken in a word that I'd said. She rose from the chair, eyes blazing and nostrils distended. A warrior queen ready for battle.

I had to get her out of there. "I'll walk you to the front door."

As I came around from behind my desk, she drew herself up to her full height, which meant she came up to my shoulders. "You haven't heard the last from us, Pat. Russell and I are going to bring up our grandchild. That little boy or girl needs a father and a mother who are living under the same roof."

She turned on her heel and strode down the hall.

I locked the front door behind her. I was hanging the Closed sign in the window when the phone on Ivy's desk rang.

"For you, Pat," she said.

"I'll take it in my office." I hurried down the hall.

"Daniel Laughton here. Sorry I missed your call. I understand it was concerning our mutual friend."

I was caught off guard. "Yes, I'm looking for—"

"Not on the phone, please," he said sharply. "Let's discuss this in person. Can you come out to our home on Raven Lake?"

"I can come right now."

"My wife, Frances, has gone into town. She'll meet you at the Raven Lake boat launch. Do you know where that is?"

"Yes." The Gibsons' and Bruce's homes on Raven Lake were accessible by road, but I'd driven past the boat launch many times.

"When can you get there?"

"I'll be at the launch in thirty minutes."

I'd put Braeloch in my rearview mirror when I realized that I hadn't given the woman who'd answered the Laughtons' telephone my number, or even told her where I worked.

The only way Daniel would know where to find me was if Bruce told him. That means Bruce is either with him, or in contact with him. He's okay!

CHAPTER EIGHTEEN

I pulled into the boat launch's parking lot a little after five and claimed one of the few empty spaces. Bruce's blue Chevy was three cars down from mine. *He's with the Laughtons!*

"Are you Pat Tierney?" a white-haired woman in a navy windbreaker called from a boat as I approached the dock.

"I'm Frances Laughton," she said when I went over to her battered aluminum boat. "Careful getting in. Bottom's slippery." Her weather-beaten face held no clue to why I'd been summoned, and I had a feeling she wouldn't tell me if I asked.

When I was bundled into a life jacket, Frances fired up the outboard motor and took us out on the lake. Our progress across the water was slow, and I remembered hearing that Raven was the largest lake in the township. I wondered how far the Laughtons' place was and whether I'd make it back to my car before dark. But there was nothing I could do but sit there and take in the scenery.

I knew that a greenie like Daniel Laughton wouldn't own a speed boat. I was surprised that the Laughtons took any kind of gas-guzzler out on the lake, but a long paddle in a canoe would have been strenuous for a couple in their seventies. There seemed to be a point where even tree-huggers drew the line.

The Laughtons' retreat was on a northern arm of the lake. We entered a bay without any sign of human habitation, and Frances pointed the boat toward a wooded knoll on the far shore. As we got closer, I made out a structure tucked behind the fir trees. A sprawling log cabin, stained dark brown.

There was no dock. Frances maneuvered the boat along the shoreline to an expanse of rock that sloped into the water. An aluminum canoe was overturned on the rock. A stooped, white-haired man, who I recognized from his television show and his photos as Daniel Laughton, came down the path from the house. Frances threw him a rope, and he tied it to a cedar.

He raised a hand to me. "Take off your shoes."

I slipped off my shoes and socks and rolled up the legs of my trousers. Daniel held the boat steady as Frances and I got out. We waded through the water, and he led us up the path to the house.

On the porch, he pulled out a chair from a table covered with a red checked cloth. "Ms. Tierney."

I seated myself, and Daniel sat across from me. Frances went into the house.

Where is Bruce?

"Let me apologize for Frances's abruptness on the phone," Daniel said.

"No need. She didn't know who I was. You value your privacy."

He nodded. "There are a lot of demands on me—from supporters, fund-raisers, the media. I find it difficult to say no, but Frances can. She's my gatekeeper."

Frances returned with a tray loaded with four mugs of camomile tea and a plate of cookies studded with seeds. "Help yourselves," she said, placing the tray on the table. She took a chair between Daniel and me.

Four mugs. One is for Bruce.

"You were looking for Bruce," Daniel said as I reached for a mug.

"I was."

"He'd like to speak to you."

The door opened, and Bruce stepped onto the porch. His face was drawn, and his shoulders sagged. He didn't look at me.

"Bruce," I said, "we've been worried about you."

"Sorry." He touched my arm and sat in the chair beside me.

"Have you heard about Wilf?"

"Yes." His face contorted with pain. "Foster questioned me for hours after the fireworks. It was nearly 3 a.m. when he let me go. I knew he'd be at my cabin in a few hours, so I called Daniel. He picked me up at the boat launch around seven. I had to get away."

Now that I knew Bruce was okay, I was annoyed. Really annoyed. "You must've known we'd be worried about you."

He looked down at the floor.

"And you've dug yourself in deeper with the police by taking off," I added.

"I couldn't cope with Foster any longer."

I saw that he was still rattled. "He told you not to leave the area without telling him."

"Bruce hasn't left the Glencoe Highlands," Frances said. "We're still in the township here."

"I don't know if the police will see it that way." Then I turned back to Bruce. "You have to get back. Your team at *The Times* is reeling. They just lost Wilf, and they're worried about you."

He gave me a hangdog look. "The police have no other suspects. Foster wants a confession from me."

"Why make it easier for him?" Frances said. "Stay here."

"I'm sorry, dear," Daniel said, patting her arm, "but he can't do that. Bruce has to face Foster, and sooner would be better than later."

Frances frowned but said nothing.

"You can't run away from him," Daniel said to Bruce.

"The longer you stay away, the worse it looks," I said. "It looks like you have something to hide."

Bruce blinked, and I could almost hear his mind clicking. I hoped Daniel's words and mine carried some weight.

"Remember our plan?" I said. "We're going to find out what happened to your mother. Put up with Foster and his questions, and focus on the plan."

"She's right, Bruce," Daniel said.

Bruce bowed his head.

I stood up. "Get your things together."

Bruce looked as if he was about to protest, but he got up and went into the house.

Frances stood up. "I'll see if he needs a hand. And I'll give Rob a call. He can take them back to the launch." She gave Daniel a slight nod of her head and went inside.

Daniel turned to me. "Bruce was doing well until Vi…"

"He lost his mother, who he cared for deeply. And the police wouldn't let up on him."

"So he said."

"Bruce needs to get back to work. He has a good team at *The Times*, and he enjoys putting out the paper."

Daniel looked at me closely. "How did you find us?"

"I was told that Vi had a friend called Daniel when she was a girl. Someone who knew all about the great outdoors. When I heard that Daniel Laughton visited her at Highland Ridge, I assumed that was the same Daniel. I looked in the phone book, and I saw your son's listing."

He smiled. "I had a crush on Vi when I was nineteen. She was a few years younger than me, a lovely young woman."

"Anything serious develop between you?"

He smiled. "Nothing serious. I got up the courage to ask her out a few times. Some holding hands, a few chaste kisses. A few summers later, she'd set her sights on Ted Stohl."

"How did you connect again?"

"Years later, I bumped into her in Toronto. From then on, we had lunch once a year, just before Christmas."

"Who suggested that?"

"I did." He brought a hand up to his face. "She looked a little sad when we first met in Toronto, and I wanted to know why."

"Did you find out?"

He shook his head. "No. It was foolish, really. I'm happily married to Frances, and as she will tell you, to my work. But I couldn't let go of my memories of the teenage Vi. I was ready to have her cry on my shoulder if she wanted to. But she never did."

"Did Frances know?"

"Of course. I explained it to her, and she had no problem with it. She knows I'm devoted to her."

"Did you know that Vi worked at a bank in Toronto?"

He nodded. "Yes, but she never told me which one."

"Did she tell you there had been a problem at work?"

He looked thoughtful. "That would've been…six years ago. Her memory had started to slip. She missed our Christmas lunch that year, and we had to reschedule. When we got together in January, she said there'd been some problems at work."

"Did she say what happened?"

"Some money was missing. She thought a fellow employee had taken it and put the blame on her. I didn't think for a moment that Vi had stolen money, but with her memory problems she could have misplaced it." He held out his hands. "I gathered Ted came up with the sum that was missing, and charges were never laid."

"Did she tell you how much money it was?"

"No."

"Did she suspect anyone at the bank?"

He shrugged and looked out at the lake.

I left him on the porch and walked around the cabin. Hydro and telephone lines ran from poles at the back of the clearing to the cabin. On the other side of the lake, an internet tower rose above the trees. The Laughtons were connected to civilization at their sylvan retreat.

A speedboat zoomed across the lake, water spraying out from behind it like a rooster tail. It came to a stop in front of the Laughtons' property. Frances and Bruce came out on the porch, and I joined them there. "Our son has a cottage on the next bay," Daniel said with a wry smile. "There are times when his boat comes in handy."

"So much for saving the planet," Frances said.

Daniel led us down the path to the waterfront and introduced me to his son. "I wish there was a fast, ecofriendly boat," Daniel told him.

"You can't have everything, Dad," Rob said.

Bruce sat slumped on the seat beside me on the trip across the lake. When Rob dropped us off at the launch, we thanked him and I followed Bruce to his Chevy.

"You've got to see Foster right now," I said at the driver's door. "I'll go with you."

"I want to stop at my place," he muttered. He was stalling for time.

"Fine, it's on our way."

He grunted and got into the Chevy.

I was right behind him as he pulled out of the parking lot.

From the driveway, his cabin looked exactly as it had on Monday morning. The window shades were drawn, and the screen door on the front porch was closed. The maples between the neighboring homes waved gently in the breeze.

"As you left it?" I asked Bruce when we'd got out of our cars.

"Seems to be."

It wasn't until we were on the porch that we knew something was wrong. The door to the house was ajar.

Bruce's face drained of color.

I pushed the door open with my foot. Bruce stepped into the house and moaned like a wounded animal. Dozens of cardboard boxes had been stacked against the living room walls. Several were torn open, and papers were scattered across the floor.

"Don't touch anything," I said. "The police may be able to lift fingerprints off the boxes and papers. What are these papers?"

"Notes for the classes I taught at the University of Calgary." He gave me a weak smile. "Probably not what my visitors expected to find."

"What about your personal documents?"

"In a safety deposit box at the bank."

I checked the windows and the back door. They were all secure. Then I went back to the front door. "Your intruders either had a key, or they picked this lock."

Bruce gave me a look of pain. "I thought I'd bought a home, but there's no peace for me here. Foster shows up whenever he likes, determined to break me. Now someone's got in and gone through my things."

I put a hand on his shoulder. "Hang in, Bruce. Right now, we've got to get the police over here. Phone?"

"Landline's not connected yet."

I thought of the internet tower I'd seen across the lake from the Laughtons' property, but I didn't have my cell phone with me.

"We'll drive over to the detachment," I said, "but pack some clothes first. You're staying with us tonight."

When he was packed, I watched as he locked the front door. "Better get the lock changed tomorrow," I said.

"They'll just pick the new one."

"Talk to a locksmith. There are locks now that are supposed to be pick-proof."

Foster wasn't at the police detachment. Sergeant Roger Bouchard fixed stern black eyes on Bruce. "He'll want to speak to you. Take a seat in the waiting room."

"Bruce's home has been broken into," I told Bouchard. "He's staying at my place tonight. Detective Foster can talk to him there."

"Stohl waits here," Bouchard said.

Bruce looked ready to bolt. I had to get him to our cottage. I wrote my name, roadside number, and phone number on the back of a grocery list I found in my pocket. "Here's my contacts at Black Bear Lake." I handed the paper to Bouchard.

I gave him the no-nonsense look I'd perfected on my daughters. "Get hold of Foster, and have him come out to the lake. Bruce will be there."

Static erupted from a police radio behind Bouchard. "Fitzwilliams here," a male voice said. "Accident on Highway 36, five miles south of Braeloch. Speeding car collided with a rock cut."

"You're at the scene?" Bouchard asked.

"Yes, sir. We need an ambulance and backup."

Bouchard picked up a telephone receiver.

I inclined my head at Bruce. He followed me outside.

"Leave your Chevy at *The Times*," I told him. "We'll take my car. I'll get you to town in the morning."

We were silent on the drive to the lake. While Bruce brooded, I thought about how we should handle Foster. But those thoughts vanished when I saw the black Ferrari in the driveway. I braced myself for another confrontation with Yvonne.

We found the kids in the kitchen. Kyle was chopping vegetables at the table, while Laura stirred something in a pot. "Hello, Mrs. T," Kyle said. "Hey, Bruce."

I looked around. No Yvonne.

"You're back, Bruce!" Tommy said, coming down the hall with Maxie. "We were worried about you."

Bruce smiled and ruffled Tommy's hair.

Laura didn't look happy. "Kyle turned up half an hour ago so I put him to work. He wants to talk to you."

"Let's go down to the lake," Bruce said to Tommy.

"Can we go fishing?" Tommy asked.

"No fishing right now," I said. "We'll eat dinner soon."

Bruce held the door open for Tommy. "We won't go far," he said.

I sat beside Kyle at the table. "Finish work early?" I asked him.

He put the knife down and looked at Laura. "Mom and Dad told me last night they're going to raise our baby."

She came over to the table, her hands clenched. "What?"

"That's not their decision to make," I said.

"Who do your parents think they are?" Laura cried. "They want to arrange the world to suit themselves."

"Mom and Dad think money can buy anything," Kyle said. "I told them that you and I are going to bring up our baby, but they wouldn't listen."

"Make them listen," Laura said.

Kyle raised his eyes to the ceiling. "Easier said than done. Mom was all revved up. Talking about decorating a room, buying baby furniture."

"Your parents aren't going anywhere near my baby," Laura hissed.

"That's what I told them." Kyle looked at me. "Then Mom drove up here today to speak to Mrs. T."

Laura turned to me. "Did she?"

I nodded. "Yvonne came to the branch this afternoon, but I'm not sure why she bothered. She'd already made up her mind."

"She called me after she saw you," Kyle said. "Said you weren't cooperating. So I left work, took the Ferrari, and drove up here."

"The boss's son leaves work whenever he likes." I shouldn't have said that, but I'd had enough of the Shinglers.

"We can't let her—" Laura said.

"I wish I knew what it would take to make her back down," I said.

Kyle banged a hand on the table. "I do." He jumped to his feet and grabbed his windbreaker from the back of the chair. "Gotta go!"

He was at the door in three strides. We heard the Ferrari start up and roar down the drive.

A car came up the drive while we were eating dessert.

"Kyle's back!" Tommy cried. "He'll take me fishing in the morning."

I could tell by the sound of the engine that it wasn't the Ferrari. I went to the door with Tommy, and we watched Foster get out of a gray Chrysler sedan.

"Go down to the lake with Tommy," I said to Laura.

I held the door open for Foster. "Bruce is here."

Foster brushed by me. His face was a thundercloud. "Give me one good reason why I shouldn't take you to the detachment and lock you up," he said when he saw Bruce.

Bruce slumped in his chair. "I told you he's after me."

"I'll give you a good reason," I said as Foster took a chair at the table. "You have nothing to go on. A lawyer would tear your case to shreds, and you know it."

Foster leaned back in his seat, but said nothing.

"You can't charge Bruce with anything," I continued. "You've questioned him since his mother was found, but you don't have a shred of evidence against him. And don't bring up that cardigan. If Bruce had killed Vi, he would hardly display her clothing on his porch."

I took a deep breath and went on. "Now Wilf Mathers has been murdered, and you can't pin that on Bruce either. I was with Bruce at the fireworks when Wilf was killed."

Foster ignored me. "I told you not to leave the township," he said to Bruce.

"He didn't leave the township," I said. "He was with his friends, the Laughtons, on Raven Lake. In this township. He's been with them since early Sunday morning. I met him there this afternoon—"

Foster turned to look at me. "You knew where he was all along."

"I didn't. Daniel Laughton called me this afternoon. I went out to their place and brought Bruce back with me."

"You knew we'd want to speak to you again about Saturday night," Foster said to Bruce.

Bruce's eyes flicked away.

"We stopped by Bruce's cabin on the way to the detachment," I said. "Bruce?"

He told Foster about the unlocked front door and the ransacked boxes.

"When I went out to the cabin yesterday morning," I said, "the door was locked."

"That's how I left it," Bruce said.

Foster scribbled in his notebook then got up from the table.

"Are you going to the cabin now?" I asked. "I'll drive Bruce."

"It can wait till morning." Foster snapped his notebook shut. "Meet me there at nine."

Then he turned to me. "I wasn't speaking to you."

When Tommy was tucked into the twin bed beside mine, I handed Bruce clean sheets and a pillowcase and pointed to the hall. "Room to the right with the *Star Wars* poster. The light is on."

It had been a long day, and I needed time to myself. I pulled on a canvas hat and a long-sleeved shirt. I didn't bother with DEET.

Outside, the stars illuminated my little corner of the world. The lake was calm and ringed with cottage lights. An owl gave a series of quavering whistles, descending in pitch. I stretched out on the expanse of rock that sloped into the water; it was still warm from the sun. I swatted at the occasional blackfly, but their numbers had dropped since the barbecue the previous Friday night.

The sound of rippling water caught my ears. Paddle strokes. A figure in a canoe glided from behind the bushes at the property line.

"Good evening," I called out.

"Pat?" A woman's voice. She eased the canoe closer to the shoreline.

"That's right, Zoe. What brings you out on the water at this time of night?"

"It's lovely out here. Mist on the water. And you see things you don't during the day. Beaver and mink. One night, I saw a bobcat drinking at the edge of the lake."

I nodded, although I didn't think she could see me. "And no speedboats."

She gave a throaty chuckle. "Not many, thank God. Still, I keep close to shore where it's safer. And where I see the wildlife."

"Shouldn't you carry a light?"

"I wouldn't be part of the night with a light." She paused for a moment. "Nate told me you have a kayak. We should go out together some evening."

"I'm just getting the hang of it. I'd slow you down."

"At night, it's not about speed, and it shouldn't be during the day either. Give me a call if you want to join me."

She raised an arm and continued on her way, her paddle making small splashes as it dipped into the water.

CHAPTER NINETEEN

Foster be damned, I thought as I drove to Raven Lake in the rain the next morning. Bruce's car was in Braeloch, and he needed a lift to his cabin. Foster couldn't keep me away.

We were the first to arrive. "We'd better wait here," I said when I'd turned off the ignition. "We don't want Foster to say we've contaminated a crime scene."

"We certainly wouldn't want *that*."

We stared at the rain on the windshield for a few minutes. "Where is he?" Bruce asked. "I said I'd be at the ten o'clock meeting. We go to press tomorrow night."

"The newspaper will still come out if you miss the meeting."

Fifteen minutes later, Foster turned up. He glared at me as he stepped out of his Chrysler. "I thought I said you weren't invited."

"Bruce needed a lift, so here I am."

He frowned. "Let's get on with it." He turned to Bruce. "Let us in, Mr. Stohl."

Bruce unlocked the front door, and we followed him inside. It was a warm summer day, despite the rain, but the cabin felt chilly.

I'd brought a thermos of coffee, and I asked Foster if he wanted a cup. He waved off my offer. He did a quick tour of the cabin and returned to the front door.

"No splintered wood on the door or jamb, and the dead bolt isn't bent." He knelt beside the door, and took a magnifying glass from his raincoat pocket. I didn't think anyone used magnifying glasses outside of Sherlock Holmes movies.

"Scratch marks." He looked up at me, standing beside him. "See the scratches on the key plate? They're shiny, which means they were made recently."

"Keys can leave scratches," I said.

"Not fine ones like these." He stood up, and wiped his hands on his raincoat. "No call for a forensic locksmith. Someone picked this lock with a shim."

He looked at Bruce. "Piss off someone at the newspaper?"

He went into the kitchen. "I'll have that coffee now. Black, two sugars." He took a cardboard box off a chair, set it on the table, and sat down.

"The lock on Frank Prentice's storage unit," I said as I put a mug of coffee in front of him. "Had it been picked?"

I expected him to tell me that was police business. He stared at me for a few seconds then said, "No."

He took a sip of his coffee. "So why am I here?"

"Someone picked the lock and came in," I said. "I believe that's a crime called breaking and entering."

"Anything taken?" Foster asked Bruce.

"Not unless they helped themselves to my lecture notes."

"That's what those papers are?" Foster asked.

Bruce nodded. "Yup."

"Some missing?"

Bruce smiled. "I doubt it. There's not a big market for Philosophy 101."

"Will you dust the boxes for fingerprints?" I asked Foster.

He shrugged. "Nothing's been taken." He turned to Bruce. "You might consider a home security system with a camera. Anyone who tries to get in will be caught in the act."

He looked into the box he'd placed on the table. "Speaking of cameras. Is this yours?"

He tilted the box so we could see into it. It held a camera with a large zoom lens. To my untrained eyes, it looked like the one Wilf was carrying on Saturday night. "Well?" he asked.

Bruce went over to the box. "A Nikon D4. Could be Wilf's."

"The missing camera turns up here." Foster pushed his mug aside and stood up.

In no time, he had Bruce and the box with the camera out of the cabin. I followed them to the Chrysler.

Inside the car, Bruce held up a set of keys. He turned to say something to Foster. The passenger window slid down.

"Will you lock up, Pat?" Bruce handed me his keys.

"Bruce didn't know about the camera," I shouted into the car. "If he'd killed Wilf, he wouldn't have left his camera in an open box when he was expecting you here. Just like the cardigan on his porch—"

The window closed. Foster revved the motor, and the Chrysler charged down the lane.

As I locked the front door, I thought about where a home-security camera could be mounted to capture the image of an intruder. On the doorframe? Or above it?

That made me think of the surveillance cameras at Glencoe Self-Storage. The cameras hadn't captured any people in the yard the night before the auction. When had Vi's body been dumped in the locker?

I burned rubber when I left the cabin. Not a smart way to navigate a narrow, winding lane in the rain. I slowed down on the side road and came to a full stop at the highway, wondering whether to turn left and drive into Braeloch. But what more could I say to the police?

I pulled a right onto the highway. Five minutes later, I braked in front of Glencoe Self-Storage's office. The Open sign was in the window. Noreen Andrews was behind her desk.

She looked up at me and adjusted the Toronto Blue Jays cap on her head. "What's the matter with the cops around here? It's been two weeks since a body was found on our premises, and they still haven't figured out how it got here."

I held out my hands palms up.

"They got any suspects?" she asked.

"They haven't told me." I pulled up a chair and sat down in front of her desk.

"And now Wilf Mathers has been killed," she said. "That's got to be related."

"I'd say so."

"Folks are gettin' knocked off around here, and the cops are just scratchin' their heads." She groaned. "What do we pay them for?"

"Ms. Andrews, you said the surveillance cameras didn't capture any unusual activity in the yard the night before Vi Stohl's body was found."

"A family of racoons and a fox came through that night. But they didn't put that body in the locker."

"So it wasn't put in that night. When could it have got in there?"

"The cameras go on at six when we close the office. They turn off at eight in the morning when we open up again."

What are you saying? "They're not on during the day?"

"What'd be the point? People break in at night. We got someone here in the office all day."

"You can't watch every locker from here."

"No, but renters come and go all day long. No one breaks into a locker when people are around."

"Someone got into Frank Prentice's locker during the day." I remembered what Foster had told me. "And that person had a key. The police said the lock hadn't been picked."

"Frank had been dead for weeks by then," Noreen said. "That's why he hadn't made his payments."

"That's right. Vi's killer—I assume that whomever put her in the locker killed her—knew that Frank wouldn't be using the locker. And other renters wouldn't think twice about seeing someone going into the locker."

Her eyes shifted, and I could see that she was processing what I'd said.

"The killer wouldn't have needed a keycard because the gate is open during the day," I continued. "But he probably had one because he was familiar with your business and its hours of operation. Who had activated cards two weeks ago?"

Noreen whipped the cap off her head and flung it on the desk. "Can't tell you that. If word got out that I ratted on clients, my business would tank."

I wanted to shake her. She was running a storage business, not a high-level military operation. But I kept my cool. "Can you show me what the cards look like?"

She pondered that for a few moments, then opened a desk drawer and took out a stack of plastic cards. She handed one to me. On one side was the company's name, Glencoe Self-Storage, a photograph of its two buildings with their orange metal lockers, its location, and an URL to its website. A magnetic strip was on the back of the card.

I put the card on her desk and thanked her for her time.

I slipped into our first client meeting of the day minutes before it ended. As I'd expected, Nate had things well in hand.

We met with three more clients before we broke for lunch. When I left Nate's office, Ivy called out to me. Bruce was seated in the reception area.

He hasn't been charged! I was elated.

"I'll grab my handbag and we'll get some lunch," I told him.

He was chatting with Ivy when I returned and handed him his keys. His smiling face and relaxed posture told me everything I wanted to know about his visit to the detachment. But I couldn't resist asking a few questions.

"What happened?" I asked as we left the building.

"I gave a statement about what we found at the cabin."

"Then?"

"Foster asked me what Wilf had been working on recently. We'd already gone over that on Saturday night, and I couldn't think of anything else to tell him."

"And that was it?"

"That was it. Foster told me to go to work. He'll have the cabin dusted for fingerprints this afternoon."

I saved the rest of my questions for Joe's.

"Was there a memory chip in the camera?" I asked when we'd given Sue our orders. "With the photos Wilf took at the fairgrounds?"

"If there was, I wasn't told about it," Bruce said.

"Whoever left the camera in your kitchen may have removed the chip."

We said nothing for a minute or two. I was thinking about who or what Wilf might have photographed before he died.

"The camera was Wilf's?" I asked.

"I think so, but I'm not certain. Darlene, Wilf's widow, will know. She helped Wilf with his freelance photography business."

Sue set mugs of coffee on the table. I smiled my thanks and turned back to Bruce.

"When we stopped by your place yesterday was the box with the camera in the kitchen?"

"I didn't notice," he said. "I was too upset about the break-in at the time."

"Whoever picked your lock must have left Wilf's camera there."

"If it is Wilf's camera."

"An expensive camera turns up in your home after a photographer has been murdered. Who else would it belong to?"

Our sandwiches arrived. I was halfway through mine when something niggled at the back of my mind. "Don't I need to give a statement to the police? That I was with you when you discovered the break-in?"

"Foster didn't mention it, maybe because I said you were with me in my statement."

Well, it was Foster's call. I was happy that he seemed to be letting Bruce get on with his life.

"How is everyone at *The Times*?" I asked.

"Shaken. Wilf was well-liked."

"When is the funeral?"

"Friday morning at the Anglican church here in town." He looked down at his mug. "Maria's writing the obit for this week's paper. The article on the funeral will run next week."

"You have a good team."

"I'm lucky to be part of it." He took a sip of coffee. "What Laura was saying about her baby last night... She and Kyle are right to stick to their guns."

"I think so."

"If I had a child, I wouldn't let anyone take that kid away from me," he said. "If the mother and I weren't living together, I'd want us to have equal time with our son or daughter."

I stared at him, surprised. It had never occurred to me that he might like to be in a relationship or have a family. But he'd clearly given it some thought.

I left Bruce tucking into a piece of blueberry pie. I'd covered a block on Main Street when Chuck Gibson hurried down the sidewalk toward me. "Pat!" he said when he saw me. "Something terrible's happened!" His breath came out in ragged gasps.

I took his elbow and guided him to a bench in the parkette between Stedmans and the bookstore. "Catch your breath."

He drew a deep breath and held it for a few moments. "This morning I went to Canadian Tire to buy oil for my lawnmower. I don't usually leave Gracie alone in the house now that these renters are showing up, but she was tired. She didn't sleep well last night. I told her not to let anyone in."

He took a few more deep breaths before continuing. "When I got back around ten thirty, the side door we use was unlocked, but Gracie wasn't in the kitchen or on the porch. I called her name, and I heard banging in the basement. She was lying on the couch in the rec room. Her wrists and ankles were tied with rope, and she had a gag in her mouth. She'd banged her feet against the wall when she heard me upstairs."

"Is she okay?" I asked.

"She was terrified."

"Of course she was. Was she hurt?"

"Rope burns on her hands and a cut on her leg."

"You called the police?"

He tipped his head to one side. "Bouchard and a deputy came out right away. They told me to take Gracie to the hospital."

"And?"

"Doc gave us a prescription for the rope burns and another for some sedatives. He said she was lucky—no broken bones, no head injuries. She just needs to rest."

"And she's resting—"

"At her friend Sally Beaton's place here in town."

"What did Gracie say happened at the house?"

"Not long after I left, a woman came to the side door. Gracie opened it, but kept the screen door locked. The woman waved a piece of paper and said she'd rented the house for two weeks. Gracie informed her it wasn't for rent. She told her about the internet scam, and she said she was very sorry but we had nothing to do with the con."

His face was drawn with worry. "The woman asked Gracie if she could have a glass of water. She was polite and nicely dressed so Gracie didn't think there'd be any harm in letting her in." He shook his head. "As soon as she was in the door, she grabbed Gracie from behind and shoved her down the stairs to the basement. Then she tied her up."

Gracie was a tiny woman. It wouldn't take much muscle to get her into the basement, but why did this woman want to frighten her?

"Did Gracie say whether this was one of the renters who came to your home in the past few weeks?" I asked.

"She said she'd never seen her before."

"Did she tell you or Bouchard what she looked like?"

"No, and we didn't ask her. Bouchard didn't think it was a good time to question her further or get a statement."

"Was anything taken or damaged?"

He shrugged, and I knew he was beyond caring about that.

"You've both had a terrible day," I said.

He ran a hand over his brow. "I don't know what we'll do, Pat. We can't stay there any longer. The next renter could really hurt us. Or worse."

I was angry. Whoever had rigged the scam had put this elderly man and woman out of their home. Chuck and Gracie couldn't afford two residences, and with their property on Raven Lake targeted in a rental racket, it wasn't a good time to try to sell it.

"Can you stay with Sally Beaton a while?"

"We'll stay there tonight," he said, "but we don't want to impose on her any longer."

I racked my brains as we left the parkette, but there was nothing I could think of to help them. Not a single thing.

I took out a business card and scribbled down my phone number at the cottage. "I'll be leaving Norris Cassidy at the end of the week. This is the number where I'm staying." I handed him the card. "Let me know where you'll be."

Nate was waiting for me in his office. I closed the door and collapsed in the chair across from him. "What's happened?" he asked.

"Remember Chuck and Gracie Gibson, the elderly couple on Raven Lake?"

"Of course."

I told him about the renters who had been turning up at the Gibsons' place. And what had happened to Gracie that morning.

"Can't the police do anything?" he asked.

"Apparently not."

"Is there anything we can do?"

I shook my head. "Maybe this will spur the police on...before something really bad happens."

CHAPTER TWENTY

I stopped at Joe's the next morning for a latté. From the lineup at the short-order counter, I scanned the tables and booths and spotted Bruce at the back of the room. A woman with a mane of wavy red hair was seated across from him. *Crystal!*

Bruce waved me over to their booth.

"You again," Crystal said. "Why do I always meet Pat Tierney when I'm in Braeloch?"

I smiled at her. "Maybe because Braeloch is a very small town."

"Join us, Pat?" Bruce asked.

"Sure." I slid into the booth beside him.

Crystal puffed out her substantial chest. "Bruce is interviewing me for an article. We have a lot to talk about."

"Nothing Pat can't hear," Bruce said. "And the entire township will read about it next week."

Her face fell. "I won't be in this week's paper?"

"Afraid not," he said. "This week's issue is just about wrapped up. It goes to press tonight."

But there was no keeping her down. "Can I see the article before it runs?" she asked. "I want to make sure everything is okay."

Bruce shook his head. "No can do. If we showed articles to everyone we talked to, we'd never get the paper out. Now, if you don't want to be interviewed—"

"No, no. I was just asking," she said.

I was impressed by how he was handling Crystal. She'd bullied her way into this interview, but he was running the show.

"Now where were we?" He scanned his notes. "Right. You were saying the antiques weren't in the locker. What made you think there'd be antiques in there?"

"My friend stored some pieces at Glencoe Self-Storage last fall."

"Your friend, Frank Prentice."

"Yes. Frank was killed in a motorcycle accident in April. Two months later, I saw that Glencoe was holding a contents auction. It had to be Frank's locker."

"But you couldn't be sure, could you?" Bruce said.

Crystal sat up straight. "Sure enough to sink $900 into it."

Bruce gave her a half-smile and waited for her to go on.

"I get a newsletter that lists storage auctions," she said. "It was the first auction Glencoe held this year. It had to be Frank's locker."

"But he'd taken the furniture out of it," Bruce said.

She snorted. "No way. Frank was counting on me to find a buyer, but I'd just opened my shop last fall. I was busy. He told me it could wait till spring."

"What do you think happened to those pieces?" Bruce asked.

"Frank's mother took them," she said.

I nodded. Ella had been lying when she'd told me she didn't know her son had rented a storage locker. But why? She was Frank's beneficiary. She was entitled to whatever was in that locker.

"We can't put that in the paper," Bruce said. "It's speculation."

"Speculation?" Crystal cried. "It's common sense."

"Why did you bid on the locker?" I asked. "You knew that a notice about the auction had been sent to Frank's home. You knew that his mother would have checked out the locker and probably removed anything of value."

Crystal heaved a sigh. "When a locker is opened, bidders can look at the contents from the door, but they can't go inside. I spotted one of Frank's end tables so I thought the other pieces would be there as well." She sighed again. "They weren't."

"Nothing else of value in there?" Bruce asked.

"I made a few hundred dollars on some old comic books," Crystal said. "But, even with the end table, that didn't cover what I put out."

"You were disappointed," I said.

Bruce slipped his notebook into his briefcase. "That's it. We'll run the story next week."

"With my photo?" Crystal asked.

"With a photo," he said. "We'll drive over to Glencoe Self-Storage now. I'll get a shot of you with the lockers in the background."

I was getting up to leave when Crystal said, "I saw Frank's mother at the fireworks last weekend. I almost asked her about the antiques she'd taken, but I knew there was no point."

And I'd seen Ella on Main Street. For someone who hadn't been in Braeloch in years, she was making up for lost time.

"You know Frank's mother?" I asked.

"Not personally," Crystal said, "but everyone in Newmarket knows who Ella Prentice is. She has a Sunday afternoon radio show. *Ella's Beauty Spot*. There's a billboard with her photo downtown."

Just before noon, Laura and Tommy appeared at my office door. "We've been at Ronnie's place," Laura said.

"How is she?"

Laura flung herself into the client's chair. "She seems to be doing okay. Jamie has a caregiver spending a few hours with her every day. She arrived as we were leaving."

"That's good." My eyes were on Tommy who was drawing a pattern in the dust on the windowpane. He wasn't having much fun this summer, I thought. I wished I had friends in the area with kids his age.

"Yeah. Now Jamie can get out a bit."

When Laura and Tommy had left, I picked up the telephone and dialed Ronnie's number. Jamie answered. She updated me on her mother's condition and told me about the caregiver.

"Can you take a break before she leaves?" Nate and I had our last two client interviews scheduled for later that afternoon. I'd be at loose ends until then.

"I like to eat lunch with Mom. How about one o'clock?"

"Are you up for a walk?" I asked. The sun was shining after the previous day's rain.

"A walk is just what I need. We'll go up to the lookout."

Ronnie's house on Prince Street was halfway up the hill behind Main Street. A park with a lookout over the town and the lake was at the top of the hill, with a network of walking trails behind it.

Jamie was waiting on the porch. I went into the house to say hello to Ronnie and give her a gentle hug.

Back outside, Jamie handed me a bottle of water and we set off along Prince Street, then up Pine Avenue. The higher we climbed, the swankier the houses became. The last house was the elaborate bungalow made of stone and stained wood where Ted Stohl had lived. A For Sale sign was on the front lawn.

We climbed the stairs to the park and sat on a bench with a magnificent view of Serenity Lake. I looked around, thinking that this was where Vi and Ronnie had met Daniel Laughton.

"I'll stay with Mom another week. I hope she'll be okay by the time I leave." Jamie sounded worried.

"Your mother should be back to normal soon." A friend in Toronto had had her gallbladder removed by laparoscopic surgery earlier that year.

"Lainey Campbell is the only one who's dropped by or called since we got back from the hospital." Jamie bit her lower lip. "I never realized that Mom doesn't have many friends. She must be lonely."

She was starting to see Ronnie in a new light, as a lonely widow rather than an interfering mother. I hoped the time they were spending together was bringing them closer.

"A few Christmases ago, I signed Mom up for a flowers-of-the-month plan with the florist here in town," Jamie said. "I gave her something else the next Christmas, and I didn't renew the plan. But when I was going through her desk the other day looking for some papers she wanted, I found invoices from the florist. She'd renewed the subscription. She's still getting flowers every month."

"They brighten her life."

"I feel terrible that I didn't renew the plan." She sighed. "It was a substitute for spending time with her, but still..."

"It's not too late for the flowers, or to spend more time with her."

"I envy Tracy's relationship with you."

I gave her a wry smile. "All parents screw up at some point. I've botched things up, as you well know."

I'd handled it badly when I first learned about Tracy and Jamie's relationship. I hadn't realized my daughter was a lesbian, and I was surprised—shocked—when she introduced her sweetheart to me. Yes, I'd bungled things royally, and it had nearly cost me my relationship with Tracy. But I'd tried my best to make amends. Thankfully, the girls had been willing to move on with me.

"Go easy on your mom," I said. "She loves you."

Jamie stood up. "Let's walk."

I took a swig from my bottle and followed her to the trailhead at the edge of the park. We hiked a short loop through the trees then descended the stairs to the street.

"Can I get a ride with you downtown? I need to buy a few things," Jamie asked outside Ronnie's house. "I'll make my own way back here."

I drove downtown—as the locals called the Main Street strip—and parked in my spot behind the Norris Cassidy branch. We walked over to Braeloch Bread and Buns. I'd just paid for a loaf of bread when the door opened with a tinkle of bells and Zoe walked into the bakery.

"Hi, Zoe," I said.

"Hey, Pat," she said. "And Jenny!"

"Hey, Zoe," Jamie said.

Zoe appraised Jamie and me. "You two know each other?"

"We do." Jamie handed a bill to the clerk. "What brings you up this way? On vacation?"

"I live here now, Jenny. You remember, Nate, my husband? He's the manager of the Norris Cassidy branch."

Jamie looked at me. "That explains how you two know each other. Zoe and I are…cousins three or four times removed."

"That sounds complicated," I said.

"Cousins three or four times removed," Zoe said. "Never heard that one before."

"We're related by marriage," Jamie explained. "Zoe's Aunt Ella married my Uncle Harlan. Their son, Frank, was our first cousin."

"And that makes us cousins three or four times removed. Hmm…" Zoe opened her handbag and gave a little yelp. "I left my wallet in the car. See you later, Jenny. You, too, Pat." She slipped out the door.

When Jamie and I left the bakery, Zoe was nowhere in sight. Jamie burst into laughter.

"What is it?" I asked.

"I'm glad you called Zoe by name. I saw her and an older woman— her mother, probably—at the fireworks, but I couldn't recall either of their names. Couldn't think of her name today, either."

Jamie had mentioned that on Saturday night. "Your mother said her sister-in-law has a large family," I said.

"There are several sisters. Tracy told me you've met Ella. Zoe's mother is another sister."

Zoe's mother is a Filipina, which explains her exotic good looks.

We walked down Main Street. "Your grandmother's funeral last fall," I said.

"Yes?"

"Was Zoe there?"

Jamie thought about that for a few moments. "Yes. We talked briefly, but I couldn't remember her name."

"What did you talk about?"

"I don't know. I was grieving for Gran, and the entire day was a blur. I must have been introduced to Zoe's husband, but I don't recall it."

"Was Zoe there when your mother showed Frank the furniture?"

"No. Mom drove Frank and Crystal to Gran's apartment when the reception was over. I walked out to the parking lot with them, and they got into her Mazda. Is that important?"

"Probably not. I'm just trying to connect some dots."

Jamie continued on to the pharmacy. As I walked back to the branch, I thought about Zoe and Frank being first cousins. *Did Zoe know he had valuable antiques in a storage locker?*

I was walking up the front steps when Bruce called my name. "The camera is Wilf's," he said when he came up to me.

"Foster told you that?"

He gave me a crooked smile. "I'd be waiting a long time to hear it from him. No, Darlene Mathers called me. Foster brought it over to her home last night, and she recognized it right away."

"It looks like the same person killed Wilf and Vi. He left personal belongings of both of them at your home."

"And he's trying to finger me. But why?"

"You had a motive for killing Vi. Now that she's dead, you've inherited Ted's entire estate."

"What was my motive for killing Wilf?"

"I haven't figured that out." I'd been racking my brains about that, but I hadn't come up with anything.

"He knows me pretty well if he knows about Ted's estate."

"Not necessarily well. He knows you were Ted and Vi's only child, and he assumes you are their beneficiary."

"So he lives around here."

"Or he's plugged into what's going on around here."

It was little after five when I got back to Black Bear Lake. Laura told me that Tracy had called. "She's taking the bus to Braeloch on Saturday morning. She'll drive her Honda back to the city on Sunday, and I'll go with her."

I smiled, pleased by the arrangement. I could spend the weekend relaxing at the lake instead of chauffeuring Laura into Toronto.

I took a pasta dish from the freezer and told Laura when to put it in the microwave. Then I got the kayak out of the shed.

I travelled close to the shoreline, focusing on the rhythm of my paddle strokes. But when I spotted Nate and Zoe's chalet through the trees, my mind clicked into high gear. Nate was sitting on the end of the dock, his feet in the water.

"Hello," I said, coming up behind him.

Startled, he turned in the direction of my voice. "Pat!"

"I love being on the water in the late afternoon. It's a golden time of day."

He smiled. "I'm waiting for Zoe. She spends most afternoons on the lakes between here and Braeloch. She's usually back by now."

"Does she fish when she's out there?"

"She doesn't fish. She just likes being on the water. The rock formations, the wildlife, she finds all fascinating. She wants to get a snowmobile this winter."

"Make sure she knows what she's doing," I said. "The lakes can be treacherous in the winter."

CHAPTER TWENTY-ONE

Friday was my last day at the Norris Cassidy branch. And I hoped that it would be my last day as an employee.

It was also the day that Wilf's funeral was held at Holy Redeemer Church in Braeloch. I wanted to attend it, but I knew I should spend my last morning at the branch. I packed books and papers into cardboard boxes. And I cleared files from the computer, sending several to Nate and downloading a few to my flash drive.

Soupy and Ivy returned from the church just before noon. Nate and I were waiting for them at the reception desk. "How did it go?" I asked.

"It was so sad," Ivy said. "Darlene cried through the entire service."

Nate put the Closed sign in the front window. We trooped out the back door to the parking lot and got into Nate's van. He drove us to Pickerel, an upscale eatery that had just opened on Twelve Mile Lake.

My goodbye lunch wasn't easy to sit through. My focus had already moved to the next stage in my life. I found myself gazing at the lake, thinking that I'd rather be out in the kayak than at that table. When my colleagues toasted me with champagne cocktails, I wanted to shrink into my jacket. I've never been comfortable with compliments, and compliment me they did—with a lot of cheering and clapping thrown in. The other diners turned to see what was going on at our table.

I thanked them and made a toast of my own to the success of the Braeloch branch.

Finally, it was time to leave, and Nate called for the bill. He took several cards from his wallet and placed them on the table while he searched for a credit card. The orange color of one card caught my eye.

"I see from your keycard that you have a locker at Glencoe Self-Storage," I said as he put the extra cards back into his wallet.

He placed his credit card on the tray the waitress had brought to the table with the bill. "We sure do. All our furniture is in it. The place we're renting is furnished."

"They found Bruce Stohl's mother in one of those lockers," Ivy said.

"That locker might have been ours if it was chosen randomly," Nate said. "But they would have had trouble getting into it. The padlock we bought is guaranteed to resist picks, bolt cutters, and saws."

I didn't think Frank's locker had been chosen randomly, but I kept that to myself.

Ivy looked impressed by what Nate had said. "How would they remove a lock like that for an auction?"

"If those claims are true, which I doubt, they'd have to contact the manufacturer," Soupy said.

I watched Nate hand the tray to the waitress. I'd found someone else who had a keycard to the storage yard gate. Nate Johnston.

But did that matter? Vi's body had been put into the locker during the day when the gate was open, so the murderer hadn't needed a card to enter the yard.

Back at the branch, I said my goodbyes to the Norris Cassidy team.

"I'll see you at my wedding," Soupy said.

"Looking forward to it." I gave his hand a squeeze.

"We'll have you and Laura over for cocktails on the dock," Nate said.

I saluted them and escaped through the back door.

I was now self-employed, I thought as I crossed the parking lot. I corrected that to unemployed. Until I started up my business in the fall, I was out of work. And you know what? I didn't mind a bit.

I was in the Volvo when I remembered a piece of unfinished business in town. I went back into the branch.

"Seems you can't get rid of me," I said to Ivy. "I thought you might know Sally Beaton. She lives here in town."

A smile lit up Ivy's face. "Of course, I know Sally. She's my granny's friend. Lives up on the hill on Newcastle Street. Pink house. You can't miss it."

I thanked Ivy, grateful for once that everyone knew everyone else in a small town. Something I hadn't always appreciated.

Sally's house was indeed a startling shade of pink, and a flock of plastic flamingos grazed on the front lawn. Sally came to the door in an oversized pink T-shirt and baggy jeans, a pink headband holding her white hair back from her face.

"I'm looking for Chuck and Gracie Gibson," I told her. "Chuck said they were staying with you."

"The fools went back to Raven Lake," she said. "They were welcome to stay here till they got their problem sorted. I've got plenty of room."

"Not very wise, what with disgruntled renters showing up."

"I'll say!"

The Gibsons' home was a good half-mile from the highway. The Raven Lake internet tower across the lake from the Laughtons' property kept them connected to the rest of the world; nonetheless, they were pretty isolated on this stretch of the lake. A Wetlands, owned by the local conservation authority, was on one side of their property. Their neighbors, on the other side, owned a large tract of land, and trees screened their buildings from view. Chuck and Gracie could be dead in their home for days without anyone knowing. My heart went out to them, remembering how isolated I'd felt in Norris Cassidy's executive home the previous winter.

Chuck came around the side of the house holding a black pistol.

I got out of the car. "That looks pretty lethal," I said, but it was Chuck I was really looking at. He had dark circles under his eyes. A muscle twitched beside his mouth.

He looked at the weapon in his hands. "Air pistol. I bought it to keep the rabbits down." He inclined his head toward the house. "Let's take a seat on the porch."

"How's Gracie doing?" I asked when we were seated at a wooden table.

"She's having a rest before dinner." He placed the pistol on the plastic table. "Her nerves are shot."

That didn't surprise me. "But you decided to come back here."

"We had no choice. We could have stayed with Sally, but we didn't want to leave the house empty. Renters might arrive and assume that the place was theirs for a week or two. They'd break a window to get in."

"So you're holding the fort with an air pistol." It was lunacy to think he could protect his wife and his home on his own. He might scare off one person, but what if a group arrived?

"Nothing else I can do," he said.

"You should have an alarm system."

"Alarm system? How would that work?"

"It would have a panic button you'd hit to call for help. And some alarms can be set to go off on unauthorized entry—during the night or when you're away."

"Where can I find out about them?"

"We can do a search on your computer right now."

He shook his head. "Gracie's lying down in the room where we have the computer. I don't want to disturb her."

And I didn't have internet access at Black Bear Lake. "Do you talk to your daughter in Toronto every day?" I asked.

"Terry's busy with her kids and her job. We don't want to bother her."

"Right now, it would be a good idea if she called at a set time every day. If you don't pick up, she'd know there could be a problem."

He shook his head. "We don't want her to know about...this situation. She's got enough on the go without worrying about us."

The stubborn old man was afraid he and Gracie would lose their independence if their daughter knew they were in danger. I'd probably feel the same if I were in his shoes.

"Then I'll call you," I said. "What would be a good time?"

He didn't answer at once, no doubt pondering the implications of my offer. "We're here in the evenings," he said tersely. "Don't like driving in the dark."

"If I call at seven will you be indoors where you can hear the phone?"

"Oh, yes. By seven, we're locked up for the night."

"You'll hear from me at seven." It was the best I could do.

A framed poster on the wall caught my eye. It was a larger version of a map of the chain of four lakes that I had at the cottage. I'd used that map as my guide when I took a snowmobile across the frozen lakes the previous winter. I went over to the wall. Black Bear, Raven, Paradise, and Serenity where Braeloch was located. Raven was by far the largest lake in the chain. And it was the lake I'd paddled into on Sunday afternoon.

"It's a great chain of lakes," Chuck said. "When we had our motorboat, Gracie and I took it to Braeloch every week for groceries."

I ran a finger over the lakes on the poster. When I'd crossed them on the snowmobile, they'd been covered with ice and snow with few distinguishing features.

I decided that when I was out in the kayak in the weeks ahead, I'd drop in on Chuck and Gracie. Raven was the lake right after Black Bear in the chain.

At the cottage, I called Bouchard at the OPP detachment. I told him that Chuck and Gracie were determined to stay in their home and that I was worried about them. He said he would arrange for a cruiser to stop by once a day.

"Could one of your officers talk to them about alarm systems?" I asked. "I suggested they have an alarm installed."

"We can't endorse specific companies," he said, "but we can tell them how they work."

"The rental sites that carried the bogus ads," I said.

"What about them?"

"Did they send you the IP addresses of the computers that posted the ads?"

"That's the first thing our Anti-Rackets Branch would ask for."

It sounded like the police were on top of it. So why wasn't I convinced?

Twenty minutes later, I had the kayak skimming over the lake. I paddled to the bay where the Johnstons' cottage and Norris Cassidy's executive vacation home were located and turned into the creek that connected the two lakes.

A short paddle down it, and I was on Raven Lake.

Directly across from the mouth of the creek, a low granite outcropping rises out of the water to form a rocky beach. There were no cottages on this stretch of Raven so I assumed that the beach was Crown land. I paddled over to it, tied the kayak to a poplar, and stripped down to my bathing suit.

The water was delicious—cool and silky. Clear, too. Diving into it, I could see the granite bedrock, sparkling in the sunlight, sloping down toward the middle of the lake. Small fishes swam over it.

I was about to pick up my towel from the rock where I'd left it, when I saw a snake basking in the sun beside it. I jumped back. The snake sounded its rattle and slithered across the rock and into the grass.

I poked at the towel with a stick before I picked it up.

A silver canoe emerged from the creek as I was drying myself off. Its sole occupant was a woman, whose short, dark hair was cut in the same style as Ella Prentice's.

"Ella!" I called as she paddled past the beach.

If it was Ella, she didn't hear me because she kept on paddling.

CHAPTER TWENTY-TWO

I tossed and turned in bed for the better part of the night, thinking about Nate's keycard and Ella's appearances around the township. *Did they have any bearing on Vi's murder? Probably not.*

But my subconscious mind didn't buy it. Ella, Zoe, Nate, and orange keycards floated in and out of my disjointed dreams. Just before I awoke, Ella plowed through Glencoe Self-Storage's gate in Nate's gold van.

"Okay," I muttered as I dragged myself out of bed. "Nate and Zoe have a van large enough to transport a body to the storage locker. But why would they kill Vi?"

I glanced at the clock on my bedside table. On my first day of freedom I was still programmed to rise at seven.

I was picking at a bowl of cereal when Tommy and Maxie joined me on the porch. "What're we doing today?" Tommy asked as he slipped into the chair beside me.

"I'm going to the library in Braeloch this morning. Want to come? You can borrow some books."

"Can Maxie come, too?"

"She won't be allowed in the library. We'd better leave her with Laura."

Tommy's mouth turned down in a pout.

I reached over and put an arm around him. "We'll be back here for lunch."

"Can I sit in the front of the car?"

I shook my head. "You know the answer to that. You're too small." When Tommy turned eight two months before, I gave away his booster seat. And he'd been pushing to ride in the passenger's seat ever since.

Tommy and I were waiting outside the front door when the Braeloch Public Library opened at nine. We introduced ourselves to the librarian, Ruth Cameron, and I told her that Tommy needed a library card. When she found out that we were cottagers, she said he could have a temporary card that he could use for the next two months, and he could check out five books at a time with it.

"Do I need a reservation to use a computer?" I asked her.

"Not this morning," she said. "Our first booking is for one o'clock. But you'll need a library card to log onto a computer."

While she made up our cards, I took Tommy over to the children's section. I returned to Ruth for the cards then sat down at a computer terminal. Fifteen minutes later, I'd printed out pages from the websites of three security firms that served Ontario cottage country.

I went over to Tommy, who was seated on the floor surrounded by books.

"Decide on which five you want?"

He drew five books toward him. "These."

Ruth showed him how to check out his books at the electronic checkout counter. I picked up a pamphlet on the library's kids' program.

"Let's go, Mrs. T." Tommy tugged on my arm. "We gotta get back to Maxie."

On the way out, we nearly collided with Zoe who was about to enter the building with an armful of books.

"Summer reading," I said.

"Can't read enough murder mysteries," she said. "Nate says I should write one."

"I saw your Aunt Ella yesterday," I said. "She must have been visiting you."

Zoe laughed and shook her head. "Not Ella. She never comes up here."

"Where are we going?" Tommy asked when I turned into the side road that led to the Gibsons' lane.

"A quick stop. I have something for Chuck and Gracie."

"Who?"

"Chuck and Gracie Gibson. They live on Raven Lake, and they're thinking about having an alarm installed. I have some information that may help them."

"Like the fire alarm at school?"

"That's one kind of alarm. There are also alarms that go off when somebody comes into a house where he shouldn't be."

"A bad guy!"

"That's right."

"We have an alarm in Toronto," he said. "Is there one here?"

"Not at the lake."

"Maybe we should get one."

I thought of Bruce's cabin after the break-in. Cardboard boxes torn open, papers scattered around the room. A tingle ran down my spine.

Chuck came around the side of the house.

"That man's got a gun!"

In the rearview mirror I saw that Tommy's brown eyes were shining with excitement.

"That's Chuck Gibson," I said. "He uses that air pistol for target practice." I didn't tell him that Chuck's favorite target was rabbits.

I pulled up beside Chuck and hit the button that lowered the window. "Everything okay?" I asked him.

"It's been quiet." He looked like he hadn't slept well.

"Quiet's good," I said. "Chuck, that's Tommy in the back seat. Tommy, meet Mr. Gibson."

"Mr. Gibson," Tommy said, "can you show me how your gun works?"

"I sure can, son." Chuck opened the back door for Tommy.

I followed Tommy out of the car.

"This is a spring pistol with a break-barrel design," Chuck said. "Each time you want to shoot, you have to break the barrel to pop the spring inside."

He cocked the pistol and loaded a metal pellet. He took aim at a tin can that was nailed to a post about ten feet away. "Here goes."

He pulled the trigger, and the pistol made a cracking sound.

We squinted, trying to see the damage he'd inflicted on the can.

"You didn't hit it, sir," Tommy said.

Chuck sighed. "I need more practice."

"And a good alarm system." I opened the car door and took out the photocopies I'd made at the library. "Take a look at what these companies offer. I've circled the URLs so you can look up their websites on your computer."

"You think bad guys will come here, Mr. Gibson?" Tommy asked. "Is that why you've got a pistol?"

"Tommy," I said.

Chuck stooped to look at Tommy. "A man has to be prepared to defend his home."

Tommy nodded solemnly.

"I'll call you tonight at seven," I said to Chuck.

He held up the papers I'd given him. "Thanks!"

"Can we get a pistol?" Tommy asked as we drove down the lane.

"We're not getting a pistol or any other firearm."

"What if..." Tommy sounded worried. He'd been through some frightening experiences in his short life, and he needed reassuring.

"We'll just mind our own business and lock our doors at night." It didn't sound as reassuring as I'd intended.

"Laura said you can't mind your own business."

I looked at Tommy in the mirror. He had a grin on his face.

"Is Laura right?" he asked.

"Laura has been known to exaggerate."

We were sitting down to lunch on the porch when Tracy's Honda came up the drive.

"Just in time for lunch," I said when we'd exchanged hugs with Tracy and Jamie.

"Thanks, but we ate at Ronnie's," Tracy said.

They joined us at the table and poured themselves tea.

"I'll stay at Ronnie's tonight," Tracy said. "Jamie doesn't want to leave her alone."

Laura rolled her eyes. "And you two haven't seen each other in what? Five whole days?"

"Dinner here tonight?" I asked hopefully.

"I don't think Mom's up for that," Jamie said. "She hasn't left the house yet."

She knew I was disappointed because she added, "We'll come over for lunch and a swim tomorrow if you'll have us."

"Ask Ronnie if she'd like to come," I said.

"I will, but I don't think she'll take you up on it."

Another vehicle arrived as we were changing into our swimsuits. "Can't people phone before they drop in?" I grumbled.

"They're in the neighborhood, and they want to say hello," Laura answered from the room beside mine. The cottage's thin walls offered no privacy.

"Kyle's here!" Tommy cried.

From the porch, I saw Yvonne and Kyle getting out of the black Ferrari. I gritted my teeth, gave them a wave, and went back inside to tell Laura.

Laura flopped down on the living room sofa. "This is my last full day of vacation. I don't want to be around that woman."

"Be polite," I said. "Say hello, and take the air mattress out on the lake."

Laura flounced out of the cottage with a beach towel tied at her waist. "Hi, guys," she said to the Shinglers and continued down to the lake.

Tommy followed her out. "Kyle, let's go fishing!"

I slammed a hat on my head and grabbed a towel and a tube of sunscreen. I knew the reason for Yvonne's visit, and I didn't feel up to another argument. "I hope you brought your swimsuits," I said, going over to the Shinglers.

"Pat, we have to talk," Yvonne said.

I gave her my best smile. "Later. I'm going for a swim."

I took two reclining lawn chairs out of the shed and set them up near the edge of the water. "Have a seat, Yvonne."

Yvonne took off the linen jacket that matched her shorts and sat down.

"No bathing suit?" I asked.

"No. Pat, we really must—"

I followed Kyle and Tommy to the rowboat that was chained to the dock. I handed Kyle the key, and Tommy ran into the shed to get his fishing rod and two life jackets.

Laura took an air mattress out of the shed and brought it down to the water.

"How are you feeling, Laura?" Yvonne called out.

"I'm good," Laura said as she stepped into the water.

I held the mattress while she climbed onto it. I spread sunscreen over her back, legs, and arms, and pushed the mattress out into the lake. Then I put sunscreen on Tommy and fastened his life jacket. Kyle helped him into the rowboat, and Maxie jumped in.

I stayed in the water for a good half hour. I practiced my breaststroke, my backstroke, my butterfly stroke, and my sidestroke. If I'd followed that routine every day, I would have been in top shape by the end of the summer.

"Impressive, Pat," Yvonne said when I came out of the water. "Have you given some thought to the arrangement Russell and I proposed?"

I took the chair beside her, leaned back, and closed my eyes.

"It makes good sense," she went on. "Laura will want to get back to school after the baby is born, and you'll be busy with your business. But I have all the time in the world to devote to the little one."

I opened my eyes and looked at her. "That's what brought you here today?"

"It's always best to talk in person."

Kyle steered the rowboat close the shore. I went down to the water and helped Tommy and Maxie out of the boat. Kyle threw himself into the lake and swam over to Laura on her mattress.

Tommy and I waited by the water until Laura and Kyle came in. Kyle picked up Laura's towel and draped it over her shoulders.

"Kyle, your shorts are soaking wet," Yvonne said.

"They'll be dry in no time," he said, spreading the towel over the grass for Laura.

Maxie ran up from the lake and shook the water off her coat, spraying us all. Yvonne yelped.

Laura rolled off her towel and handed it to Yvonne.

"Tommy, get yourself a Popsicle in the house," I said.

He took Maxie by the collar, and they went up to the cottage.

"We're all here," Yvonne said as she dried herself off, "so we should talk about the baby. What hospital did you say you'll be in, Laura?"

Laura looked away, saying nothing.

"Our family doctor referred Laura to a midwife," I said. "The baby will be born at the Toronto Birthing Place unless there are complications."

"A midwife!" Yvonne looked horrified.

"That's right," Laura said.

"And what has this midwife told you?" Yvonne probed. "Does she think there will be complications?"

She was beyond endurance. "Laura hasn't seen her yet," I said. "She has an appointment on Thursday."

"I'll be sure to call you Thursday evening, Laura. You'll be in Toronto then?"

"I start my job on Monday," Laura said.

"Kyle, you never told me about Laura's summer job," Yvonne said. "What will you be doing, my dear?"

"Laura will be looking after a little girl," I said. "Good practice for her."

Yvonne cleared her throat. "That's where I was heading. Laura, you and Kyle don't want to marry, but you must agree that the baby needs a mother and a father. Russell and I can provide that."

Kyle sat up on the grass. "Our baby *will* have a mother and a father. He'll live with Laura and Mrs. T—until we get married. In the meantime, I'll be very involved in my kid's life."

"Kyle will definitely be involved." Laura smiled at him. "I wouldn't have it any other way."

"This child needs a mother and father under the same roof. A solid family unit," Yvonne said. "Kyle and Laura, you may start dating other people, which would create all kinds of complications. Would that be any way to raise a child?"

"Mom, I told you and Dad to back off." Kyle turned to Laura and said, "And I'm not going to date anyone else."

Yvonne gave a little snort. "Back off on how my grandchild is raised?"

"Mom, I'm warning you."

"Warning me?" She turned to face her son. "Warning me that if I don't allow my grandchild to be raised in a loosey-goosey fashion, you'll do what?"

"Don't make me do it, Mom," Kyle said.

Yvonne laughed. "Do what?"

Kyle sighed. He looked at Laura, then at me. "Mom has a…habit."

"Don't you dare," Yvonne said.

"A habit she finds difficult to break," Kyle continued.

We were all ears.

"Kyle!" Yvonne said.

"Mom can't resist taking things that don't belong to her. One time she tried on an expensive pair of shoes and walked out of the store with them on her feet. Another time she slipped a bracelet into her pocket."

Yvonne stared at him with her mouth open.

"She's not very good at this because she keeps getting caught," he went on. "Dad managed to get some charges dropped, but last year she was found guilty of theft under $5,000 and put on probation."

"How could you, Kyle?" Yvonne's voice shook.

"I told you," he said, "and now I'm telling you again. If you don't give up trying to take our baby, I'll let the rest of the world know why I don't want you raising him."

Yvonne turned to look at me. Her face was wet with tears. "My therapist says I'll be okay."

I felt sorry for her. She was a bored, wealthy woman who needed a project to keep her busy. "I'm sure you'll be fine," I said.

"I understand, Mom," Kyle said in a softer tone. "And you'll have to understand what Laura and I want for our baby."

I went over to Yvonne and placed a hand on her shoulder. "Let's go inside and make some tea. You'll want a cup of tea before you drive back to the city."

Laura and I served our guests tea and cookies on the porch. Nobody said much at the table, and Yvonne didn't say a word. "Goodbye, then," she managed to croak out as she got up to leave. She looked sad and broken.

"Goodbye, then," Laura said as we watched the Ferrari drive down the lane. "What did that mean? Is that the last I'll hear from her?"

"I wouldn't count on it. She'll want to see a lot of the baby. It's her grandchild, after all." I gave Laura a sidelong look. "But she may have given up the idea of raising him...or her."

"I hope so," Laura said fervently.

Tommy went down to the lake with Maxie. Laura and I stayed at the table, watching the loons teach their chicks how to fish. We sat there, deep in our thoughts, until our reverie was interrupted by the sound of a vehicle coming up the lane.

"Damn it!" I said. "They're back."

But the vehicle was a green sedan, not a black Ferrari. It pulled up beside the cottage, and a man and a woman in their thirties, along with two small children, got out.

"Hello," the man called out, "I'm Steve Matthews. You must be the Simpsons."

I stepped onto the deck. "I'm sorry. You have the wrong place."

He came over and thrust some papers at me. "We've rented this cottage for two weeks."

I looked at the papers. One of them was a printout from Cottage Getaways' website. A thumbnail photo of the cottage where we were staying was circled in red ink.

I looked at Steve. "I'm sorry, but I think you've been scammed. Ross and Maria Dawson own this place, and I've rented it from them for the summer."

"We've been scammed?" Steve ran a hand through his short ginger hair.

"Yes, and you're not the first," I said. "There's been a rash of phony rental listings in cottage country. The police are investigating them, but so far they've come up empty-handed."

By this time, Steve's wife, Pauline, and their kids had joined him on the deck. They looked so lost and bewildered that I invited them onto the porch.

"Rest a bit," I told them. "I'm going to call the owners. And the police. They may want you to give a statement."

I went into the cottage and tried the Dawsons first. Maria picked up and said she'd be over in ten minutes. I reached Bouchard at the OPP detachment, and he said he was on his way.

Back on the porch, Pauline was saying, "We should have gone down to Maine with Mom and Dad."

The little girl, a blonde cherub, began to cry. She and her brother were hot and tired and didn't know what was happening.

"Why don't you get the kids into their swimsuits and take them down to the lake while we get this sorted out?" I said to Pauline and held the door to the house open for them. "Bathroom's at the end of the hall."

I told Laura and Tommy to take the Matthews down to the water when they were ready.

"This Donald Simpson you wired money to," Maria said to Steve when she'd joined us on the porch. "You answered an ad he placed on the internet?"

"That's right, on Cottage Getaways. He offered a discount if I sent him the full amount, so I did."

"I've never heard of Donald Simpson," she said. "And we don't advertise on the internet or anywhere else. We only rent to people we know."

Bouchard arrived and told Steve about the rental scams. "There've been a number of cases in other parts of the province. They just started around here."

Steve looked skeptical. He probably thought we were all in it together.

"You're the first people to show up here," I told him. "But a couple on another lake have had several groups come to their cottage."

"They're elderly, and their home is isolated," Bouchard added. "They're afraid."

"Why should they be afraid?" Steve asked. "Renters like us are the ones who get hurt. We sent our money in good faith, and we lost it. We lost our vacation, too."

"Cottage owners are afraid that a renter who's been duped will take out his frustration on them," I said.

"The chances of getting your money back are pretty slim," Bouchard told Steve. "The guys who place these phony ads seldom get caught. They use burner phones and generic e-mail addresses."

Steve looked at each of us in turn. "It took us four hours to get here. We're not going back tonight."

I wondered if he expected me to put them up. "The Sandy Cove Inn is across the lake," I said quickly. "I've heard good things about it. Shall I see if they have a room?"

I went inside to make the call. Nothing was available at the Sandy Cove so I tried the Dominion Hotel.

"The Dominion Hotel has a double room," I told Steve. "It's on Main Street in Braeloch. You can't miss it."

Looking none too happy, he went down to the water to round up Pauline and the kids. The family had been looking forward to two weeks at a lake, and they were headed for a hotel in town instead. I thought of Bruce's room at the Dominion and grimaced.

"I'm going to get to the bottom of this," Steve said when they came up from the lake.

His daughter began to cry again. He picked her up, scowled at us, and walked over to his car. Pauline took her small son's hand and followed her husband.

It wasn't my fault. So why did I feel like I'd ruined their vacation?

CHAPTER TWENTY-THREE

The next morning, I woke up much too early again. More weird dreams, and Ella was in all of them.

I lingered in bed, mulling over the events of the previous day. I now knew exactly how Chuck and Gracie felt—like sitting ducks. I threw off the bedcovers and slipped my feet into my sandals.

When will the next group of renters show up?

Ruth Cameron unlocked the front door of the Braeloch Public Library on the dot of nine. "You're back," she said.

"There's no internet access where I'm staying."

I logged into a computer, called up Cottage Getaways, and typed in "Glencoe Highlands, waterfront." I skimmed over images of homes on lakes and rivers. There it was, our gray clapboard cottage with its red shutters. The rent that was listed was considerably more than I was paying the Dawsons.

I clicked on the thumbnail photos of the cottage's interior: the living room, the kitchen, the master bedroom with my canvas carryall bag on the chair in the corner. *My bag!* The next shot was of Tommy's room. His brown teddy bear sat on his nicely made bed. *Tommy's teddy bear. And he never makes his bed.*

The hair on the back of my neck stood up.

The photographer had taken those pictures in the past week—after we'd moved into the cottage. The photographer had been watching us, waiting until we'd left.

A search for vacation rental scams in Ontario brought up an article dated three weeks earlier. It quoted a police spokesman who said that seventeen properties were known to have been targeted in Muskoka and Georgian Bay that season. No mention of the Glencoe Highlands, but

Chuck and Gracie's renters started arriving after the article had been published.

I made printouts of the photos and drove over to the police detachment.

I showed the photos to Bouchard and pointed out my carryall and Tommy's teddy bear. "These were taken after we moved in last weekend," I said. "Someone broke in when we were gone."

"I spoke to our Anti-Rackets Branch yesterday," he said. "I thought the ad would be down by now. I'll fax them these photos."

He unclipped his walkie-talkie. "Ten minutes," he said into it. "Something's come up here."

I swung by Chuck and Gracie's place on the way back to the cottage. Chuck came out of the house with the air pistol.

"All's quiet," he said.

"How's Gracie?"

"The same. She's taking the sedatives and sleeping a lot."

"She needs the rest." I paused. "I didn't want to get into it on the phone last night but...the cottage where I'm staying has been targeted. A family came by yesterday, saying they'd rented it for two weeks."

"It's an epidemic," Chuck said.

But my news seemed to cheer him up. Misery likes company, I've noticed.

"Keep Sergeant Bouchard's phone numbers handy," I told him. "My number, too."

Gracie came out of the house in pajamas and a housecoat. Her white hair stood up in tufts, and her walk was unsteady. "Hello, Pat."

"Renters showed up at Pat's place," Chuck said.

Gracie's eyes lit up. "You, too!"

"What will those con men think of next?" Chuck said.

"The woman who came here," I began.

A look of pain crossed Gracie's face.

"Did she think you were behind the rental fraud?" I asked.

She thought about that for a few moments. "She seemed to accept what I told her about the fake internet ads. When she asked for a glass of water, I assumed that she was about to leave. So I let her in."

"What did she look like?"

"She was wearing sunglasses that covered part of her face, but I'd say she was in her fifties. Had one of those turban things on her head so I couldn't see her hair color."

Tracy's Honda bounced up the lane just before noon. Veronica's Mazda, with Jamie at the wheel, was right behind it.

"Ronnie wasn't up to coming?" I asked when the girls got out of the cars.

"She's doing a bit more every day," Jamie said, "but she has to lie down frequently."

They changed into their swimsuits, and Tommy took them down to the lake. When they returned, Laura fired up the barbecue. I put salads and buns on the table.

As soon as we sat down, Laura began to tell Tracy and Jamie about the Matthews' visit the previous day. I touched her arm and inclined my head toward Tommy. "Later."

I took Tommy inside when he'd finished his burger. I put on a *Harry Potter* video and settled him on the sofa with a bowl of chocolate ice cream.

When I returned to the porch, Laura had finished her story.

"You've been targeted by the Cottage Con," Tracy said to me.

Jamie nodded. "That's what the Toronto media is calling whoever's behind these frauds. Of course, there may be more than one person."

"The police can't seem to stop them," Tracy said. "Renters should deal directly with cottage owners."

"That didn't help me," I said. "The Dawsons don't advertise, and this place still got hit."

Tracy placed a hand on mine. "Mom, people will be turning up here at all hours. If you're not around, they'll force their way inside."

"And what if they don't believe you had nothing to do with the scam and become aggressive?" Jamie said. "A woman and a small boy out here…"

Variations of that scenario had been flashing through my mind since the Matthews arrived. My dream vacation had become a nightmare.

Laura put an arm around me. "You and Tommy have to get out of here."

"Why don't you stay with my mother while you look at other options?" Jamie asked.

Ronnie didn't need visitors while she was recovering. "We'll be fine here," I said. "If renters show up, I'll call the Dawsons and the police. And I'll take anything valuable with me when we're out. If someone breaks into the house when we're not here…well, there'll be a broken window to fix."

The girls didn't look convinced. I was glad I hadn't told them about the photos of my carryall and Tommy's teddy bear.

"Hey," Laura said to Tracy and Jamie. "Yvonne may have backed off."

They looked puzzled, so I told them about the Shinglers' plan to raise Laura and Kyle's child. Laura capped that with a detailed account of how Kyle had handled his mother.

"Are you sure Yvonne cares that much about people's opinions?" Jamie asked. "Is that more important to her than raising her grandchild?"

Laura grinned. "She cares a lot what people think. And I'm counting on it."

"I saw Ella Prentice at the supermarket yesterday," Jamie said to me. "She pulled into the parking lot as I was leaving. In a white Corvette convertible. I asked Mom if she'd rented a cottage, but she said Ella never comes up here."

"She must've changed her mind about the Glencoe Highlands," I said, "because I've seen her around, too."

Jamie left for Braeloch right after lunch. I was helping Tracy and Laura load up the Honda for their trip to Toronto when a blue Chevy drove up the lane.

Tommy grabbed my arm. "Bruce is here! He'll take me fishing."

Bruce got out of the car, and Tommy rushed up to him. Bruce put an arm around his shoulders. I gave my daughters one last hug, and the three of us stood waving as they drove away.

"Let's go fishing," Tommy said to Bruce.

"Bruce just got here," I told Tommy. "He'd probably like a piece of apple pie."

"That sounds good," Bruce said.

"Aww," Tommy said and took Maxie down to the lake.

"I heard that Wilf's funeral went well," I said to Bruce.

He took a chair on the porch. "The church was packed, and there were a lot of heartfelt tributes. Wilf would have liked the send-off."

We looked at each other with sad eyes. Wilf would have preferred to have more time with his family and friends.

"Has Foster been on your case these past few days?" I asked.

"He seems to have backed off. For now."

"He must have another suspect."

"He has no evidence against me. Only what was planted at my place."

Bruce leaned forward in his chair. "Maria told me about the renters who were here yesterday. I want you and Tommy to stay with me until this guy is shut down."

Bruce would be doing home repairs in the evening and on his days off. I didn't want to live in a construction zone. "We'll be fine," I told him.

"You don't know who'll turn up," he said. "They may not be as accommodating as the Matthews."

"As I said, we'll be fine."

He saw that my mind was made up, and he moved on. "My phone will be hooked up tomorrow. I'll get you the number. If renters come by, call me at home or at *The Times*. You've got Maria's numbers?"

"I do," I said, and I went to get him a piece of pie.

When he'd scraped his plate clean, he pushed his chair back from the table. "*The Times* will run an article on the rental scams this week."

I knew where he was going.

"Maria and Ross are willing to be interviewed," he said. "And I talked to the Matthews this morning. Steve Matthews is game. He thinks an article might help catch this guy."

Tommy opened the porch door. Maxie ran in and Tommy followed her. "What's *interviewed* mean?" he asked.

I put an arm around him. "Bruce asks people questions. That's called an interview. Then he writes up what they tell him into an article for the newspaper."

"Are we going to be in the newspaper?" Tommy wanted to know.

"Maybe." I patted his shoulder and turned back to Bruce. "You want to interview me for the article?"

"The Dawsons and Steve Matthews should be enough," he said. "The story will focus on Steve because he lost his vacation money."

"Interview me. I'll give you an earful about how these con men are messing with the people who live in these cottages. They see pictures of their homes on the internet. They don't know who'll be at their door next."

"Is that wise?" he asked. "It would draw attention to your situation."

"I'll live with it."

"Has it occurred to you that this guy may know who you are? That he targeted this cottage because you're staying here?"

I'd been pushing that thought to the back of my mind. "But why? I don't know anything that could shut the scam down."

"It may be connected to my mother's murder. You've been looking into that."

"And I haven't gotten very far."

"Be careful, Pat."

"I should get myself an air pistol."

"We're getting an air pistol?" Tommy asked.

I had to watch what I said around that kid. He didn't miss a thing. "I was joking, Tommy."

"Grab your fishing rod and life jacket, Tommy," Bruce said. "I'll meet you and Maxie at the boat."

It was a beautiful day, and I wanted to get out on the water, too. Away from my worries. "I'd like to go for a paddle while the two of you are fishing. I won't be more than an hour."

"Take your time," Bruce said. "I'm in no rush."

I sat straight-backed and centered, and focused on thrusting my paddle deep into the lake. As the kayak skimmed over the water, I tried to purge my mind of thoughts and worries.

But the image of Ella in a silver canoe popped into it. *What is she doing in the township if she doesn't like this part of the world?*

Ten minutes later, I found myself in front of Nate and Zoe's home. Nate was seated on a wooden chair on the dock, his eyes closed, a paperback on his lap. A silver canoe was tied to the dock beside Zoe's yellow one.

"Nate," I said.

He jerked awake and looked around him.

"Down here," I said. "Sorry to startle you."

He peered over the edge of the dock. "It's Pat Tierney in her kayak. A nice surprise."

"Is Zoe at home? I have something to ask her."

"She's in the house with her aunt. Come on up."

I tied the kayak beside the canoes and followed him up the path.

"They're watching a video," he said when we were on the veranda. He opened the door, and I heard the voice of Tom Hanks.

"*Sleepless in Seattle*," he said. "One of Zoe's favorites."

Zoe was curled up on a sofa, a bowl of popcorn in front of her, her eyes fixed on a wide-screen television. A woman sat with her back to me. Her dark hair was stylishly cut. *Ella!*

Zoe turned to look at us. "Pat! Come in. We'll be with you in just a moment. The movie's nearly over."

The other woman turned around as well. She had the same hairstyle and hair color as Ella, but she wasn't Ella. She had a leathery face and neck, and well-defined muscles in her arms.

The woman in the silver canoe.

When the credits started to roll, Zoe turned off the DVD. "Pat, this is my Aunt Riza." She turned to Riza. "Pat Tierney ran the Norris Cassidy branch before Nate took over."

Riza smiled at me. "Rizalina Santos. I am pleased to meet you, Pat Tierney. I hear you've met my sister, Ella."

"Pat told me she'd seen Ella around here," Zoe said to her aunt. "It must have been you she saw. Ella never comes up here."

Riza chuckled. "We look alike, Ella and me. But poor Ella, she's terrified of bugs and bears."

"Riza has a cottage on Raven Lake," Zoe said. "She's alone there so we hang out together. We Filipinas run in packs, don't we, Riza?"

"I come over in my canoe," Riza said. "Across the lakes."

She'd been paddling home when I saw her on Raven Lake on Friday.

"Pat has something to ask you, Zoe," Nate said.

I blurted out the first thing that came into my mind. "My son and I will be alone this week, and we'd enjoy some company. How about coming over for dinner? The three of you. Tuesday, Wednesday, Thursday, whatever works best for you. Talk it over and give me a call."

Running in packs. The words lingered in my mind as I paddled back to the cottage. I pictured Ella, Riza, and Zoe cruising down a highway in a white convertible. Laden with bags and boxes in shopping malls. Pampering themselves at spas and beauty salons.

My thoughts turned to Ella. Her first visit to Frank's house after he died would have been heartbreaking. She would have been grieving, and going through all his things would have been terribly upsetting for her. She wouldn't have gone there alone.

I found Bruce and Sergeant Bouchard sitting on the low stone wall near the waterfront, watching Tommy trying to catch a frog.

"The listing on Cottage Getaways is down," Bouchard said as I climbed out of the kayak.

"That's good news," I said, "but how many other people have wired money to stay here?"

He nodded.

"The ad may be on other rental sites." I named a few that I knew. "Can you check those out and have it taken down if you see it?"

He didn't reply, so I wasn't sure if I could count on him to do that.

They got up to leave, and I walked them to their vehicles.

Bouchard turned to me at the door of the police cruiser. "You and the kid shouldn't be here. As you said, how many people have already sent their money? Pack your bags and get out. Now."

With that, he climbed into the cruiser.

"Have you come across a Riza Santos?" I asked Bruce when Bouchard had driven off. "She's a cottager on Raven Lake."

"Never heard of her. Should I have?"

"No reason to, I guess."

He took a ring of keys from his pocket. "Bouchard's right. You and Tommy need to get out of here. You know that."

I shrugged.

"You're a stubborn woman, Pat. But think about Tommy."

"What about me?" the boy asked, coming up beside me.

I ran a hand through his hair. "Maybe it's time you visited your grandmother again."

They were right, I thought as we watched the Chevy disappear down the lane. We couldn't stay there any longer.

CHAPTER TWENTY-FOUR

I was wondering where we could go when the telephone rang.

"I've been trying to reach you for the past hour." Tracy's voice was pitched higher than usual.

"What's happened?"

"We're at St. Justin's Hospital. It's Laura."

My heart beat in my throat. "What's the matter?"

"She started to hemorrhage when we were on the road. I took her straight to the hospital when we got to Toronto. She's having an ultrasound right now."

"I'm on my way. I'll drop Tommy with his grandmother."

"Mom," Tracy said, "Laura may lose the baby."

Ten minutes later, we were headed south on the highway, pushing the speed limit. In the rearview mirror, I saw Tommy nod off to sleep with his arm around Maxie. I put in my iBuds, and thoughts of Laura flooded my mind as Glenn Gould played Bach's *Goldberg Variations*.

Is my little girl okay? I was well aware that bleeding during a pregnancy can signal a number of problems, some of which are life-threatening.

And there's the baby. She might lose it.

Over the past few weeks, I had come to accept that my daughter would be a mother in a few months and that she and her child would be with me for several years. The baby would have Tracy's old room, and I had planned to help Laura decorate it in the fall. I had also been thinking about childcare arrangements for the following year when Laura would be at school. My grandchild already had a place in our family. *We can't lose this baby!*

Two hours later, Norah Seaton greeted us at the front door of her Rosedale home. She enveloped Tommy in a hug. "We're going to the zoo tomorrow," she told her grandson.

I couldn't picture Norah, dressed to the nines, visiting the lions and the polar bears. But I kept that thought to myself. "You don't mind taking Maxie tonight?" I asked. "I'll pick her up tomorrow."

"Maxie is welcome to stay here as long as you like."

Mr. Bonokowski, Norah's chauffeur and general factotum, came down the hall and took Maxie's leash. Then I was back in the Volvo, driving too fast into the city's downtown core.

I asked for Laura Tierney at the reception desk in St. Justin's emergency wing. The clerk spoke to a woman wearing a badge with the word Volunteer on it. She went down the hall and returned with Tracy.

"Mom!" Tracy kissed my cheek.

I hugged her. "Laura?"

"She's okay. She and the baby are both okay. Come with me."

Laura was in a bed behind curtains across the hall from the main emergency room. She opened her eyes at the sound of our voices. "Momma!" she cried. She looked younger than her 18 years, and very frightened. I gave her a kiss and took a chair beside the bed.

"I told you that Mom would get here," Tracy said as she took the chair on the other side of the bed.

"I started to bleed in the car," Laura said.

I reached for her hand.

"I was sure I was going to lose the baby." She closed her eyes for a few moments. "They did an ultrasound. The baby has a strong heartbeat, and they said he—or she, I didn't want to know the gender—seems to be fine."

"Do they know what caused the bleeding?" I asked.

"A subchorinoic hemorrhage," Tracy said. "A tiny tear in the placenta. The doctor said it will heal on its own."

"She said many women have had healthy babies after bleeding like I did." Laura gripped my hand hard. "I don't want to lose this baby."

I leaned over and hugged her. "I want this baby, too."

"Mom?" Her eyes were pleading.

I nodded. "I do."

Tracy said the doctor would look at Laura in the morning. If all seemed to be well, she could go home. "She's booked for another ultrasound in two weeks," she added.

"Will she go upstairs tonight?" I asked.

Tracy shook her head. "No beds. She'll be right here."

"I have to stay in bed for two days and take it easy for the next week," Laura said. "I'll need to tell the Harrisons that I'll be taking another week off."

"I'll call them when I get home," Tracy told her.

"Everything will be fine," I said to Laura.

She held up both hands with all the fingers crossed. "I sure hope so!"

CHAPTER TWENTY-FIVE

Tracy dropped me off at the hospital early the next morning, and I was with Laura when the doctor told her she could go home. I bundled her into a taxi, and it whisked us across the city.

We found Farah Alwan, our housekeeper, stretched out on the living room sofa, a mug of coffee and a stack of magazines on the table beside her. She jumped to her feet when she saw us.

"I finish bathrooms, now I take break," she said.

I nodded at her and helped Laura upstairs. I put her in my room, which has an ensuite bathroom. I wanted her off her feet as much as possible.

I made tea in the kitchen, noting that Farah had her work cut out for her there. Dishes were stacked in the sink, and the floor still needed scrubbing.

Laura was asleep when I brought a mug of tea up to her. I took my tea into my study and turned on the computer. After I'd scanned and deleted dozens of e-mails, I picked up the telephone.

"Have you found out who was working with Vi Stohl at the Bank of Toronto six years ago?" I asked Foster when I reached him at the Braeloch detachment.

"Ms. Tierney—"

"I know. I should let you get on with your investigation. But money was missing then, and Vi took the blame. Now she's been murdered, and it stands to reason the two might be related. A mild-mannered homebody like Vi... It would be a huge coincidence if two people had it in for her."

"Let it go, woman. You're obsessed with this missing money."

"Did you find out who was working with her at the bank?" I asked again.

"That's police information, Ms. Tierney," he said and hung up.

I found the web page for the Bank of Toronto's branch in the Beach. I punched in the phone number that was listed and asked for Irene Hounsell.

"I wanted to talk to you again, but I didn't catch your last name," Irene said when I'd told her who I was.

We arranged to meet at a Queen Street bistro at 6 p.m.

I reached Bruce at *The Times* and told him about Laura. I said I'd be in Toronto for a few days.

"I hope everything goes well for Laura and the baby," he said. "While I have you on the line, can I ask you a few questions for the article?"

"Fire away."

"What was your reaction when would-be renters showed up at your cottage last weekend?"

"Surprised, shocked, horrified. But what really blew me away was when I saw the listing on the internet with photos of the cottage's interior. There was a photo of my son's bedroom with his teddy bear on the bed. The photographer broke in when we weren't there."

When I told him how vulnerable I felt, I was speaking for Chuck and Gracie as well as myself. "I don't know who'll turn up at the cottage," I said, "and they may think I'm behind the scheme. I don't feel safe there."

I spent the rest of the morning at home. After lunch, I did a grocery run and bought magazines for Laura.

"The kitchen floor needs washing," I told Farah when she was about to leave for the day.

She threw me an injured look, and I knew the floor would stay dirty for days.

At five forty-five, Kyle arrived, and I took him upstairs to Laura.

"I'll be out for a few hours," I told them. "Kyle, make sure that Laura stays in bed."

"I will, Mom," she said. "I want this baby."

At 6 p.m., I was seated at a window table at Café Quatre Saisons with a glass of merlot in front of me. The door opened with a tinkle of chimes, and Irene hurried in, patting her halo of gray hair.

I waved at her.

"Am I late?" she asked as she approached the table.

"Right on time."

She took the chair across from me. "I'm so glad you called. When you were at the bank, you asked if I'd kept in touch with Vi."

"I thought you might've stayed in contact."

"I called her every month or so, and we met for lunch a couple of times. Then she had trouble remembering me when I called. When her home phone number went out of service, I assumed that she and her husband had moved."

The waiter came over, and Irene asked for a glass of chardonnay. I pointed to the menu and told him to bring us an appetizer plate.

"You don't need to buy me dinner," Irene said.

"It's just a snack. I'm keeping you from your family."

"My cat's the only one waiting for me. I live alone."

"Have the police spoken to you about Vi?" I asked.

"Two officers came to my home last week. They asked me about Vi, and they wanted to know who worked at the branch when she was let go."

"You gave them their names?"

"Yes."

"Money was missing," I said. "Do you know how much?"

"We were never told, but the rumor mill put it at $10,000."

The waiter brought Irene's wine to the table. When she'd taken a sip, I continued. "Did Vi take the money?"

"No way." She wrapped her hands around her wineglass. "It never would have occurred to her. She didn't need the money." She frowned. "And she couldn't have pulled off something like that. I assume that small amounts were taken over several months, maybe even a few years. Probably from clients who didn't look at their bank statements. That would have required planning, and Vi was too scattered to do that."

"Why was she blamed?"

"I don't know. Something must have pointed to her, but I don't know what it was."

"Someone at the branch framed her," I said. "Who was there at the time?"

"There were six full-time tellers, three part-timers." She dug a notebook out of her purse and flipped through the pages. "The full-timers were Vi, Susan Smith, Nico Pappas, Serge Junot, Deb Petrovic, and myself. Vanessa Thompson, Fran Reardon, and Doug Thomas worked part-time. Ed Patterson was the branch manager." She tore the page out of the notebook and handed it to me.

I'd never heard any of those names before. "Did Vi get along with all of them?" I asked.

"Vi got along with everyone."

"What about the manager? What was Ed Patterson like?"

"Ed was a good manager. He was fair, and he liked Vi. He felt badly when she was let go."

Before we left the bistro, I wrote down Irene's home phone number and her e-mail address.

On the way home, I stopped at Norah's house to pick up Maxie. Mr. Bonokowski came to the front door, dressed in chinos and a polo shirt instead of the navy blazer and gray trousers he usually wore. Tommy greeted me as if he hadn't seen me for a year, and he gave me a detailed account of his visit to the zoo.

"Did you enjoy it?" I asked Norah.

She gave me a half-smile. "I wasn't up for it today. Mr. Bonokowski took Tommy."

Tracy and I had just sat down to dinner when the telephone rang. I was about to let the call go to voicemail, but something whispered to me to pick up.

Bruce was on the line. "I went over to your cottage this afternoon," he said. "Two women were sitting on the porch, waiting for Donald Simpson to let them in."

More disgruntled renters. The image of Tommy's teddy bear flashed through my mind.

"I drove to town and brought Maria back," Bruce went on. "Bouchard came out as well. They explained the situation to the women."

"How did they react?"

"They weren't happy, but they went away."

It's no longer my problem. Tommy and I are out of there.

"How is Laura?" Bruce asked.

"She seems to be okay. She's taking it easy this week."

"What are your plans?"

"I'm not sure."

"I now have a phone at Raven Lake."

I wrote down the number he gave me.

"I won't have internet service at home for a while," he said, "so if you want to e-mail me, send the message to my address at *The Times*."

Back at the table, I told Tracy that more renters had arrived at the cottage. "I'd like get back up there," I said.

"Bad idea." She shook her head. "Renters are turning up every other day. It's only a matter of time before someone takes his frustration out on you."

CHAPTER TWENTY-SIX

"I'm going back," I told Tracy the next morning. "Bruce offered to put us up. I'll take him up on it, but Tommy will stay with Norah. You and Laura can look after Maxie. Kyle can help you walk her until Laura gets back on her feet."

"Mom, there's a killer up there. You've left your job so you can spend the summer here. Why go back?"

"It's something I have to do."

"For Bruce?"

"Yes."

"Bruce is okay, but…Mom, you're not…?"

I smiled. "Bruce and I are not romantically involved. He's like a younger brother. He's made great progress in the past few months, and I want to make sure he doesn't slide back to where he was before."

And until Vi's murder was solved, I couldn't be sure how well Bruce would do. He needed to know who killed her and why before he could move on with his life.

"Call it unfinished business." Then I changed the subject. "I'm counting on you to see that Laura takes it easy this week."

"Don't worry about that," Tracy said. "She has my number at work. Farah will make her lunch, and Kyle will be here every evening. And she'll follow the doctor's orders because she wants that baby."

"I'll say goodbye to her when she wakes up. Then I'll head out."

Driving up the Don Valley Parkway, I debated whether to call Ella on my cell. I didn't like people dropping in on me unannounced, but there was a good chance she would hang up when she heard who was calling. I didn't make the call.

There was no answer when I rapped on the front door of the bungalow. I went around to the back of the house and found Ella on the deck. She was stretched out on a chaise longue, massaging cream into her hands.

"Hello, Ella."

A frown creased her attractive face. "What do you want?"

I took the chair beside her. "The first time you went to Frank's home to get things in order—"

"Go away."

"—must have been distressing. Your son had just died, and you had to go through his belongings. You had to get the house ready to sell. You didn't want to go in there alone so you took someone with you. Who was it, Ella?"

Her face smoothed itself into a mask.

"You weren't there alone. Not that first time."

She closed her eyes, and I knew I'd hit a nerve.

"The rental contract, the keycard to open the gate, and the key to Frank's locker were somewhere in that house. You never found them. But while you were in another room, the person who came with you did. Who was with you that day?"

She turned her head away from me. "I was alone."

"A woman's body was found in Frank's locker, Ella. She'd been murdered."

I took a business card from my wallet, scratched out the office phone number, and scribbled down Bruce's new number at Raven Lake. "Give me a call." I put the card on the table beside her and returned to the Volvo.

Zoe and Riza were likely candidates, I thought as I drove back to the highway. They didn't have jobs, so they were available to go to Frank's place with Ella.

And Zoe had told me she visited another aunt at Highland Ridge. She was familiar with the building and its garden. That aunt was Riza's sister, so Riza visited her at Highland Ridge, too.

But why would Zoe or Riza want to kill Vi?

My next stop was the cottage at Black Bear Lake. I found a telephone message that Zoe had left the day before. She thanked me for the dinner invitation and said that Tuesday would work well for them.

Tuesday... Today is Tuesday.

I took a business card that I'd picked up at Pickerel from my wallet and made a dinner reservation for that evening. I tried Nate's home and office numbers and got voicemail at both. I left messages saying that I had a problem at the cottage and asked the Johnstons and Riza to meet me at Pickerel at six.

I sat in the Volvo, looking at the cottage that I had rented for a relaxing summer vacation. The rental scamster knew the area, but he could have been running his con from anywhere. From Toronto, or Ottawa, or Montreal. Anywhere. And he could have been watching the cottage—and me—as I sat in the car.

I glanced around the property. The trees on both sides of the house waved gently in the breeze. I shivered.

I turned the key in the ignition. *The summer's not over. I may be back.*

The security guard buzzed me into *The Times* building and picked up the telephone on his desk. "Ms. Tierney is here to see you."

He lifted his head to smile at me. "Go on up."

Bruce met me at the elevator and took me to his office. "I didn't expect you back for a while," he said when we were seated.

"There's nothing more I can do for Laura. Maybe I can..."

He smiled. "Find Mom's killer and the rental scamster?"

I flashed him a grin. "Why not?"

"I hope you're not at Black Bear Lake."

"No, I'm taking you up on your offer. I'd like to camp out in your spare room. I've brought bedding from Toronto."

"Glad to have you." He opened a desk drawer. "Here's a key."

Maria came into the office. "I'm sorry about the cottage, Pat. We'll give you a refund, of course."

"I'll stay with Bruce for a few days, but I may be back at your cottage yet."

When she turned to go, I said, "Can I take the kayak?"

"By all means," she said. "That's the least we can do for you."

Bruce walked me back to the elevator. "What are you up to today?" he asked.

"I'll take the kayak over to your place. And I've invited Nate Johnston and his wife for dinner at Pickerel this evening. I hope you can join us."

"Not tonight. I have an appointment with Dr. Reynolds."

"You're seeing him again."

"Once a week."

I was happy to hear that. "Bruce, I'd like to talk to Wilf's widow. You said she helped him with his freelance business."

"Darlene lives at 17 Newcastle Street." He pointed a finger in the direction of the hill behind the Main Street strip. "Next to the house with the pink flamingos."

I was back at Black Bear Lake a lot sooner than I'd thought. I went down to the lake and dragged the kayak over the lawn to the driveway. I hoisted it onto the Volvo's roof, secured it with ropes, and stowed the two-bladed paddle in the car.

Then I drove over to Raven Lake.

The spare room in Bruce's cabin held a battered dresser and a single bed covered with a colorful throw. Dozens of boxes were stacked against two of the walls. I put the food I'd taken from the cottage into the fridge and the kitchen cupboards. Then I made up the bed, hung my clothes in the closet, and draped my paisley shawl over the dresser.

I hoped my stay there would be short. The cabin was small, and I wasn't sure how Bruce and I would get on in close quarters. But it would be foolish to return to the cottage I'd rented.

I took the kayak off the car roof and headed back into town.

Number 17 Newcastle Street was a brown clapboard bungalow. It looked like a dowdy wren beside Sally Beaton's pink house with the flamingos. A woman with long brown hair streaked with silver came to the door. Dark half-moons underlined eyes that had run out of tears.

"Mrs. Mathers?"

She looked at me without saying anything.

"I'm Pat Tierney, a friend of Bruce Stohl's. Could I talk to you for a few minutes?"

She held the door open. "My parents took the kids for a week," she said. "I'm not myself right now."

"That's understandable. I'm very sorry for your loss."

Darlene took me into the kitchen. We sat at a table covered with empty coffee mugs and a sprinkling of crumbs.

She raised her eyes to my face, telling me to go on.

"Your husband's colleagues feel terrible about what happened."

"Wilf worked at *The Times* for years. Since he got his journalism diploma."

"He had a freelance business as well."

She looked at me defiantly. "He did his freelance work on his own time. Plenty of newspaper people freelance."

"Of course. And you helped him."

"I'm winding up the business—or I will as soon as the police return his computer. Exactly what do you want to know?" There was a shrewdness in her mild blue eyes that told me she didn't miss a thing.

"What kind of freelance photos did Wilf take?"

"Mostly wedding pictures and kids' portraits."

"Did he take any pictures of Riza Santos or Zoe Johnston? Or for them? Family photos, maybe?"

"No. And I would know because I did the billings."

"Any of his recent assignments stand out in your mind?"

"One does."

I wanted to know more. "What was it?"

"He'd just finished a portfolio of photos for Daniel Laughton. He's the—"

"Environmentalist. Has a place on Raven Lake."

"That's the one."

"What kind of photos did Daniel want?"

"A variety. Candid shots of him at the lake. Head-and-shoulders shots for a new website. Some family photos."

"How did Wilf get to the Laughtons' cottage?" I asked. "There's no road to that part of the lake."

"Daniel's wife came for him in the boat."

"Did Wilf finish the job?"

"He gave Daniel some prints and a flash drive with digital images the day before—" she paused, and a shadow crossed her face, "he died."

"Did he think the job went well?"

She toyed with a spoon on the table. "No."

"No?"

"Wilf had a falling-out with Daniel. He was excited when Daniel hired him. He'd always admired him. But he lost interest along the way. He wanted to get the work done and move on."

"What happened?"

"No idea. Wilf clammed up whenever I asked how the assignment was going."

"Why did Daniel hire your husband? Had they already met?"

"They met at the township's Sustainable Living Day two years ago. Daniel was the guest speaker. Wilf was taking pictures for the newspaper, and he talked to him afterwards." She paused again. "My husband was big on saving the planet—recycling, renewable energy, ethical investing. All that green stuff."

"He and Daniel had a lot in common. Did they keep in touch?"

She shrugged. "Probably saw each other at the township's council meetings when something came up about the aggregates."

"Aggregates?"

"Gravel pits. Stone rubble the glaciers left behind during the ice age. There are a few extraction operations around here. All the greenies turn out whenever anything about the aggregate companies comes up before council."

"Do you think the falling-out with Daniel had something to do with your husband's death?"

Darlene looked startled. "Can't imagine what. You don't kill someone over some photos."

But I had a feeling she didn't really believe that.

"Did the police talk to you about this?"

"They wanted to know about Wilf's assignments at the newspaper, not his freelance work. But they've got his home computer. There must be e-mails from Daniel on it."

I logged onto a computer at the Braeloch library and found a wealth of material about Daniel Laughton. The man was in his seventies, but he hadn't slowed down. Since he had left the university a few years before, he'd increased his public appearances and publications. I skimmed reviews of his latest book, *Planet in Jeopardy*, and reports of his talks at colleges, universities, and conferences. A newspaper article that ran a few months before quoted him on the subject of ethical or responsible investing—buying shares in companies with good environmental and human rights records. It caught my attention because I'd wanted to know more about ethical investing. Its premise was great, but did building a better world mean sacrificing investment returns?

"Responsible investments are among the world's fastest-growing asset classes, with about $34 trillion in assets managed globally," the article quoted Daniel telling business students at a Toronto university.

The month after that, *The Toronto World* ran a piece about Daniel signing on to do celebrity endorsements of The Green Funds, a family of mutual funds operated by Green Unlimited Corp., an ethical investment firm. The article said the ads would start running on national television the following week.

I called up Green Unlimited's website. "We invest in companies that obey or exceed laws for environmental concerns, safety, and public disclosure," it stated. "We expect them to reuse and recycle, pursue clean and efficient production methods, and have a deep concern for the welfare of animals."

It certainly sounded good.

"The companies we look for provide fair, sustainable compensation for their employees, extend opportunities to the disabled, and respect workers' rights to negotiate, organize, and bargain collectively."

I wrote down the names of all the companies held by The Green Funds.

I returned to the articles on Daniel, this time focusing on the photographs. Head shots; photos of him in a canoe, on snowshoes, standing beside a marsh; with high school and university students; and with his wife, Frances Reardon Laughton, president of Toronto's Sustainable Living Society.

I made printouts of several articles.

My guests were already seated when I arrived at the restaurant. We ordered drinks, and they asked about the problem I had at the cottage.

"I've had a few issues," I said, "but I want to forget about them tonight and enjoy myself."

"Country living," Riza said. "Mice in the winter, ants in the summer. Problems with the septic. You get used to it."

We studied our menus for a minute or two and placed our orders.

"Have you been on Raven Lake long?" I asked Riza.

"Twenty years. I sold the house in Toronto after my divorce, and I bought my place on Raven. I rent an apartment in Toronto."

"Riza has a great place." Zoe glanced at Nate. "I'd love to find something like it."

"Keep looking," he told her.

"Do you come up in the winter?" I asked Riza.

"The odd weekend, that's all. I thought I'd live there full-time when I retired, but when I left the bank last year, my heart was no longer in it. Winters are lonely up here when you're on your own. In the city, I have my sisters, my bridge group, and my art classes. I've decided that summer is my season here."

"If you paddle into Raven, you'll see Riza's place," Zoe said. "It's not far from the creek that connects Black Bear to Raven. Her house has a bright red roof."

"I'm not on Black Bear right now," I said.

"Where are you staying, Pat?" Nate asked.

"With a friend on Raven Lake."

"Whereabouts on Raven?" Zoe wanted to know.

"The other end of the lake. Not far from the creek that connects it to Paradise Lake." I smiled at Riza. "But if I'm ever paddling near you, I'll drop in."

"Please do," she said.

"What bank were you at?" I asked her.

"Bank of Central Canada. A branch in Scarborough."

A different bank, and a different part of Toronto than where Vi worked.

Our appetizers arrived. When conversation resumed, Nate told us about two new clients at the branch. I asked him how Soupy was doing.

"He has his nose to the grindstone."

"Soupy?" Zoe said. "That's—"

"The guy who's getting married." To me, he added, "Zoe and I are invited to his wedding."

"So you're friends now," I said.

"I wouldn't say that we're friends," he said with a smile, "but we're invited to his wedding."

The meal was a pleasant one. The food was excellent, and Riza told us about some of the local events we could look forward to in the coming weeks. The summer fair and rodeo on the first weekend in August. The garlic festival in Donarvon the following weekend. And the tour of artists' studios throughout the township on Labor Day weekend.

"I enjoyed the Canada Day fireworks," I said. "Until its abrupt end."

"When that man was murdered," Zoe said. "The newspaper photographer."

"That was terrible," Riza said. "His poor family. He had young kids."

"You were at the fireworks?" I asked.

"All three of us," Nate said. "We had dinner at Riza's then we drove into town for the fireworks show."

We sat on Pickerel's porch after dinner and watched the sailboats on Twelve Mile Lake. I was the first to get up to leave. Nate and Zoe thanked me and said they'd have me over to their place soon.

"I hope no more renters show up at that cottage of yours," Riza said.

I looked at her, stunned. "How—?"

"Word gets around up here," she said with a smile.

I thought about what Riza had said as I drove back to Bruce's cabin. *How does she know that my cottage is a target of the rental scam? The article in* The Times *won't be out until Friday.*

Riza had retired from a Bank of Central Canada branch the previous year, but where was she when money went missing at the bank where Vi worked? She might have changed jobs.

And she was at the fairgrounds the night that Wilf was killed.

Bruce hadn't arrived home when I got in. I switched on the lamp beside the sofa and took the page Irene had given me out of my wallet. I scanned the names of the people who had worked at the bank with Vi. Riza or Rizalina Santos was not one of them.

But one name caught my eye: Fran Reardon, one of the part-timers. Fran was probably short for Frances.

I went to my room to get the articles I'd printed out that afternoon. The cutline under the photo of Daniel and his wife identified her as Frances Reardon Laughton.

It was a little after nine. Not too late for a phone call. I punched in a number, and Irene answered at the other end of the line.

"Pat Tierney here," I said. "Fran Reardon was a part-time teller when Vi was at the bank. I assume that Fran was short for Frances."

"Probably, but I only knew her as Fran."

"Is she still there?"

"She left a few months after Vi was let go."

"What did Fran look like?"

"Tall, shoulder-length white hair that she often wore up in a chignon. Weathered face. Probably in her early sixties back then."

"Was she married?"

"She mentioned her husband now and then, but I never met him."

"Did she say what kind of work he did?"

"I don't think so. I remember they had a place in the country. Went there most weekends."

"Did she say where it was?"

"She may have, but I don't remember."

"Well, thank you—"

"Wait! The name had something to do with a bird."

"Raven Lake?"

"That's it. Their place was on Raven Lake."

CHAPTER TWENTY-SEVEN

At breakfast the next morning, I asked Bruce about Wilf's crusade to keep the planet green.

"Wilf was definitely a greenie," he said, pouring coffee for us. "He was talking about buying a hybrid car."

"Tell me about the aggregate operations around here. Darlene said the greenies show up at council meetings whenever anything about the aggregates is on the agenda."

He took his coffee mug to the table. "There are seven aggregate operations in the township. The greenies claim they're driving the planet into extinction, and Wilf was leading the fight against them. He wasn't shy about addressing council on this issue."

"Didn't he cover council for *The Times*?" I asked.

"Janet Bailey covers council. We can count on her to write unbiased reports."

I nodded and pressed on. "Darlene said Wilf was looking into ethical investing."

"He talked about putting money into green funds, but I don't think he did much of that. Not while they were raising two kids."

"He had some freelance work."

"The occasional wedding helped out, but weddings didn't come along as often as he would have liked. The locals tend to take their own pictures."

"He did some work for Daniel Laughton recently."

"Wilf was excited about that. Considered it an honor to photograph a man he admired."

"Did he say how it was going?"

Bruce shook his head. "He didn't talk about it all, which was curious seeing as how pleased he'd been to get the job."

"Darlene said Wilf and Daniel had a falling-out."

"Wilf never mentioned that." He looked thoughtful for a moment or two. "A few weeks ago he sent me an e-mail about a pharmaceutical company. Can't recall the details, but I'll show it to you."

"I'd like to see it."

"I'm meeting an advertiser at ten. Come in with me now and I'll give you a printout."

I sipped my coffee while he finished his breakfast. "When you went to the Laughtons' place after the fireworks, Daniel picked you up at the boat launch. Why not at your cabin?"

"I suggested he come to the boat launch. It's a shorter trip in the outboard."

"Didn't Frances usually come for you?"

"Yeah, she usually did, but she was visiting their daughter that weekend. Rob, their son, brought her back to the cabin on Sunday afternoon."

"Where does the daughter live?" I asked.

"Toronto."

Frances was away from home on the evening of the fireworks.

"Did you know that Frances worked with your mother at the bank?"

Coffee sloshed over the rim of Bruce's mug. "No way!"

I told him about the photograph that identified Daniel's wife as Frances Reardon Laughton. "She went by the name of Fran Reardon at the bank. Vi may not have known she was Daniel's wife."

"Frances has never said anything about knowing Mom," Bruce said. "Are you sure about this? There wasn't another Fran Reardon at the bank?"

"An employee who worked with your mother told me Fran Reardon had a place on Raven Lake. What are the odds of two Fran Reardons being on this lake?"

We drove to Braeloch in separate vehicles and went directly to Bruce's office in *The Times* building.

"One of Wilf's animal rights friends gave him a tip about a company called Spadina Pharmaceuticals," he said, his eyes on his computer screen.

"I've heard of it. Its headquarters are in Toronto."

And it's one of the companies held by The Green Funds.

"Wilf was hot to trot on this," he said.

The printer across the room began to rumble. Bruce went over to it and handed me a sheet of paper.

I read the message aloud. "Buddy of mine at AnimalPals says the big pharma outfit, Spadina Pharmaceuticals, is illegally trapping cats and using painful, invasive methods on them in its experiments. This is a BIG story. Let me follow up on it. Wilf."

I looked up at Bruce. "What did you say to him?"

"I told him—whoa, we're a small-town paper, and local news sells local papers. Toronto is outside our coverage area." He paused. "And we don't have the resources to tackle this."

"You were worried about a lawsuit."

He nodded. "A lawsuit could put us out of business."

"How did he take it?"

"Called me a chickenshit. I told him he was welcome to pursue the story on his own, as a freelancer. Sell it to one of Toronto papers or one of the TV networks. That was the last I heard of it."

"But why wouldn't his friend, or this AnimalPals group, approach the Toronto media to blow the whistle?"

"Good question. Maybe they don't have much clout and they'd be shown the door without a second thought." He paused. "Or maybe they weren't as ready to go public as Wilf thought they were. Needed proof to back their claims and wanted him to poke around and be the lightning rod if things went sour."

"You met the friend?"

"Nope. Don't even know his name."

"Darlene said the police took Wilf's home computer. I assume they have the machine he worked on here?"

Bruce nodded. "That's right."

"Then they'll find Wilf's friend and see what he knows."

He didn't look happy about that.

"Last month, Daniel signed a contract to do television endorsements of The Green Funds. You've heard of them? Green Unlimited's four mutual funds. Spadina Pharmaceuticals is one of their holdings."

Bruce whistled. "Holy shit! Wilf must've told Daniel what he'd heard about Spadina. That's exactly what he would've done."

"Hence the bad blood between them," I said. "Darlene couldn't put a finger on what it was."

"It would certainly sour their working relationship."

"Daniel may not have known about Spadina's mistreatment of animals. He may have toured its facilities, but everything would have been squeaky clean on that occasion. But if the claims turn out to be true, the fallout will badly tarnish his reputation."

As I waited for the elevator, I watched Bruce join Maria at a desk in the middle of the room. Another issue of *The Highland Times* was taking shape.

At the library, I did an internet search for the Sustainable Living Society of Toronto. Frances Reardon was listed as its president emeritus and a member of its board of directors. A search for her name brought up three articles that referred to her as Daniel Laughton's business manager.

Back on Main Street, I crossed paths with Jamie. "How's your mother?" I asked after I'd given her a hug.

"She's coming along nicely. Yesterday was the caregiver's last day, and I'll go back to Toronto on Sunday. How are you doing? I hear you had more renters at the cottage."

"I'm staying with Bruce."

"Tracy told me that. It was a smart move."

I had something to run by her. Jamie is the greenie in our family. She walks and bikes wherever she can and voices her concerns about greenhouse gas emissions and endangered species.

She's also a lawyer who specializes in investment issues.

I steered her over to the bench in the parkette and showed her the e-mail that Wilf had sent Bruce. I told her about Daniel Laughton endorsing The Green Funds on television.

"I caught a few of those ads," she said. "Laughton is very convincing, but I was surprised to see him doing endorsements. There must be a whack of money in it for his foundation."

"Would he know that Green Unlimited's funds may not be as green as it claims?"

"He would have done his homework, but he wouldn't know everything that goes on at a company unless he actually worked there."

"I'd like to talk to him," I said.

"Be careful. That's what Wilf did. He must have confronted Laughton with what his friend told him. And look what happened to him."

Something cold rattled down my spine.

My next stop was the OPP detachment. Foster grunted and didn't look up when the sergeant on duty brought me to his office.

I ignored his bad manners, sat myself down, and told him about Wilf Mathers' freelance assignment. And that his widow had the impression that it hadn't gone well.

Foster scribbled notes on a pad and gestured with his other hand for me to continue.

I told him about the e-mail Wilf had sent Bruce, Daniel's TV endorsements of The Green Funds, and that the funds held Spadina Pharmaceuticals' stock.

I pushed my printout of the e-mail across his desk.

He grabbed it. "I'll keep this. Why the hell didn't Stohl show it to us?"

"He only thought of it today when I told him about Daniel's endorsements."

"I'll bet he did. He's been thwarting this investigation at every turn."

It was just bluster. He had no evidence against Bruce. That's why he'd eased up on him.

"At the time, Bruce dismissed it as a pitch from an over-eager reporter," I said. "When he called up the e-mail this morning, I remembered that The Green Funds were invested in Spadina Pharmaceuticals. Bruce said Wilf would have confronted Daniel about the claims against the pharmaceutical company."

"And you rushed right over to tell us."

"That's exactly what I did. There should be e-mails from Wilf's buddy at AnimalPals on his computers. You have them, so you may be able to locate him."

"You have more to tell me?"

I told him Daniel and Vi were friends when they were kids and that Daniel had visited Vi at Highland Ridge in recent years.

Foster put down his pen. "Where can we find Laughton?"

"He has a place on Raven Lake. On one of its northern arms."

"Thank you for bringing this to our attention. We'll talk to Laughton, and we'll take another look at Mathers' computers. We need to find his animal rights friend."

I couldn't believe my ears. A thank you from Foster. I took the opportunity to slip in a question. "Have you got the test results for the cardigan you found on Bruce's porch?"

"There's a backlog of evidence at our labs. What's important is that we get results in time for a court appearance."

I sighed. They still had no idea whether the cardigan was Vi's.

"Let us worry about it, Ms. Tierney."

"If you need me," I said, "I'm at Bruce's place. The rental scamster is sending his victims to the cottage I rented."

He grunted. "This township is a hotbed of crime."

I was thinking about how I'd get the kayak down the steps to the lake, when Ronnie's Mazda roared up the lane. A blue kayak was strapped to its hood.

"Like my boat?" Jamie called through the open window. "I rented it for a few days. Figured you'd be heading over to Raven and you'd need company."

She handed me a brown paper bag. "Lunch."

I must have looked wary because she smiled. "I passed up the kelp wraps for tuna and egg salad sandwiches," she said. "We can have a picnic."

Ten minutes later, we were on the water. The lake was calm, the water sparkling in the sunlight. Jamie took the lead. I reminded her that it was my lake, because I was staying at Bruce's cabin, and that I should be in front. Our laughter echoed over the water.

We paddled steadily until we came to a sandy beach. I pointed to it, and Jamie nodded. We made soft, smooth landings, tied the kayaks to a tree, and spread a blanket on the sand.

While we ate, I told her about my visit to Foster. I took my map of the chain of lakes out of my pack. "The Laughtons' cabin is up here." I pointed to a bay on the north side of the lake. "Here's where we are."

"That's a long paddle on this big lake." She glanced at me. "But you want to visit the Laughtons."

"Not today. Foster said he'll be talking to Daniel. He may be there this afternoon."

She bent over the map. "We can check out the old-growth hemlocks at Cat Lake. There's a portage into Cat from Raven."

"Portage?" I wasn't up for hauling a boat across the township.

She showed me where Cat Lake was on the map. "We'll leave the kayaks on the shore and walk to Cat. It's not far."

"Can we drop in on Chuck and Gracie Gibson on our way?" I told her that their home had been one of the rental scamster's targets. I pointed to its location on the map.

I'd been calling the Gibsons every evening, but it had slipped my mind the night before.

We got back into our kayaks and headed east. We passed Riza's place—a handsome two-storey log affair with bright red shutters that matched the red metal roof. The lawn sloped down to the waterfront and was completely given over to a woodland garden with flowering plants nestled among the rocks. A motorboat was moored at the dock, but Riza's silver canoe was nowhere in sight. She was probably out on the lakes with Zoe.

We passed the creek that connected Raven to Black Bear, and I led the way across the bay to the Gibsons' dock. Chuck hurried down the path, brandishing his air pistol.

"Chuck, it's Pat Tierney with a friend," I called out.

He lowered the pistol. "Pat, thank goodness. We were worried when we didn't hear from you last night."

I introduced him to Jamie and told him I was no longer at the cottage on Black Bear Lake.

He sat on the edge of the dock. "More renters turn up?"

I gave him a wry smile. "Another group arrived when I was in Toronto. It seemed best to get out. I'm staying with a friend."

He looked down at the pistol he'd placed on the dock. "Is this ever going to end? I don't know how long Gracie and I can hold on here."

"More renters came by?" Jamie asked.

"It's been quiet this week, but we're gearing up for the weekend. That's when they show up."

His face broke into a grin. "I was interviewed by *The Highland Times*. For an article on the rental frauds. It'll be out on Friday."

"I'll look for it," I said. "But, Chuck, tell me you've had an alarm installed."

"Not yet. We're having trouble deciding between two companies."

"Don't wait too long."

I was about to push my boat away from the dock when I thought of something. "Do you know Riza Santos across the bay?" I asked. "Big house with a red metal roof? She's out in her canoe a lot."

"Riza?" Chuck said. "Never met anyone with that name. And since we sold the boat we're not down at the water much. Especially not this summer."

"I'll call you tonight," I told him.

Jamie took us into a bay farther east on the lake. It was ringed by trees and bushes, with not a building in sight. As we approached the far shore, I spotted a yellow sign on a tree. Closer still, I made out a black stick figure on the sign holding a canoe over its head. Under the figure were the words: Cat Lake, One Mile.

We tied the kayaks to trees at the waterfront and hit the trail. Sunlight filtered through the trees, illuminating the forest like light from a cathedral window. We were well past the height of blackfly season, and I only had to slap a few suckers off my neck and arms.

At Cat Lake, Jamie led me down a path to our left. "This is a protected area because of its old-growth ecosystems." She pointed at a tree that was growing over a large rock. "Yellow birch. Pretty rare around here."

She looked up at a magnificent tree that reached into the sky. "Hemlock, hundreds of years old. How did these giants manage to hide from the loggers?"

She went up to the tree and wrapped her long arms around its trunk. I went to its other side and did the same. The tips of my fingers just managed to brush hers. "We're tree huggers," I said.

"How many years would it take for another tree to grow to that size?" she said as we returned to the trail. "We need to preserve places like this."

A breeze had picked up when we got back to Raven Lake, and waves were slapping the rocks. The stony beach was empty. The kayaks were gone. I glanced at the tree we'd tied them to. Two pieces of nylon rope dangled from it.

Jamie was looking at the lake. "Out there." She pointed to two shapes, one red and the other blue, on the water.

She stripped down to her swimsuit and pulled a length of rope from her pack. "Stay here with the backpacks."

She dove into the water and swam hard with sure, even strokes. She circled each kayak, attached the rope to it, and swam back to shore towing the boats behind her.

"The paddles are gone," she said as she waded out of the water.

"We're stranded here," I said.

"It would be a long swim back."

I must have looked worried because she added, "A boat will come by."

"When? Next week?"

Then worry gave way to anger. "Why would anyone do that?" I was thoroughly ticked off.

She shrugged. "We should've taken the paddles with us."

"Someone wanted to frighten us. Or worse."

She began to gather pieces of wood. "If nobody comes for us by nightfall, we'll light a fire. This isn't a designated camping spot, and the rangers will be here to make us clear out."

My heart sank at the idea of being stranded on the shore of that isolated bay after dark. If the rangers didn't see our fire, we'd be dinner for hungry animals. Or rattlesnakes.

A few hours later—neither of us had watches, but the sun was sinking low in the sky—a boat entered the bay, water spraying out from its sides. We took off our shirts and waved them. The boat headed in our direction. It pulled up in the deeper water several feet from shore.

Riza took off her aviator glasses. "Pat Tierney! What's the problem?"

I have never been so happy to see someone I hardly knew. I introduced Jamie to her and explained our predicament.

Riza gave a hearty laugh. "I'm sorry. It's not a laughing matter," she said, "but you never leave your paddle in your boat. It's like walking away from your car with the key in the ignition."

Jamie's face reddened. "I know," she said.

"Tie the kayaks to the back of my boat. I'll get you home," Riza said briskly.

We waded into the water. Jamie tied the kayaks to the motorboat, and we climbed into it.

I gave Riza my heartfelt thanks when she dropped us off at Bruce's beach, grateful that we wouldn't be out in the wilderness after dark.

"Glad I could help you out," she said.

Jamie and I beached the kayaks and made a date to go out on the lakes the following day if the good weather held. "I'll rent two paddles at the outfitters in town," she said.

We were halfway up the stairs to the cabin when it hit me. "Riza knew exactly where to drop us."

"You're right," Jamie said. "She did."

"I told her at dinner last night that I was staying with a friend on Raven Lake. But I didn't say who the friend was, or where his place was on the lake."

I had a pot of spaghetti sauce simmering on the wood-burning stove when Bruce got home. I told him about our misadventure that afternoon, and how Riza had come to our rescue. "She brought us right to your beach. She knew where I was staying."

"Weird."

"It certainly is."

He picked up a spoon and tasted the sauce. "Nice and spicy. How did you know that's how I like it?" He took another taste. "Frances called me at work today. I was in a meeting, so she left a message. Said we needed to talk."

"Did she say what she wanted to talk about?"

"No. I thought I'd call her this evening."

She wants to find out what you know about The Green Funds' holdings.

"I went to the police detachment this morning," I said. "I told Foster about Daniel's connection to Wilf and showed him the e-mail he sent you. He kept it."

He heaved a sigh. "Why did you do that? He'll say I withheld evidence."

"The police need to know. They'll find Wilf's friend who told him about Spadina Pharmaceuticals." I paused for a moment. "Will you meet Frances tomorrow?"

"No time tomorrow. It's our busy day."

"Bruce, how well do you know the Laughtons?"

"I met them a few years ago. I went to see Mom at Highland Ridge and found Daniel with her. He told me they were friends when they were kids. He started inviting me over to Raven Lake."

"Did he talk to you about his work?"

"A little, but mostly he talked about me. Wanted me to see a therapist, send out job applications, that kind of thing. He's a good guy."

"What about Frances?"

"She doesn't say a lot, but she's the driving force behind Daniel. Now that he's left the university, she's getting him gigs on the lecture circuit."

"She's his business manager."

"Yeah."

"She probably got him the endorsement contract."

"I'm sure she did."

"An unusual couple. I wonder how they met."

"She was the department secretary when Daniel was a young lecturer at the university. His first book had just come out, and she knew he was going places."

Frances sounded like an unstoppable force. "She told you this?"

He smiled. "In one of her more talkative moods."

"Foster asked me where he could find Daniel, and I told him he had a place on Raven Lake. He must've gone out to see him."

"Yeah."

"He showed him Wilf's e-mail. That's what Frances wants to talk to you about."

"Probably."

"Meet with her on Friday. Meet with both of them, but in Braeloch. At Joe's or at the Dominion Hotel. Not at their place on the lake."

He thought about that for a few moments. "I'll give her a call after we eat," he said. "But I don't know anything other than what was in that e-mail."

CHAPTER TWENTY-EIGHT

The next morning, Jamie drove over with two paddles. "You'll be on your own on the lakes today," she told me. "I'm taking Mom to Bracebridge."

I lost no time getting the kayak into the water. I wanted to talk to Riza.

Movement on her dock caught my eye. As I came closer, I saw that she was tinkering with the engine of the motorboat.

"Hi there!" I called out.

She turned and flashed me a grin. "You're back for more."

"I hope I won't need to be rescued again."

"Hop in and we'll go for a spin. I'll take you to a cool spot that would be a long way for you to paddle. Raven's Nest."

I saved my questions for later and tied the kayak to the dock. I took my paddle with me when I climbed into the motorboat.

I dug my map out of my pack and followed the course that Riza was taking. As we approached the Laughtons' bay, an aluminum boat chugged out of it, headed in the direction of the boat launch. A figure in a navy windbreaker sat by the engine, white hair fluttering out behind her. Frances. Had she talked Bruce into visiting their cabin even though it was his busy day at work? I hoped not.

I shook my head at the irony of warning Bruce not to go out on the lake with Frances, yet there I was flying over the water with Riza. I had misgivings about both women, but Riza's upbeat personality had been disarming.

We sped along for a good ten minutes until Riza pulled up in front of a wall of rose-colored stone. She tossed an anchor overboard. "We'll wade to shore." She pointed to the top of the cliff. "There's a path that will take us up there."

"I'll never make it up there." I was wearing water shoes, not sturdy hiking boots.

"It's a piece of cake."

On shore, we followed a path that brought us to the back side of the cliff where the land sloped down gradually from the summit. A trail, with a couple of switchbacks cut into it, led us to the top. It wasn't quite the piece of cake Riza had said it was, but it was less difficult than I'd thought it would be.

At the summit, we sat on a log with the serpentine lake stretched out below us. A large black bird swooped through the air, sunlight glinting on its feathers. Keeping my eyes peeled for snakes, I thought about how to broach the questions that were swirling in my mind.

"Native people came up here to throw tobacco on the water," Riza said. "They believed ravens were the guardians of the spirit world."

"The raven is a trickster in some native myths. He doesn't play by the rules."

"I didn't know that." She paused for a few moments. "You must've been scared when those renters showed up at your place."

"You mentioned that on Tuesday evening." I tried to keep my voice neutral. "How did you know that my cottage had been targeted?"

She didn't miss a beat. "My neighbor's daughter, Maria, owns some rental cottages. Maria told her mother that you'd taken one of them, and that you moved out when renters arrived."

It was possible, just possible that she'd heard about it that way so I let it go, but I had another question. "When you took us back yesterday, you dropped us at my friend's place. How did you know where I was staying?"

She gave me a cheeky smile. "From my neighbor again."

Of course, the neighbor.

"Maria works at *The Times*. She told her mother that the guy who owns the newspaper bought a place on this lake. Last week, my neighbor and I drove over to take a look at it. No one was around so we walked down to the beach."

"And Maria told her mother that I was staying at her boss's place."

"Exactly."

"I never realized I was so interesting."

"Of course, you are," she said with a wink of an eye. "Have the police found out who's behind the rental frauds?"

"If they have, they haven't told me."

"You were smart to leave that place."

When we got back down to the lake, Riza announced that she was going for a swim.

I stripped down to my bathing suit. Riza splashed into the lake in her birthday suit. Her hard, muscular body would have done justice to a woman half her age.

The water was cool and silky, and we lingered in it for a while. I was the first to get out, and I pulled on my clothes. An outboard with two fishermen passed close to shore while Riza was wading out of the water. She turned and waved jauntily at them. They stared at her with open mouths.

I howled with laughter.

Riza threw back her head and laughed, too. "They got an eyeful," she said.

She was almost dressed when I heard her say, "Massasauga rattler."

I jumped off the rock I was sitting on. "A rattlesnake?"

"Just a baby," she said. "Massasaugas won't bother you if you leave them alone."

I waded out to the boat and waited for her there.

"That woman who was murdered a few weeks ago," she said when she joined me. "She was the newspaper owner's mother."

"Yes." I wondered where this was going.

"A terrible thing." She shook her head. "And putting her in a storage locker."

"It was terrible," I said. "Vi Stohl lived at Highland Ridge. She was elderly and confused and no threat to anyone. Yet somebody strangled her and put her in that locker."

"When I heard the news reports, I wondered if I'd met her."

"Met her?"

"At Highland Ridge. My sister, Lucy, lives there. I visit her once a week when I'm at my cottage. I may have spoken to Vi on one of my visits."

As I left the boat, I noticed two two-bladed kayak paddles on Riza's dock. The blond wooden one looked exactly like the paddle I'd lost the day before. I picked it up. White Owl Paddle Co. Made In Canada was on the back of both blades. Just like on my paddle.

"Something the matter?" Riza asked.

"This looks like the paddle that was taken from my kayak. And the same company made it."

"I've had that paddle for years," she said. "I always buy White Owls."

"Why have a kayak paddle if you don't have a kayak?"

"I had a kayak," she said. "I sold it last month."

When I was seated in mine, she untied the rope and threw it to me. "I like you, Pat," she said, "but you question everything I say."

"Don't be so sensitive," I said with a smile. "I always ask a lot of questions."

I pushed away from the dock and gave her a wave.

But I was uneasy as I made my way back to Bruce's cabin. Very little of what Riza said rang true.

CHAPTER TWENTY-NINE

Jamie handed me a copy of *The Highland Times* the next day. "Front-page interview with Pat Tierney," she said with a smile.

"Cottage con hits the Highlands," the banner headline read.

I scanned the article. "Only a few lines about me. That's a relief."

The accompanying photo was a long shot of the cottage I'd rented with the maple tree partly obscuring the front of the building. From a distance, it looked similar to many summer homes in the area, and the article didn't give its location.

Chuck Gibson was quoted as saying, "My wife and I don't know who will turn up at our door thinking that they've rented our place for their vacation. They paid their money, and they may think it was us who ripped them off. We're afraid it could get nasty."

Chuck and Gracie were terrified in their own home.

I read the article more carefully. As far as the police knew, only two properties were targeted in the township: the one I'd rented and the Gibsons' home. *Why those two?*

"D'you mind if we stay on Raven today?" I asked Jamie as we took the stairs down to the beach.

"Fine with me. Somewhere in particular on this lake?"

"Riza's place."

I told her my misgivings about Riza. "She knew I was staying here. She knew my place was targeted by the rental fraudster. And she has a paddle that looks like the one that was taken from my kayak."

"Do you think she's involved in the rental scam?" Jamie paused for a few seconds. "Or Vi's murder?"

"I don't know. What I do know is there's more to her than meets the eye."

Riza's canoe and motorboat were moored at her dock. We climbed the path to the house, took the stairs up to the second-story veranda, and knocked on the screen door. Flamenco music was playing inside.

"She can't hear us," Jamie said.

I walked across the veranda and banged on the door to the house.

Riza opened it. She was wearing cut-off jeans, a tattered shirt, and a white turban over her hair. "Well hello, Pat and Jamie!"

"We saw your boats at the dock and thought you'd be in," I said.

"I read about you in the newspaper this morning," Riza said. "The man who was interviewed in the article has a place on this lake. That's too close to home for me."

She looked down at her clothes. "I look a sight. I put on these old duds and crank up the music when I clean the house. Come in."

Inside, the air smelled like lemons. Riza picked up a remote and turned down the sound.

"You like my little country home?" She had a big smile on her face.

"Who wouldn't?" I said. The house was a showpiece. Cedar paneling covered the living room and dining room walls. The rooms had vaulted ceilings, and large windows let in lots of light.

She cleared magazines from the leather sofa that faced the stone fireplace. "Have a seat, ladies. I'll get some refreshments." She bustled into the kitchen.

I went over to Jamie, who was standing beside a slant-top desk. She looked troubled. "What is it?" I whispered.

She pointed to the desk. "My grandmother had a desk exactly like this. One of the pieces that Mom gave Frank. In fact, I'm almost positive it was this desk."

My mind moved into overdrive.

Riza came out of the kitchen, carrying a tray with a bottle of white wine and three glasses. She put the tray on the coffee table.

"Not for me, thanks," I said, seating myself on the sofa.

Jamie sat beside me and shook her head.

Riza shrugged and poured a glass of wine for herself.

I took a deep breath and plunged in. "Frank Prentice was given his grandmother's antique furniture last fall. He put it in a locker at Glencoe Self-Storage, and after he died this spring, the contents of the locker were auctioned off. The woman who bought the contents was Frank's friend, and she knew the value of the antiques that he'd stored in the locker. But they weren't in it."

I waited to see how Riza would react. She took a sip of wine and nodded at me to continue.

"Ella lost her only child when Frank died," I said. "She wanted company the first time she went to his home after his death, and she asked you to go with her. You found the rental contract, the keycard for the gate, and the key to the padlock. And you took them."

Riza had a defiant look in her eyes. "Ella had enough on her hands. She had to sell Frank's house and his truck and wind up his roofing business. His locker was up here so I took care of it. Saved her a trip into the Canadian wilderness."

"You checked out what was in the locker," I said.

"Of course, I did. Frank had some lovely pieces in there. I kept the desk, and I sold the rest." She finished her wine and poured herself another glass.

"You had help moving the furniture. You couldn't do it alone," I said. "Was it Zoe?"

Riza shrugged.

"I bet Ella doesn't know you took her antiques," Jamie said.

"Hey, I did her a favor. When Frank's house sells, she'll have to clear it out. The last thing she needs is more furniture."

"Why did you kill Vi Stohl?" Jamie asked.

Riza scowled. "That's a terrible thing to say. I didn't kill anyone."

"Her body was in Frank's locker, and you had the key," Jamie said.

"Frank's card had been deactivated, but you didn't need it," I said. "You put the body in the locker during the day when the yard was open. You hid it in a rolled-up rug."

The security cameras hadn't captured Riza putting the rug into the locker because they were only switched on after office hours. The same reason they hadn't caught her removing Frank's furniture.

"Yeah, Frank's card no longer worked." Riza gave an elaborate shrug. "I have my own locker there and my own card. But I didn't do anything wrong."

"The police will want to know who had access to Frank's locker." Jamie stood up. "Let's go, Pat."

"Wait!" There was a hint of panic in Riza's voice. "I had nothing to do with the old woman's death. Here's what happened."

Jamie eased herself back onto the sofa. "Let's hear it."

Riza had regained her composure. "One afternoon two, three weeks ago, I put a box of clothes in my locker. After I locked up, I left my car in the yard and walked over to the variety store."

I pictured the businesses on the northwest side of the highway intersection. Glencoe Self-Storage was at one end. The miniature golf course beside it had gone out of business the year before, and the property was a field of weeds. The variety store was on the other side of the golf course.

"On my way back to the car, I cut across the little golf course," Riza said. "I saw a rolled-up rug by the fence. Someone had abandoned it, and I thought I could use it somewhere. I put my shopping in my car and went back for the rug with one of the dollies in the storage yard. I stashed the rug in Frank's locker, thinking that I'd take a good look at it another day. I had a friend coming for dinner, and I had to get back to the lake."

"Why Frank's locker?" Jamie asked. "Why not put it in yours?"

"As I just said, I didn't take a good look at the rug. I didn't know what condition it was in, only that it was really heavy. There was only crap left in Frank's locker, so I put it in there."

"You didn't want to risk contaminating your locker," I said.

"That was my thinking. Two days later, I found out why that rug was so heavy. It was all over the news."

"The police must have questioned you along with the other people who'd rented lockers," Jamie said.

"They did," Riza said.

"You didn't think finding the rug was worth mentioning?" I asked.

"I had nothing to do with that woman. I didn't want them to waste time on me when they could be looking for her killer."

"How thoughtful of you," Jamie said.

Riza sat comfortably in her seat, sipping her wine. Her posture was relaxed, her tone of voice was light. But, for a moment or two, her eyes skittered around the room. She wondered whether we believed her.

I didn't. I didn't buy her story about stumbling upon the rug on the miniature golf course. But Riza was a trickster who didn't play by the rules. It was time for the police to step in. I caught Jamie's eye and inclined my head toward the door.

As I got up from the sofa, the turban covering Riza's hair reminded me of something Gracie Gibson had said. The woman who'd assaulted her had worn a turban.

At the door, I turned to Riza. "You read the article in *The Times* today. The Gibsons' place on the other side of the lake has been a target in the rental scam."

"That's what it said."

"Strangers have been turning up at that elderly couple's door, thinking they rented the property for their vacation. It's scaring the daylights out of the Gibsons."

"You were smart to leave your place on Black Bear Lake."

"So you told me," I said.

"This con is pulling a nasty trick," Jamie said. "It's bad enough to steal people's vacation money, but it also puts homeowners and legitimate renters in danger."

"It's very nasty." Riza looked genuinely concerned. "And now renters are showing up at your friend's place on this lake."

A shiver ran down my spine. "What do you mean?"

Riza's eyes shifted away from mine. "Nothing."

The Gibsons, me, and now Bruce. She has to be stopped.

"You posted the ad for the Gibsons' home on Cottage Getaways," I said.

"What are you talking about?" Riza said.

"You sent strangers to the home of an elderly couple," Jamie added, "and to Pat's place on Black Bear."

"And renters will be coming to Bruce Stohl's cabin, too," I said.

"That's ridiculous." Riza tossed her head. "You ladies have been out in the sun too long."

"You committed fraud, theft, breaking and entering, and assault on Gracie Gibson," Jamie said. "All indictable offenses. You'll be looking at some serious jail time."

"That's quite a story," Riza said with a laugh, "but you can't prove any of it."

"Gracie will identify you," I said. "You wore that turban and sunglasses when you assaulted her, but she'll recognize your face and your voice."

Riza picked up a telephone from the end table. "I'm calling my lawyer. Get out!"

Jamie and I made a beeline for the door, and we didn't stop until we were on the dock.

"How did she do it?" I asked.

"Opened e-mail accounts under other names," Jamie said. "Posted the ads under those names."

"Donald Simpson was one of the names she used. The family who came to our place last weekend said they'd rented the cottage from a Donald Simpson."

"Riza figured she had everything covered."

"But taking interior photos was overkill," I said, thinking of Tommy's teddy bear. "Our cottage would have rented without them."

My heart had stopped racing. "It has something to do with the Gibsons. She sent several groups of renters to their place."

"Nate told her they were your clients and that you were helping them," Jamie said. "She broke into your cottage and took the interior shots to frighten you into returning to Toronto."

"She wanted me out of the way, but what about the Gibsons?"

Jamie shook her head.

Then it came to me. "Zoe wants a home on a lake. Riza must have heard that the Gibsons were planning to put their place up for sale next spring. She wanted to pressure them to sell sooner than they planned, and at a low price."

"That's carrying family love too far," Jamie said.

"I can't figure out why she killed Vi," I said.

"You don't believe her story about finding the rug either."

"Not for a moment," I said. "But what did Vi have to do with the rental scam? It doesn't fit."

We heard a door slam, an engine start up, and tires squeal on pavement. We ran up the path, up the stairs, and into the house. The room we'd just been in was empty. The telephone was on the sofa where Riza had been sitting.

"Riza!" I called, but there was no answer.

We ran through the house to the door that opened onto the driveway. There was no vehicle in sight. The garage beside the house was locked, but a glance through a window told us it was empty.

"She's gone," Jamie said. "We have to call the police."

CHAPTER THIRTY

Bouchard sat down in a plastic chair on Riza's veranda. "So Santos went for a drive in her vehicle," he said. "That's not a criminal offense, but what are you two doing here at her home?"

"We just *told* you," I said from my perch on the veranda railing. "We paddled over here and came up to see Riza. She invited us inside."

"I recognized a desk in there that my mother gave Frank Prentice," Jamie said. "I asked Riza about it, and she told us that she'd taken the antiques out of Frank's storage locker. She didn't seem to think anything of it."

Bouchard gave us a lopsided smile. "And while she was being so talkative, she admitted to killing Vi Stohl and running the rental frauds."

"She didn't come right out and confess," Jamie said, "but you should take a look at her computer. You'll probably find something on it that will link her to the frauds."

"And she knows that Gracie Gibson could identify her," I said. "The Gibsons need to be warned."

Bouchard just sat there, smiling at us.

"Is Detective Inspector Foster at the detachment now?" I asked.

He glanced at his watch. "Couldn't say."

"Tell him I want to speak to him." I motioned to Jamie that we should leave. "He knows where to find me."

"Any idea where Santos went?" Bouchard called out as we walked down the path to the dock.

"She's close to her sisters," I said. "She may go to one of them."

It was almost five thirty when we got back to Bruce's cabin. I helped Jamie carry her kayak up from the beach and strap it onto the roof of Ronnie's Mazda.

Lainey and Burt had invited Bruce to an afternoon barbecue, and I knew he wouldn't be home yet. As I unlocked the cabin door, I was thinking about what I could rustle up for my dinner.

The window shades had been drawn, and when my eyes adjusted to the dimness, I saw someone seated in an armchair. A woman with long white hair. *Frances Laughton.*

"What a surprise," I said. "How did you get in?"

"I turned the knob, and the door opened."

I'd locked up when I left so I knew she was lying. She was waiting for Bruce. She wanted to know what Wilf had told him.

And now she had me to deal with.

I decided to play it friendly. I'd treat Frances as a visitor who'd dropped by to see Bruce then I'd leave as quickly as I could.

I went over to the floor lamp and turned it on. "I'm staying here for a few days. There were some problems at the cottage I rented."

"I wondered whose cars those were outside."

"One is mine. The other belongs to the friend I was paddling with this afternoon."

"When will Bruce get home?"

"Not for a while. He's at a barbecue."

"Dear Bruce has come a long way in the past few months, hasn't he?" She bared her teeth in a smile. "Friends, a job he enjoys, his own home. You've helped him a lot."

"I can't take credit for any of it."

"You're too modest, Pat."

I shrugged. "I'm going to run into town for groceries before the stores close. I don't have much to offer you, but I can get you a bottle of water."

"Sit down for a minute."

"Sorry, but the stores will close soon." I moved toward the door.

"Sit down!"

It was both a command and a threat. I hesitated then perched on the end of the sofa.

"Did Bruce tell you about the article Wilf Mathers wanted to write?"

"Article? I haven't seen much of Bruce since I got here two days ago. He's been busy at the newspaper."

She stared at me with cold gray eyes. She didn't believe me.

"What was the article about?" I asked.

There were three loud raps on the front door.

Frances started at the sound. "Who's that?"

I figured anybody was welcome under the circumstances. I jumped off the sofa, sprinted to the door, and flung it open. Frances was right behind me.

Two young men, in their late teens or early twenties, stood on the porch. A black car, with a canoe on its roof, was parked in the driveway. "Mrs. Wynne?" one of them asked.

"Nobody here by the name of Wynne," I told them.

"We've rented this cottage for a week," the second young man said. "David Wynne, the owner, said he'd meet us here with the key."

I invited them inside. Frances shot me a dark look, which I returned with a smile. The rental con had come to my rescue.

When the boys were seated, I told them about the rental scam.

"You mean we can't stay here?" asked the one who'd introduced himself as Sean.

"We lost our money?" his friend Matt said.

"Yes to both your questions," I said. "The police will need to talk to you. They're investigating the rental frauds in the township." I went to the telephone in the hall and called Bouchard.

"An officer will be here shortly," I said when I returned to my guests.

Frances snatched up her handbag. "I have to go."

Bruce arrived while Bouchard was talking to the boys.

"It's my fault that your place has been hit," I said when Bruce had been told why Sean and Matt were there. "Riza knew I was staying here, and she wanted to scare me away."

"We'll find her and put an end to it," Bouchard said.

"So you've decided to look for her," I said.

Bouchard ignored my remark and turned his attention back to the boys.

They were college kids who had saved up for a week's summer vacation. "We were going to camp in Algonquin Park," Sean said, "but when I checked Cottage Getaways early this morning, this place had been posted. The price was right. Seemed too good to be true."

"It was too good to be true," Matt intoned mournfully.

I signaled to Bruce that I wanted to speak to him, and we went into the kitchen. I told him about Frances's visit.

"When you were staying with the Laughtons, did they ask you about the article that Wilf wanted to write?"

"No, they didn't. But Wilf must have told Daniel what he'd heard about Spadina Pharmaceuticals."

Then it hit me. "He didn't tell Daniel. He told *Frances*."

Bruce whistled. "That could be. She looks after his business affairs."

"She'll be back here, looking for you. Why don't you let these kids have the cabin for a week?" I said. "Riza took their vacation money."

"Frances might hurt them."

"Why would she? They didn't know Wilf, and they don't know you. They're complete strangers."

"This is my home, Pat. I won't leave it."

"It won't be for long. Frances showed her cards by coming here. She's desperate."

Sean and Matt nearly jumped for joy when they heard that the cabin was theirs for a week. While they were taking their canoe down to the beach, I told Bouchard that Frances had broken into the cabin that afternoon, and she was waiting when I returned. "She asked me about an article that Wilf Mathers wanted to write for *The Times*," I said. "Detective Foster was going to speak to her husband about it."

Bouchard went over to the table in the hall. "Does this telephone work?" he asked.

"Yup," Bruce said.

"Where will we stay tonight?" he asked me as Bouchard picked up the phone.

"I'll try the Dominion Hotel when he's made his call," I said.

Bouchard hung up the phone and came over to us. "Detective Inspector Foster will meet you at the detachment at eight."

As soon as he'd left, I called the Dominion Hotel. All the rooms were taken. I tried the Winigami, and that was completely booked, too.

"No luck," I said. "Well, there is Ted's place."

I knew Bruce wanted nothing to do with his father's home, but it was a place to spend the night.

He heaved a weary sigh. "Okay."

"It will just be for tonight. We'll find someplace else tomorrow."

"I told you to let us handle the Laughtons," Foster said when we were seated across from him at the Braeloch detachment.

His tie was loosened. I smelled cigarette smoke and beer on him.

I smiled at him. "I was out all afternoon. When I got back to Bruce's cabin around five thirty, Frances was there. She'd broken in."

"She was waiting for me," Bruce said.

"She asked if Bruce had told me about the article that Wilf wanted to write," I said. "Have you talked to the Laughtons?"

"We spoke to Daniel Laughton," Foster said. "We went out to Raven Lake yesterday. Asked him about those green funds he's advertising. And about the pharmaceutical company that Mathers was concerned about."

"You showed him Wilf's e-mail?" Bruce asked.

"Yes. It was apparently new information to him," Foster said. "He seemed genuinely surprised and upset."

"What did Frances have to say?" I asked.

"She wasn't there," Foster said. "Laughton said she'd gone into town to take care of some business."

He scribbled something in a notebook. "What else did she say to you at the cabin?" he asked me.

"The renters showed up, and she left."

"Renters?"

"Two college kids came by, thinking that they'd rented my place for a week," Bruce said.

"More victims of the rental scams," I said. "Can't you arrest Frances for breaking and entering?"

Foster tightened his tie. "Leave the Laughtons to us. Riza Santos, too. I heard you scared her off today."

I was about to protest, but I saw a twinkle in his eyes. "Are you following up on Riza?" I asked. "Sergeant Bouchard didn't seem to believe what Jamie Collins and I told him."

"We're waiting for a court order to go through her place. Should have it tomorrow. We have an officer stationed outside the house."

As Bruce and I got up to leave, he added, "Find somewhere else to stay tonight."

It was a little after eight thirty. Bruce ducked into *The Times* building to check his voicemail. I parked my Volvo in the public parking lot and went over to the library.

The listing for Bruce's cabin on Cottage Getaways carried a photo of its exterior and several interior shots, including one of the bedroom I'd been using—with my paisley shawl draped over the dresser. Sean had said he'd found the listing early that morning. Riza must have gotten into the cabin on Wednesday afternoon, after she'd stranded Jamie and me on the lake.

I took another look at my shawl in the photo and shivered.

CHAPTER THIRTY-ONE

Bruce drove us up the hill to Ted's house in his Chevy.

He had tensed right up. The idea of spending the night in that house had rattled him, so I didn't tell him what Riza had said about putting the rug in Frank's locker. Her story seemed so far-fetched that I didn't think it was worth upsetting him further.

I took charge as soon as we were inside. I made sure the front and kitchen doors were locked. In the living room, I closed the drapes over the wall of floor-to-ceiling windows that looked out on the lights of Braeloch. Then I opened a few windows. The house had that musty odor buildings get when they've been closed up.

I found a box of herbal tea in the kitchen. The kettle hadn't been packed and there were still a few mugs in a cupboard, so I brewed some tea. We sat sipping our drinks at the kitchen table for a while, not saying anything. Then I took the guest bedroom across the hall from the living room, and Bruce bunked down on a living room sofa.

I had trouble falling asleep. My mind was buzzing with thoughts of Frances and Riza. I'd finally drifted off when voices jolted me awake.

"I thought I'd find you here," I heard Frances say. "Where's Tierney?"

"Pat's with a friend," Bruce said. "Why don't you put the gun down?"

"Not on your life." She gave a wicked laugh.

I was glad I'd left my car down the hill. I needed to keep out of sight.

The streetlight outside bathed the room in a half-light. I eased myself out of bed and pulled on the clothes I'd arrived in.

"You hightailed it out of your place," Frances said, "but you never thought I'd look for you here."

Bruce made no reply.

I straightened the bedcovers carefully, slid my carryall and my handbag under the bed, and gently opened the closet door. Empty. It wouldn't be much of a hiding place if Frances went on the prowl. I hovered near the door and listened to the conversation in the living room.

"I knew you'd come here," Frances said. "To Ted's place, the home of the man who never wanted you."

Frances was hitting below the belt, bringing up the tortured relationship that had dragged Bruce down for years.

"He shaped your life," she went on, taunting him. "Gave you his name and an education you wouldn't have had if you'd been raised by your real parents. You tried so hard to please him, but you never could. Now he's dead, and you're still begging for his approval. Running his newspaper. Staying in his home. What a loser you are."

I wanted to charge into the living room and throttle her. But I forced myself to remain quiet and think about how to get us out of there.

"The detective showed Daniel an e-mail that Wilf sent you," Frances said. "You tipped them off."

"Not me. The cops took Wilf's computer from the newsroom. His home computer, too, his wife said. They went through his e-mail."

Bruce sounded defiant, not scared.

"The fool. He was going to write an article on Spadina Pharmaceuticals."

"It wasn't something we'd run in *The Times*. He should've known that. He'd worked at the newspaper for years."

"You expect me to believe that was the end of it?"

"It certainly was. We have crackpots calling us every day with harebrained ideas. If we took half of them seriously, we'd never get the paper out."

Bruce was definitely holding his own with Frances.

"How are you going to explain this to Daniel?" he asked. "Talk your way out of murder?"

"Daniel does what I tell him, and he believes what I tell him. I'll figure something out, and he'll take it as gospel."

I slipped over to the closet and grabbed the metal pole that served as a clothing rack. It fit into supports on the walls, but came away easily. Couldn't compete with Frances's gun, but it was the best I could do.

"It goes back a long way, doesn't it?" I heard Bruce say. "Back to the money Mom was blamed for taking at the bank. No, back even farther. Back to Daniel's friendship with Mom when they were kids."

"Vi Stohl, the mouse who squeaked." Frances's voice was scathing. "It was so easy to set her up at the bank."

"Daniel didn't know that you and Mom worked at the same place?"

"No. I wasn't about to tell him, and she never did."

"You took the money and made it look like Mom did it," Bruce said. "You hated anyone coming between you and Daniel, so you framed her for a criminal offense."

"I couldn't resist giving her some grief," she shot back. "I made Daniel what he is today. *Me*, not Vi. Forty years ago, I talked him into making a pitch for *The Wonders Around Us*. His career took off with that kids' show. And I was behind him every step of the way."

"You're a real piece of work, Frances. But your scheme at the bank didn't put an end to his friendship with Mom."

"He told me about the date they had every December," she said. "Then he visited her up here."

"She had dementia, that's why she was living at Highland Ridge. Mom was no threat to you."

"I assumed she was ill, like my friend Lorraine who lives there," Frances said, "but I didn't know she'd lost her marbles until I heard it on the news. One day I was visiting Lorraine and I saw Vi in the hall. She recognized me. 'Fran,' she said, 'you took the money.'"

My grandmother, who'd suffered from Alzheimer's, had similar flashes of lucidity. Very few and far between.

"And you panicked," Bruce said.

"I did not panic."

"If she told Daniel what you did at the bank—"

"I couldn't let that happen."

She killed his mother!

"You knew Highland Ridge. You lured Mom into the garden when she got off the bus. You got her into your van in the parking lot, and you strangled her." His voice broke. "Why did you—"

I heard a gunshot and the sound of something shattering.

"Sit down and don't move. The next one will be for you."

"You put her in a storage locker. How could you?"

"I don't know how she got into that locker. I rolled her up in a carpet I had in the van and tied rope around it. I was going to take it into the woods and let wild animals deal with it."

"You psycho!" Bruce said.

"Daniel was coming up from Toronto that afternoon," she continued, "and I was meeting his bus. He would have put his luggage in the back of the van. He would have seen the carpet, might have even looked closely at it. I decided I'd take him out to the lake and come back for the carpet later."

"Where did you leave the carpet?" Bruce asked.

"On the miniature golf course beside the storage business."

And Riza found it when she cut across the golf course.

"You went back for it?" Bruce asked.

"Just before it got dark, but it was gone. I heard on the news the next day that it had been found in a storage locker."

I was horrified by her story. And I knew there was only one reason she was confiding in Bruce: she was going to kill him.

I slipped off my shoes and padded to the bedroom door with the metal pole in my hands. I assumed that Bruce was still on the sofa, but where was Frances?

I tiptoed down the hall, hugging the wall until I was close to the mirror that faced the archway into the living room. In the mirror, I saw Frances standing behind the armchair, her back to me. I tightened my grip on the pole and raised it to my shoulder like a baseball bat. As I stepped toward the archway, the wooden floor creaked.

"What was that?" Frances asked.

"It's just the house," Bruce said. "The sounds old houses make."

"This place isn't that old. Twenty years, maybe." She paused. "Hmm, I wonder…"

In the mirror, I saw her step away from the armchair, holding a gun in her right hand.

"What are you doing?" Bruce asked.

"Looking at your friend."

She smiled at me in the mirror.

I sprang at her, swinging the pole.

Bruce yelled, "No!" He jumped off the sofa and tossed an ashtray at Frances. She ducked, spun toward him, and fired. He fell to the floor, clutching his left leg.

As she turned toward me, I hit her left shoulder with the pole. She stumbled backward and fired as she fell. The shot shattered the mirror.

I brought the pole down on her left arm as she staggered up. She got off another shot, this time hitting the floor. I stepped back and struck her right arm as hard as I could. She screamed in pain. The gun fell from her hand and clattered across the floor. She dropped to her knees.

I kicked the gun toward Bruce. He picked it up and trained it on Frances. He clutched his leg with his other hand, trying to stop the bleeding. He looked up at me and tried to smile. "Just a flesh wound."

I handed him a cushion, which he pressed to his thigh. "Your cell," I said.

While Bruce kept the gun pointed at Frances, I dialed 911 and asked for an ambulance. Then I called Foster and told him where we were.

"What about me?" Frances whimpered from the floor. "I'm seriously hurt."

I ignored her and took the gun from Bruce. "Can you get over to the sofa?" I asked him. "You can stretch your leg out on it."

"There's not a lot of blood," he said as he limped to the sofa. "Bullet just grazed the thigh."

I sat on the other end of the sofa, and we looked down at Frances. "Wilf was going to blow the whistle on The Green Funds," I said.

She remained silent.

"He told you what he'd heard about Spadina Pharmaceuticals," I went on.

"I told him not to bother Daniel. I said I'd deal with it," Frances said.

"Daniel didn't know the company was mistreating animals?"

"He had no idea."

"When nothing happened, Wilf said he'd write an article about it unless Daniel stopped the TV endorsements. You had to shut Wilf down."

A muscle in Frances's face twitched, but she didn't reply.

"You didn't want to lose the endorsement money," Bruce said, hatred in his eyes.

Her eyes flickered. "The money goes to a good cause."

"The Daniel Laughton Foundation," I said. "Promoting clean energy and protecting Canada's ecosystems."

"That's where it goes," Frances said.

"But it wasn't just about money," I said. "It was about Daniel's image. Daniel Laughton, Canada's national treasure."

"An image you worked so hard to build," Bruce said.

"You wouldn't understand how important that is," Frances said. "A lot of people, all the climate-change deniers, would love to see Daniel brought down. I couldn't let that happen."

Banging sounded on the front door. Before I could go over to it, Foster, Bouchard, and two paramedics strode into the room.

"Officers, arrest Pat Tierney," Frances cried. "She assaulted me."

Foster came over to me. "A gun, Ms. Tierney?"

"Her gun." I waved it in Frances's direction. "It's safer in my hands."

"I'll take it." Foster removed a paper bag from his jacket pocket and held it open. I dropped the gun into the bag. Foster handed the bag to Bouchard.

The paramedics moved Bruce onto a stretcher.

Foster looked at Frances, then at me. "Well, Ms. Tierney?" he said. "Care to fill me in?"

"Frances broke in here an hour ago," I said. "Wanted a word with Bruce. At gunpoint."

"That's a lie," she said. "I came here to talk to Bruce. You crept up and whacked me with a piece of metal."

"Frances picked the lock on the door," Bruce said from the stretcher. "I woke up and found her standing over me with a gun."

"I knocked on the door, and you invited me in," she said.

"Like hell, I did," Bruce said as the paramedics wheeled him out.

"Frances killed Vi Stohl," I said. "Wilf Mathers, too."

"More lies!" Frances cried. "Officers, she's making all this up."

Foster took a pair of plastic handcuffs from another pocket. "I'm sure we'll get to the bottom of it."

Frances eyed the cuffs and crossed her arms over her chest. "Please, not those. She hurt my arms."

"Hold out your hands, Mrs. Laughton," Foster said.

"You'll want to check out the gun," I said to him. "I wouldn't be surprised if the bullet that killed Wilf Mathers came from it."

"You'd think we'd never heard of ballistics," he muttered.

He fastened the cuffs on Frances's wrists. Bouchard pulled her to her feet, and they marched her to the door. She didn't seem to be badly hurt.

Not that I cared.

CHAPTER THIRTY-TWO

Our table cleared as Etta James's "At Last" floated through the room, and the couples headed for the dance floor. Lainey came over from the head table and sat down with Bruce and me.

"Am I glad this wedding is nearly over," she said. "I've been almost as jittery as my son."

"The past few weeks have been a wild ride." But I wasn't talking about wedding preparations.

Lainey smiled ruefully. "I've been so caught up with the wedding that I've had blinders on for everything else. Who would have thought it was Frances Laughton who killed Vi and Wilf? The wife of the famous environmentalist."

"Poor Daniel," Bruce said. "I went over to see him in my canoe this week."

"How is he holding up?" I asked.

"He feels terrible about the murders. And he can't understand why Frances killed Mom, that she was jealous of her." He paused. "He's talking about setting up a scholarship in Mom's name."

I chuckled. "Frances will love that. Are Daniel's endorsements still running on TV?"

"He had them pulled," he said.

"A cottager on Raven Lake was behind the rental frauds," Lainey said. "Soupy told us she's related to the new manager at the Norris Cassidy branch."

"Nate Johnston," I said, nodding. "He and his wife Zoe are at this table, but they've gone for a stroll along the lake. Zoe is Riza Santos's niece."

Sergeant Bouchard returned to the table with his arm around Crystal King.

"Roger, any developments on Riza Santos?" Lainey asked Bouchard as he sat down. "I heard you don't know where she is."

Bouchard adjusted his tie. "We haven't found her yet, but we will."

"How long has she been gone?" Crystal asked.

"A week," I said.

"She could still be around here." Lainey's eyes were as round as saucers. "That's scary."

She turned to me again. "Are you back at the cottage you rented on Black Bear?"

"I found another place." I wasn't as confident as Bouchard that Riza would be caught. In case she wanted to settle the score with me, I'd taken another of the Dawsons' rental cottages. On another lake, but not Raven. I'd had enough of Raven Lake.

"I'm back at my cabin," Bruce said. "Riza won't keep me out of my home."

"Was Riza behind the scams in Muskoka and Georgian Bay?" I asked Bouchard.

"We're looking into it," was all he would say.

"Ladies and gentlemen." The disc jockey's voice filled the room. "Let's hear it from the Highlands' very own High Lonesome Wailers!"

"Everyone up to dance!" Mara called out.

With a roll of drums, the Wailers launched into Bob Marley's "One Love," with Soupy and Mara doing the vocals. Soupy was clearly having a grand time. I figured his jitters had ended now that the wedding ceremony was over.

Burt came over to the table and led Lainey into the crowd.

Bruce held out a hand to me. "Like to dance?"

"Your leg's okay?"

"Fit as a fiddle."

We joined the throng of people bopping and swaying on the floor. I doubled over with laughter when Bruce tried out some reggae moves.

We were still laughing as we made our way back to the table. The band moved into its version of "Hound Dog." Soupy was no match for Elvis, but he tried to compensate with the sheer energy of his performance. Lainey and Burt joined us at the table, and we all watched Bouchard and Crystal cut up the floor.

They returned to the table when the number ended. "Whew!" Bouchard said, wiping his face with a checked handkerchief. "I'll sit the next one out."

"You snooze, you lose, big boy." Crystal turned to Bruce. "Wanna dance, Bruce?"

Bruce stood and gave her a small bow. Crystal tucked her arm into his, and they went off.

"How are the Gibsons?" Lainey asked Bouchard. "Any renters come by since Riza's been on the run?"

"They're in Toronto," Bouchard said.

"Toronto?" Lainey asked.

"One of the wire services picked up *The Times'* article on the rental frauds, and it ran in the Toronto papers," I said. "The Gibsons' daughter saw it and talked them into putting their place on the market. They're staying with her until it sells."

"Sounds like a smart move," Lainey said. "They were terrified out there."

I nodded. "It had become too much for them. They were going to sell next spring, but they wanted one more summer at the lake."

"Some summer it's been for them," she said.

Burt and Bouchard headed for the bar, leaving me alone with her. "Soupy seems in fine form," I said. "His nerves have calmed down?"

"He was jittery as a coffee addict for weeks," she said. "But he finally settled down a few days ago. After the big announcement."

"Announcement?"

"He and Mara are going to be parents in December. He kind of freaked at the idea of getting hitched and becoming a dad as well. But he's cool with it now."

I gave her a wink. "High time they got married."

"You bet it is. Burt and I have known Mara for years. She's like one of our daughters. Another grandkid will be the cherry on top of the sundae."

It was after 1 a.m. when Bruce and I left the hotel. "I'm keeping you from a nightcap with Crystal," I said as the Chevy sped through the summer night.

"Crystal is Bouchard's date tonight." He turned his head to flash me a grin. "But, hey, I may call her in a few days."

"How did she hook up with Bouchard?"

"She went to him about finding the furniture that Frank had in the locker. There wasn't much he could do about that, but it got them acquainted."

I thought of something that had been niggling at my mind for the past week. "How did Frances know where your cabin was?"

"When I was staying with the Laughtons, I told them I'd bought a place. I said it was on Raven Lake, but that we wouldn't be neighbors. Frances asked me what the roadside number was, and I gave it to her. It didn't occur to me to wonder why she asked for it."

Frances certainly covered all her bases.

As he turned into Braeloch, he asked, "Sure you're up for driving home? I can take you there. Get you back to your car tomorrow."

"I'll be fine," I said.

In the public parking lot, he waited while I started up the Volvo. I gave him a toot of my horn and drove off.

Inside the cottage, something didn't feel right. I switched on the lamp beside the door. No one was in the living room. I went through the house, turning on lights in every room, but there was no one there.

Still uneasy, I returned to the kitchen to pour myself a glass of chardonnay. An envelope with my name on it was propped against the sugar bowl on the table. My heart did a flip-flop. Someone had come into the cottage while I was at the wedding.

I went straight to the sofa and turned on the reading lamp. Inside the envelope was a single page of creamy stationery covered with large, round handwriting. I flipped the page over and looked at the signature. *Riza!*

"Don't look so frightened," was how she began.

I had to chuckle at that.

"We could have been friends," she continued. "Too bad the way things turned out."

You mean it's too bad you got caught.

"I'm lying low. I figured my business might come to an abrupt end, so last month I put a big mortgage on my place on Raven. I have plenty of money to live on."

And you don't think the police will find you?

"The cops don't have anything that links me to my business. I've been very careful not to leave a digital footprint."

You hid your IP address, but the Anti-Rackets Branch may have other ways of connecting you to the rental scam.

"But I'll still try to stay under the radar. You know, I didn't like doing business on my home turf. I only sent renters to the Gibsons' place for Zoe."

So she could have her dream home on a lake.

"The poor girl couldn't find anything she liked that she and Nate could afford. The Gibsons were planning to leave next year, and I figured there was no harm in making them go a bit sooner."

And sell at a lower price.

"Then you started to help them."

So you sent renters to my cottage, and to Bruce's home.

"I did what I could to make you go back to Toronto, but you're a stubborn woman, Pat."

Damn right I am!

"I'm sorry if I caused you a few bad moments. Like when I took your paddles. Taught you a lesson, though, about leaving paddles in a boat. And I came back to get you and your friend."

We appreciated that, Riza.

"You won't see me again. You did what you had to do, and I don't hold it against you. Goodbye, Pat."

I glanced at the lock on the door. Riza could pick it again, but I didn't think she would. She was gone for good.

EPILOGUE

Two weeks later, I packed up my belongings. I'd had a relaxing holiday reading and paddling the kayak. With no unwanted visitors. But it was time to get back to the city. I knew that I'd miss the Glencoe Highlands and its residents, but I'd miss Laura, Tracy, Tommy, and Jamie even more if I stayed away from Toronto any longer. And I had to get down to setting up my own financial advisory practice.

I said my goodbyes to Bruce and the Campbells at a lunch at the Winigami. We promised to keep in touch by e-mail and on Facebook.

That evening, I had dinner with Nate and Zoe at their cottage. I didn't want to ask where they'd be staying that winter. I decided they could bring it up if they wanted to.

Zoe did that as soon as we sat down at the table. "We need a home of our own," she said.

She gave Nate an inquiring look, and he nodded. "We're having a baby in December," she added.

Another December baby. "I wish you every **happiness**." I raised my glass to toast the expected arrival.

After we'd clinked glasses, Zoe smiled wistfully. "I'd love to tell Riza. She would be thrilled."

"I take it you don't know where she is," I said.

Zoe smiled. "I don't where she is, but I'm sure she's fine. Riza always lands on her feet."

Nate grimaced. "And disrupts other people's lives in the process."

Zoe put a hand on his. "Now, Nate."

"She's the reason we're leaving the township."

"Leaving?" I said.

"Keith took me to lunch two days ago," he said. "Said he was sorry, but he couldn't have me managing the branch because of my family connection to Riza."

"You didn't know what she was doing," Zoe said.

"I had no idea what she was up to," Nate said, "but Keith was right. We're in the business of managing people's money, and we can't allow even a shadow of doubt to tarnish our reputation. Riza is wanted for financial crimes, and everyone around here knows that she's your aunt."

"Where will you go?" I asked.

"Keith is sending me to Vancouver. I'll take over a branch on the lower mainland."

"It's so unfair," Zoe said.

"No, Keith is being extremely fair," Nate said. "He could have sent me packing. And you'll love the West Coast, hon."

I didn't mention that Vancouver had the highest house prices in Canada, but maybe Riza would try to come to their rescue again.

"Who'll take your place in Braeloch?" I asked Nate. I would have heard at lunch if Soupy had got the job.

"Colin Peterson from Toronto. I worked with him at Optimum a few years ago. Keith will announce the appointment next week." He chuckled. "Soupy won't be happy."

"Probably not," I said.

The next morning, the sun shone down from a clear blue sky. It was early August, but there was a touch of fall in the air. I had a big smile on my face as I drove south to Toronto.

There was a lot to smile about. I was starting a new phase in my career. My family was moving forward with their lives. Bruce had mourned his mother, and he was moving on. He was happy in his new home and thriving in his new career.

And there would be three Christmas babies—Laura and Kyle's, Mara and Soupy's, and Zoe and Nate's. Three new lives at the end of the year.

I started to hum "Merry Christmas Baby."

There was a lot to look forward to.

~ * ~

If you enjoyed this book, please consider writing a short review and posting it on Amazon, Goodreads and/or Barnes and Noble. Reviews are very helpful to other readers and are greatly appreciated by authors, especially me. When you post a review, drop me an email and let me know and I may feature part of it on my blog/site. Thank you. ~ Rosemary

http://www.rosemarymccracken.com/Contact.html

Message from the Author

Dear Reader,

I hope you've enjoyed this ride with Pat Tierney. Pat thought she was going have a relaxing summer vacation in Ontario cottage country; instead, she found herself up to her neck in Raven's Lake's treacherous waters. She is now on her way back to Toronto where she plans to set up her own financial planning practice.

Because that is what she does—she takes care of her client's money; she sees that small investors are treated fairly; and she's constantly on the outlook for financial crimes committed by those who are greedy and clever enough to challenge the financial system.

Until the next Pat Tierney adventure, please keep in touch with me by visiting my blog at https://rosemarymccracken.wordpress.com/ and my website at http://www.rosemarymccracken.com/.

Rosemary

About the Author

Born and raised in Montreal, Rosemary McCracken has worked on newspapers across Canada as a reporter, arts reviewer, editorial writer and editor. She is now a Toronto-based journalist who specializes in personal finance and the financial services industry. She advocates greater investor protection, and improved financial services industry regulation and enforcement.

Rosemary teaches novel writing at George Brown College in Toronto.

Rosemary's short fiction has been published by Room of One's Own Press, Kaleidoscope Books, Sisters in Crime, Carrick Publishing and Darkhouse Books.

Safe Harbor, the first Pat Tierney suspense thriller, was shortlisted for Britain's Crime Writers' Association's Debut Dagger Award in 2010, and it was published by Imajin Books in 2012. Its sequel, Black Water, was released in 2013. "*The Sweetheart Scamster*," a Pat Tierney short story in the anthology THIRTEEN, was a 2014 Derringer finalist.

Visit Rosemary's blog, http://bit.ly/15LYn05, and her website, http://bit.ly/1FIyACM.

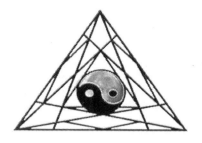

IMAJIN BOOKS ™

Quality fiction beyond your wildest dreams

For your next eBook or paperback purchase, please visit:

www.imajinbooks.com

www.imajinbooks.blogspot.com

www.twitter.com/imajinbooks

www.facebook.com/imajinbooks

IMAJIN QWICKIES ™
www.ImajinQwickies.com

56594113R00126

Made in the USA
Charleston, SC
26 May 2016